DESTINATION: DEATH

The train hit a grade and began to slow. *It was now or never.*

"My uncle is sick," Regina said. "I think his ankle is broken. You have to go without us."

"I can't leave him," James shouted. "Don't you understand that?"

"The Germans do not want him anymore," she shouted back. "They are sending us to a concentration camp. Do *you* understand that?"

James dared not take the chance of leaving the old scientist behind alive. Sooner or later, the Germans were bound to come to their senses and realize who the professor was. James geared himself mentally to do anything necessary to make sure neither the Germans nor the Russians got their hands on Professor Jahne. His palm sweated as he gripped the knife tightly.

"We must go now," one of the men crowded into the boxcar cried out.

"The next move is yours," Regina said, looking James in the eye . . .

By Charles W. Sasser

OSS Commando
HITLER'S A-BOMB
FINAL OPTION

Detachment Delta
OPERATION COLD DAWN
OPERATION ACES WILD
OPERATION DEEP STEEL
OPERATION IRON WEED
PUNITIVE STRIKE

OSS COMMANDO
HITLER'S A-BOMB

CHARLES W. SASSER

HARPER

An Imprint of HarperCollinsPublishers

This is a work of fiction. Names, characters, places, and incidents are products of the author's imagination or are used fictitiously and are not to be construed as real. Any resemblance to actual events, locales, organizations, or persons, living or dead, is entirely coincidental.

HARPER

An Imprint of HarperCollins*Publishers*
195 Broadway
New York, NY, 10007

Copyright © 2008 by Charles W. Sasser
ISBN: 978-0-06-112214-9

First Harper paperback printing: May 2008

Printed in the United States of America

Visit Harper paperbacks on the World Wide Web at
www.harpercollins.com

10 9 8 7 6 5 4 3

For my granddaughter Haleigh Foster

PREFACE

On 11 July 1941, with World War II looming on the horizon, President Franklin Roosevelt established the nation's first peacetime intelligence organization, the Office of the Coordinator of Information (COI), under the direction of William J. "Wild Bill" Donovan, a hero of World War I. Six months after Pearl Harbor, Roosevelt placed COI under the military authority of the Joint Chiefs of Staff and renamed it the Office of Strategic Services (OSS).

OSS was the approximate counterpart of Britain's MI6 (Secret Intelligence Service) and its SOE (Special Operations Executive) branch. Its primary function, truncated to a single sentence, was to obtain information about enemy nations and sabotage their war potential and morale. Thus, wartime necessity gave birth to the predecessor of both the modern CIA (Central Intelligence Agency) and such military special operations forces as the U.S. Army Green Berets and the U.S. Navy SEALs.

Also during the summer of 1941, British scientists warned Prime Minister Winston Churchill that Germany would likely produce an atomic bomb before the end of the war. A German, Otto Hahn, had developed the principle of atomic fission. Published accounts of uranium chain reaction had first come from Germany. Although both Britain and the United States were working on developing an atomic weapon, it appeared by the end of 1943 that Hitler might beat the Allies in the race to acquire the world's most powerful weapon.

Churchill cautioned that the Allies "must not run the mortal risk of being outstripped in this awful sphere"— that the consequences of Hitler's obtaining the weapon first were "horrendous" and could well result in Germany's conquering the world. Fear of such an outcome lent desperate impetus to research by Allied scientists and to undercover inquiries by Allied secret agents to find out just how near the Nazis might be to success.

OSS COMMANDO
HITLER'S A-BOMB

1

The two landing strips side by side at Amendola Airfield on Italy's Foggia Plains were made of steel mats bolted together to keep bombers from sinking in the mud. A green flare streaked a signal against the red, orange and purple veins of dawn. Deep-throated *pop*s and backfires crackled as fifty-six B-17 bombers and one B-24 started their engines.

Each of the B-17s contained nearly 3,000 gallons of high-octane gasoline, 8,000 pounds of bombs, hundreds of pounds of 50-caliber ammunition and ten crewmen. It took full power from all four engines of each aircraft to lift that much mass into the air. Takeoffs were always dangerous.

Unlike the other bombers, the B-24 Liberator was lightly loaded. Its cargo consisted of twelve Type C containers, packed with weapons and other equipment, and one OSS agent, all for delivery to Polish resistance fighters operating around Warsaw. It would be the last plane to take to the air, since it needed to conserve fuel.

Today's assigned bombing target was the Rakos railroad marshalling yard in Budapest, Hungary, which supplied German forces along the Russian front. The B-24 would accompany the other bombers to Budapest, then fly on through the target and proceed, alone, to Poland with its payload. Even the gun turrets had been removed from the Liberator's nose, waist and belly to lighten its weight, leaving only a mounting on top of the fuselage and a tail gunner. Only eight airmen from the "Carpetbaggers," the 801st/492nd Bombardment Group, which supported covert operations in Europe, flew the giant aircraft.

Planes lined up nose to tail on each of the two runways, taking off within seconds of one another. Pilots applied full throttle to their engines while standing on the brakes, and then released their big birds to pick up speed as they lumbered down the uneven steel matting. They lifted slowly, laboriously, into the air to fly circles overhead as they formed up. There would be four squadrons of seven planes each, for a total of twenty-eight aircraft in each of two flight groups. Plus the black B-24 Liberator.

Captain James Cantrell, OSS operator currently assigned to OGs—operational groups—working out of London—occupied a jump seat forward of the navigator's station in the B-24. He wore fleece-lined flight gear. His steel helmet, kit bag and flak jacket were piled on the deck at his feet for ready access as he watched the B-17s struggle to get into the air. While squadrons packed together in tight formations carried a bunch of firepower and could put up quite a battle against German fighter planes, a single plane was little more than an old crippled sheep separated from the flock and vulnerable to preying coyotes.

"A bombing mission is enough to scare shit out of the Pope," the navigator, Lieutenant Jack Myers, warned James through the plane's intercom.

"I've gone beyond that," James said. "I'm already up to scared shitless."

Lieutenant Myers laughed as though he couldn't believe a man who would parachute behind enemy lines could ever be *that* frightened.

"It'll be even scarier after we break off by ourselves past Budapest," he said, and he stopped laughing. "Better put on your helmet, Captain."

The Liberator roared and shuddered against its locked brakes. Then it took off and joined a squadron in the first group as the sun slid, red and festering, into sight above the hazy curvature of the earth.

Judging by his appearance and modest size, Captain Cantrell hardly matched his growing reputation in the OSS for getting jobs done. In his mid-twenties, he was barely five and a half feet tall, wiry and with stiffly cropped hair so red it looked orange. A generous rash of freckles across high cheek bones and pug nose gave him a cocky, slightly belligerent look. A "Dustbowl Okie" from the hills and prairies of east-central Oklahoma, he had defied his stature to become an outstanding athlete during his college years at Oklahoma A&M: captain of the baseball team, champion collegiate welterweight boxer, member of the starting-five basketball squad.

The OSS had recruited him from the robbery-homicide investigations detail of the Oklahoma City Police Department and from the 45th U.S. Army National Guard Division because he spoke both French and German fluently. His maternal grandparents were immigrants, Gramps from Germany and Grams from France. They had raised him in three languages after his parents were killed in a freakish accident when a team of farm mules bolted through the woods.

James had excelled during OSS training as he had in college and in virtually everything else he tried. Colonel "Wild Bill" Donovan, founder of the OSS and James's uncle by marriage, had corralled swashbucklers like James from all over the States and had run them through tough courses in the black arts of spying, guerrilla warfare, demolitions, secret radio broadcasting, cryptography, lock picking, safecracking and "dirty fighting" hand to hand. James had proven such a natural in special-operations warfare that within the past year he had conducted four "behind-the-lines," including the last one in support of the D-day landings, which had won him a personal audience with his hero, Winston Churchill.

This mission into Poland might well prove to be his most challenging and hazardous to date.

The OSS station chief in London had summoned James to the cramped office of "British Isle Exports" on Southwark in London for his briefing. Most OSS ops in Europe were initiated from this underground cloak-and-dagger closet.

"Thrilled to see you've recovered so chipper," Henry greeted the agent, referring to the wounds and injuries James had sustained at Normandy.

"I'm thrilled you're thrilled, sir."

James limped over and took the proffered stuffed chair in front of the desk. The permanent slight limp came from an old bullet wound he had sustained in Sicily. He casually draped one leg across the chair's arm. Henry didn't smoke, couldn't stand the stench of burning tobacco, but he said nothing when James fired up a Lucky Strike and blew smoke toward the ceiling.

"A nasty habit," James conceded. "But then, so is war."

Whether "Henry" was the station chief's true name remained unknown, secrecy of course being a trademark of the OSS. He was tall and bony with a slight Cockney accent, whether affected or not was difficult to tell. Otherwise, judging from his lanky appearance and the dirgelike quality of his speech, as unemotional as an old preacher delivering his one hundredth funeral sermon, he was as American Midwest as a Southern Baptist circuit rider from the previous century. Put him in a pair of farmer gallus overalls and an old straw hat, and he became

James's Uncle Pony, tilling the dry Oklahoma soil. For that reason, James referred to him as Uncle Henry.

Uncle Henry openly evaluated the agent through thick eyebrows. His angular face softened slightly. A bond that was more than professional had formed between the two men.

"We haven't given up, James," Henry said in response to James's unspoken question. "But we still don't know where the Germans took her."

James nodded. He smoked and gazed out through the office's single window. Something had changed in him since American GIs advancing from the Normandy beachhead had discovered him shot up, beaten up, and suffering rampaging infections in the cellar of an old beach house. Missing was a young French-Jewish resistance fighter named Gabrielle Amandine Arneau. James's only comment about their relationship was that the Allies owed as much to her as to him for saving D-day. He requested Henry put out feelers as to where the Jerries may have transported her.

At first, noting the change in James, Henry had wanted to transfer him stateside.

"Beastly, the entire affair," he had commented. "You 'ave done your share, James, more than anyone should expect. You deserve a training slot to ride out the war back home."

"It's not over until I say it's over," James shot back.

"It's daft to keep pushing your luck, James."

"When I leave Europe," James insisted, "Gabrielle will be going with me. I owe her that."

For some reason, of which he had never spoken, James obviously blamed himself for whatever had happened in that beach-house cellar the morning of the Normandy Invasion.

And now Henry was sending him out again. He sighed, chewed on the end of his pencil, sighed again. James extinguished his cigarette by pinching off the ember with his thumb and forefinger and dropping the butt in a wastepaper can. He wore British dungaree trousers, a short-sleeved blue shirt that exposed a recent scar on his arm, and a Dodger's baseball cap.

"So where am I going this time, Unc?" he asked.

"Don't call me Unc."

Henry stood up quickly, all business now, and spread a map on his desk. James leaned forward for a look.

"Poland?" There was a chance the Germans took Gabrielle to Poland.

"Most of us are out on Jedburgh assignments in France," Henry began. "You're my most experienced agent, James. This mission may be our most vital yet for the war effort."

"I may as well take advantage of the full tour."

Henry traced a jagged line across the map with a long forefinger. "The Russian offensive on the eastern front has stalled out here, east of Warsaw," he said, as deadpan as a recording. "One reason is the railroads. Old lines must be repaired and converted back to the broad Russian gauge before the Red Army can carry its offensive into Poland much deeper. We may not have much time left before the Russians resume their attacks. They're our allies, but no one trusts Stalin as far as you Oklahoma chaps can toss a Hereford bull. James, it is imperative that we—by *we*, meaning England and America—pick up a package behind German lines and get it out before the Russkies overrun the region."

"Patton thinks we may have to fight the Soviets next," James said.

"It is difficult to stop warring once we begin. Now here," he went on, jabbing a skinny finger at the map, "is where you'll be inserted, thirty miles northwest of Warsaw, near the village of Grudwald on the Vistula River. Polish resistance fighters will receive you on the drop zone. Your ground contact will identify himself and help you locate the package in Grudwald. You have roughly thirty-six hours from the time you set boots on ground to get the package to an area where an aircraft will snatch up both of you for transportation back to Italy and then London."

He produced a thick file from a desk drawer.

"This folder provides details," he said, "including codes, radio frequencies and other essential intelligence. You'll note that this mission is so critical that a flight group of bombers will remain on standby for air cover in the event you need it. All you have to do is relay a code word and give coordinates—and the bombers will scramble. Remember also, the Soviets are not your friends during this mission. Avoid them."

James took the file.

"Memorize it and destroy everything before you leave this office," Henry said.

"As always. And the 'package' is . . . ?"

Uncle Henry leaned back in his chair. "There is only one way the Germans can win this war," he said. "We Allies have long known this. The Germans have had their best scientists laboring feverishly. Gerlach. Diebner. Heisenberg. Fleischmann. Jahne. Their goal is to build a weapon that will break apart the atom, with enough power in it to blow an entire city like London or New York off the map. It is such a destructive device that it will make other weapons and techniques of warfare and military strategy in part obsolete. While an atomic bomb might weigh half as much as the largest aerial bomb ever used, it will produce as much energy as explosives stacked the height of the Washington Monument. If all the atoms in a single pound of matter were released in energy, it would result in an explosion equivalent to *ten million* tons of TNT and produce a fireball with temperatures measured in millions of degrees."

James released a long, whistling breath. *That* impressed him.

"There is a race taking place between the Germans, the Russians and the Americans," Henry continued. "Whoever builds the weapon first will rule the world.

That brings us to Professor Erwein Jahne, one of Germany's leading nuclear physicists, who was working with Professor Fleischmann at Strasbourg University prior to the Warsaw ghetto uprising. Unfortunately for Professor Jahne, perhaps fortunately for the Allies, he was exposed as a Jew and expelled from Strasbourg. To the Nazis, their ideology against the Jews trumps their celebrated Aryan practicality.

"Thousands of Jews who survived the Warsaw uprising sought refuge in the Christian sections of Warsaw, where many of them were later betrayed and hunted down. Although exiled, Professor Jahne was whisked out of Warsaw by the gestapo and taken to Grudwald, where he continues to work under their protection."

"You're saying Professor Jahne may not be a *willing* package?" James concluded. "That he is still loyal to the Germans even after all this?"

Uncle Henry shrugged. "He and Professor Fleischmann know more about nuclear energy than any other scientists in the world. It is believed they were on the threshold of finally creating an atomic bomb before Professor Jahne was expelled. The Allies need that expertise. We know where Jahne is. We know we have to bring him out to the West."

Uncle Henry's stentorian voice hardened. He summed up the briefing: "Professor Jahne must either be brought out to work with the Allies, or . . ."

James lifted an eyebrow.

" . . . or he must become further testimony to the transient nature of human life."

2

The bombers climbed out over the Adriatic to their ceiling of 30,000 feet. Temperatures plummeted to fifty below. Since the planes were neither pressurized nor heated, crews wore oxygen masks and suits that plugged into the heating system. Captain Cantrell experienced a strange sensation with the sun warm on his face through the windows while cold sweat droplets pricked the rest of his body with icy pins.

Up here, the world seemed lovely and peaceful with the amazing blue of sky above and the white billow of clouds below. Lulled, James daydreamed of long summer days back on the farm in Oklahoma, where he loafed around on the creek bank of his favorite fishing hole with a straw between his teeth and a cane fishing pole trailing a line and bobber into the water, dreaming boy fantasies of romance and adventure.

His thoughts turned to Gabrielle. Eyes so blue, hair as red as his, trussed back in a saucy ponytail. He had told her that she was something more than beautiful. She wanted to know *what* was more than beautiful, but he had never had the chance to tell her.

He shook his head slightly. A man's head had to be clear while on mission.

Out of habit and to occupy his thoughts, he opened his kit bag and gave the contents a final inspection: a canvas money belt stuffed with Polish *zloty* and a few U.S. dollars; British jump boots and a jump smock, its pockets crammed with code books and radio crystals; a radio sealed inside a briefcase; an MP-40 German automatic rifle; a .45 Colt pistol with noise suppressor in a holster; ammunition; a sharpened stiletto knife; chocolate bars for emergency energy; extra packs of Lucky Strikes; a few other personals he might need once he parachuted to the ground behind Kraut lines. In addition, he noted somberly, hollowed-out secret compartments in the soles of his jump boots concealed a clasp knife and a pair of rubber-coated L-pills of potassium cyanide. The L stood for "lethal." They were to be self-administered as a final bug-out from this old world if a situation turned hopeless.

The words of an old song played through his mind and he grinned to himself. *Pack up your troubles in your old kit bag and smile, smile, smile . . .* His kit bag always seemed to contain plenty of troubles whenever he went on mission.

The crew in another plane tuned in to Axis Sally on FM radio and opened its mike for the rest of the formation to listen to. Sally played American records between her usual claptrap about how the Allies should give up now and save themselves from annihilation. Bing Crosby crooned his way through *It Must Be True* and Harry James blew *Cherry* before the flight commander called for radio silence and ordered aircraft to prepare for battle.

Zigzagging to avoid cities and known antiaircraft sites, the bombers dropped to 22,000 feet as they crossed the Alps. They would maintain this altitude throughout the rest of the flight and bomb run. It placed them well within range of infamous German 88s on the ground.

They were now flying underneath thin, high clouds. If James unbuckled from his jump seat and stood up, he could look out past the pilots and leading B-17s to see terrain unfolding below like an elaborate typographical map. Mountains, houses and roads, farmland in contrasting blocks of greens and browns. It was summer in the valleys, but snow dusted the mountain peaks.

The skies remained friendly, and no one down there was shooting at them. Maybe this would be nothing more than a "milk run."

F*ighters! Fighters at twelve o'clock high!"*
The alert blasting over the intercom chilled James's blood. Unlike ground war, a slow, plodding monster, air war began like a horrific bolt of lightning. James had never felt so helpless, so vulnerable, in his entire life. On the ground a man could fight back. If nothing else, he could run. Up here there was nothing he could do except hold on and go along for the ride.

Maybe I ought to consult a different travel agent next time.

German FW-190 fighters came out of the sun from straight ahead and above. Half attacked from the front. The others burst from clouds on either side, swooping down upon their startled quarry four to six abreast, shooting rockets at long range and then 20mm cannon and machine guns as they got closer, brazenly blowing through the formation like hawks in a flock of pigeons. Action occurred with such rapid-fire immediacy that James caught only streaking glimpses of hostile aircraft. Shells exploded. Tracers flew, crisscrossing. The B-24 shuddered from the recoil of its two gun mounts.

In the sky off to the right, a B-17 pulled out of formation, bleeding black smoke from two engines. Enemy fighters swarmed to finish it off. Five men either jumped or were thrown from the aircraft, their bodies twisting and turning in the slipstream. The other half of the crew expired with the bomber as it rolled over on its back and exploded in a flash-ball of fire.

The bombers gave as well as they took. One Kraut fighter plummeted toward Earth, trailing oily smoke. A wing broke off and the fuselage went into a spin. Another fighter got caught in some crossfire as it slashed underneath the B-24 Liberator, exploding with such a bump that it clattered James's teeth.

Winston Churchill once remarked how there was nothing more exhilarating than to be shot at and missed. James wondered if Winston had ever been attacked by enemy fighters while on a bomb run.

The strike ended as abruptly as it had begun. The bombers were approaching their target. German fighters did not attack during the bomb run itself because they would be subjected to their own antiaircraft fire. Instead, they circled and waited for the bombers to emerge on the other side.

Barely had James congratulated himself on having survived the fighters than the sky blossomed with ugly black puffs from exploding AA shells. The next minutes of the bomb run, as Lieutenant Myers had predicted, were the most nerve-wracking of his life. No evasive action could be taken because the Americans' Norden bomb sight required stable platforms for bombardiers to do their job. The bombers leveled out, flying straight and steady through a fierce storm of ack-ack. The Carpetbaggers' B-24 had no choice but to stay in formation over the rail yards.

The German antiaircraft gunners down there were hardened marksmen. They led perfectly and placed every shot inside the formation, like a crowd of hunters firing shotguns into a flight of geese. Even above the roar of engines and the hoarse repetition of his own breath through his oxygen mask, James heard the dull and rapid *thud-thud* of explosions. Shrapnel peppering fuselages and wings sounded like hail on a tin roof. The buffeting was like racing a jalopy over a rubboard country road. The rotten-egg odor of cordite stung James's nostrils.

Flak blossomed, a frightful black flower, directly in front of the Liberator. The impact, like that of a giant hammer, knocked James from his seat. He had neglected to buckle himself back in during all the excitement. He scrambled back to his seat, securing the straps this time. Myers, his face and head encased in helmet and oxygen mask, shook his head at him in reproval. The guy appeared nonplussed. These Carpetbaggers had balls, James had to give them that.

A B-17 out of control cut across the Liberator's front, spewing guns, junk and pieces of itself from its ruptured midsection. An engine cowling and parts of the tail section sailed past. To James's horror, the top half of a human body smashed against the pilots' windshield, splattering blood.

"*My God!*" came a startled cry over the intercom.

Farther out, another plane slid out of formation as black smoke erupted from three engines. Flames lashed over its wings as far back as the tail stabilizer. The B-17 tumbled out of control and plunged toward Earth, trailing a slipstream of black smoke. As it went down, the pilot continued to yell over the radio for his copilot to pull the engine fire extinguishers.

They were really catching hell. Men screamed, yelled, sobbed, and prayed over their radios for all to hear. The hellish chatter through James's earphones seemed about to make his skull explode.

"*Feather number two! Damn it! Feather now!*"

"*Going down. This is Tennessee Twosome going . . . going down!*"

"*. . . request fighter protection.*"

"*Fire!*"

"'*Yea, though I walk through the valley of the shadow of death . . .*'"

"*I'm hit! I'm hit! Oh damn, I'm hit!*"

"Get off the radio! Get off the radio!"

At last, through the aerial hail and brimstone, the first waves of surviving bombers approached the targeted rail yards. Clusters and sticks of half-ton bombs began dropping and detonating in strings. The distant rumble of ground thunder reverberated across the sky.

Beyond the target, the B-24 separated itself from the pack. It would be on its own for the rest of the way into Poland. The pilot, named Callahan, whose demeanor as he directed his crew through the fighter and AA attacks had remained calm and controlled, suddenly sounded rattled. Every AA gun in the vicinity seemed to be opening fire on the lone Liberator. Could fighters be far behind?

"Dive! Dive!" Major Callahan ordered his copilot, reason being that the maneuver would confuse the Jerries and cause them to resume pounding the main formation rather than adjust fire on a lone bird that appeared to be hit and falling anyhow.

The big Liberator turned nose down, engines shrieking as the rpm built up. G-forces glued James to his seat. Through the pilots' windows he watched Earth zoom up toward them.

A shell burst near number four engine. The engine issued a stream of black smoke and blistered the windows on that side with hot oil and soot. The plane began to shudder like a scrap of old 'coon hide ragged on by a pair of redbone pups. It was going down for real now. Major Callahan and his copilot struggled desperately to both ease the airplane out of its dive and activate the fire extinguisher for number four. They feathered the prop to keep it from vibrating in the wind.

A frantic call from the tail gunner reported that his oxygen lines were severed and that he was about to black out from lack of air. He would be dead of hypoxia in less than ten minutes unless the plane descended to an altitude below 10,000 feet.

It was descending. Fast. It took both pilots on their yokes to bring the plane to a more reasonable rate of descent. By that time, the fire extinguisher on number four had worked its miracle and the flames were out. The engine continued to leak a thin mist of oil.

Hardly had anyone inside caught a breath of relief, however, than a blow from the mighty fist of a giant Joe Louis nearly knocked the B-24 out of the sky. Chaos erupted once again as a hole in the fuselage aft of the port wing blasted in a roar of air. The concussion left James momentarily stunned.

Recovering, he glimpsed blue sky and exploding flak through the hole, half the size of a jeep, in the airplane's side. The flight engineer, wild-eyed, had already thrown off his oxygen line and was preparing his parachute for departure. Lieutenant Myers was screeching, "I'm hit!" over and over again. Bright blood gushed from around a piece of shrapnel the size of a hoe blade sticking out of his upper arm.

The plane was shaking like a wet dog.

"*We're going down!*" yelped someone in the cockpit.

Right in the middle of a big nest of thoroughly pissed-off Krauts—and still a few hundred miles short of Poland and Professor Erwein Jahne.

3

If the B-24 went down over enemy territory, there was no way the Krauts were going to take it for an ordinary bomber. It was stripped down, painted flat black and loaded with canisters of weapons and gear for delivery to partisan fighters. Adolf Hitler had issued orders for any captured OSS, spy, or clandestine operative to be immediately shot. Every man jack of the crew, if he survived the crash, would be seized and executed.

Near-panic prevailed in the first few frenetic minutes. Teamwork came apart as it seemed the plane was about to disintegrate. Lieutenant Myers kept screaming over the interphone that he was hit. The flight engineer struggled to the gaping hole in the plane's fuselage, where he stood staring out in shock, cold wind whipping at his flight jacket. Ends of torn cables and electrical wiring snapped around the jagged edges of the wound like dying snakes. Back in the tail section, the gunner gasped for air and begged for help. James prepared to destroy his kit bag and its telltale contents.

The plane shuddered and shimmied violently as Major Callahan and his copilot reduced engine power and trimmed the craft to more or less level flight. Pieces of shrapnel and debris rattled on the floor. After his initial loss of restraint, Major Callahan came over the interphone in a calm, steady voice, ordering the crew to get off the radio.

"*Damage report?*" he demanded once order returned.

James was no expert on a plane's airworthiness, but he had heard that a Liberator could do fine on three engines and that you could knock a hole the size of a manhole cover in it and it would continue to fly as long as the controls and at least two engines remained functional. The breach in the side of this plane was much larger than a manhole cover.

"Major, we got a crack in the side of this baby I can walk through," James radioed.

The flight engineer remained frozen, looking out through the hole.

"*Pilot to crew,*" Callahan radioed back for all to hear. "*I've just consulted God. We're not going to crash after all. We are going to keep flying. Roger that?*"

The aircraft was still vibrating enough to shake out tooth fillings while wind howled in through the break with the sound of an Oklahoma tornado. But at least it had escaped the flak zone. James saw clear, uninterrupted sky all around.

"*How about casualties?*" Callahan asked.

There was only one—the navigator with the shard of steel sticking out of his arm, not counting the shell-shocked engineer and the tail gunner, who was starting to recover from mild hypoxia at the lower altitude. James unbuckled and braced himself to render first aid to Lieutenant Myers, who now slumped in his harness in a state of distress.

He was slitting cloth away from the wound with his pocketknife when the crew's medic stumbled forward, bouncing back and forth on the unstable footing. He was young, about nineteen or twenty, with a thin face that looked as pale as the underbelly of a catfish. He had removed his O2 mask and indicated it was now safe for James to do likewise. James ripped off his mask, relieved to be free of the restriction.

"I'll take him now, sir," the kid said through his voice mike.

He bent over and finished exposing the wound. Lieutenant Myers stirred, looking about.

"You'll be all right, Lieutenant," the medic assessed. *"You've got yourself a little souvenir to show the folks back home, sir."*

"If it's all the same with you, Bosco," Myers murmured through his pain, *"I'd just as soon show snapshots."*

The crew was back and taking care of business. Even the flight engineer snapped out of it and got busy inspecting the jagged edges of the plane's wound for possible repair opportunities. James felt a revived sense of confidence in the bomber and its Carpetbaggers.

"Captain Cantrell?" the pilot radioed. *"Could I see you up forward?"*

James worked his way past the radio operator's station and plugged into the jack that Callahan indicated; he could now communicate with the pilots without the rest of the crew listening in. The copilot took over the flying. Callahan twisted around in his seat. He had replaced his helmet with a jaunty soft cap and earphones that made him look like the movie actor Errol Flynn, complete with mustache. He got right to the point.

"I'll not gloss this over, Captain," he said. "We may make it and we may not. We still have over three hundred miles of flying through hostile skies swarming with enemy fighter planes. That's about an hour and a half. If we go down, chances are none of us will make it back home for another supper."

"For a fact, sir, it's a long hike."

Major Callahan paused, then said, "We can fly only

one pass over your destination, so you need to be ready to go out the first time."

"Roger that, sir. Call me Johnny on the spot."

"With only three props turning and a hole in our ribs," Major Callahan continued, "we will continue to slowly lose altitude. We'll have to jettison everything we can spare in order to lighten the load. That includes your equipment containers. If there are weapons in them, which I assume there are, I suggest you render them inoperable before you dump them along with everything else."

James craved a Lucky Strike. Something hard knotted inside his belly. The B-24 on its return flight would have to climb in order to cross the Alps.

"Captain Callahan . . . ? You and your crew are not going to make it back, are you?"

The drawn lines in Major Callahan's face held the answer. "Every man on this plane is a volunteer, Captain. Just like you. We knew the odds when we stepped forward. My orders are that your mission is so vital that I'm to get you to your drop-off point, no matter what it takes. We're going to do our job. I'm sure you'll do yours."

Jesus! It was one thing for James to risk his own life for a mission, but quite another to take an entire flight crew to their deaths with him. This guy was willing to sacrifice himself and his men for a mission the purpose of which he knew nothing. Where did America get such men?

The pilot stuck out his hand. They shook solemnly.

"Luck," James said.

"Luck," Major Callahan replied. "Shall we dare damnation together?"

His thin mustache twisted in a wry grin. He turned away to resume flying. With his back to James, he said, "Captain, do you pray?"

"Sir?"

"If you don't, it might be a good time to start."

* * *

The pilots had their hands full keeping the plane in the sky while it continued to shake and quiver, taking in air through the opening in its side like a leaky boat takes on water. A sense of urgency infected crewmen as they ripped out seats, instrument panels, emergency equipment, and anything else not essential to actual flight and hurled it all out through the fractured rent in the aircraft's flank. James broke open the cigar-shaped Type C containers intended for Polish resistance fighters and, with the assistance of the flight engineer and the tail gunner, pounded the weapon mechanisms inoperable before dragging the heavy cocoons across the unstable platform to shove them out into the slip-stream.

The crew set aside enough M1 carbines and ammo to arm itself and stacked the weapons near the "Joe hole" for ready access. There was no need for explanations; somewhere along the route back, this old bird was going down inside German lines.

"*Captain?*" Callahan interphoned to James. "*Thirty minutes. Get ready.*"

James exchanged his flight gear for British jump boots, smock, and steel helmet. He buckled on web gear rigged with the holstered .45, stiletto knife, and extra ammo pouches, then set the MP-40 aside to strap to his left shoulder just before he jumped. He gave his parachute a final check, tightening buckles, before he attached his kit bag in the place normally occupied by a reserve chute. No reserve would be needed. Although he would be jumping higher than normal combat altitude in order for the Liberator to clear the area before it had to ditch, he would still be going out too low for a reserve to be activated if his main parachute failed. Parachuting, he thought wryly, was just like life: You didn't get do-overs.

This would be his seventh jump, including five practice jumps during OSS training. The first six had been out of perfectly good airplanes.

He noticed that his hands were trembling slightly, as he snugged down his leg bands. There was a knot in his stomach. He willed himself to focus. He had a job to do, a mission to accomplish. The outcome of the war, as Uncle Henry put it, might well hinge on the success or failure of the next forty-eight hours.

A sudden tense exchange over the intercom between Major Callahan and the topside gunner caught his attention.

"*Hold your fire!*" Major Callahan rasped. "*Whatever you do, don't shoot at him.*"

"*Sir!*" the gunner protested, his voice rushed and quivery. "*He'll shoot us down, sir. I have to get him first. I have to!*"

"*Don't shoot, Johnson. Damn you, that's an order. He's looking us over. Let him. We don't have a chance if we open up.*"

James turned around. The flight engineer and the tail gunner had just tossed the radioman's seat out through the hole in the side. They remained as though frozen in time as they stared out at something beyond, fear written so huge on their profiles and in their postures that James felt it like a bolt of electricity. He scrambled to take a look for himself.

His heart hammered wildly against his chest at what he saw. A Focke-Wulf 190 flew alongside the Liberator, throttled back so that it kept pace. It was painted mottled gray, darker on top, lighter on the belly, like a shark. It had a shark's nose. It was so near that James detected the color of the pilot's eyes. Blue. Like chips from a glacier, bright and savage.

With a jolt, James recalled a night on the farm when the guineas made such a terrified racket that he and Gramps had jumped out of bed to check on them. They found the petrified fowl huddled against the side of the henhouse, while not ten feet away an owl on the ground regarded them with the same fixed gaze that the Focke-Wulf pilot now directed at the Americans visible through the hole in the B-24. The owl wasn't merely considering whether or not to take one of the guineas. That was a given. What he was deciding was which one to take, when and how.

4

The German Focke-Wulf continued to fly alongside the crippled Liberator, tucked in so close that James thought it might be possible to leap from the bomber to the fighter's stubby wing. A blast of black smoke billowed from the B-24's feathered engine and whipped past the enemy fighter. Apparently curious, the fighter jock seemed in no hurry to administer the *coup de grâce*.

Although he wore a helmet and oxygen mask that concealed most of his face, his eyes were still visible as they stared, hard and predatory, out through his canopy. James and the two crewmen stared back. They were all locked on to one another's eyes, unable to break free for what seemed an eternity. Inside the bomber, the interphone remained quiet in dead air.

The German's eyes darted upward toward the topside gunner, then back to the three Americans frozen in the jagged gap of the bomber's ribs. The B-24 was almost entirely at the mercy of the fighter. One hostile move from the topside gunner's .50-cal and the Focke-Wulf would tip a wing, dart underneath out of sight, then immediately return with power turning and guns burning.

The feathered engine belched more smoke. Incomprehensibly, the German suddenly saluted without taking his eyes off the Americans. He might even have smiled, although it was difficult to tell. Then the fighter tipped a wing and streaked away under full throttle. Everyone watched, fearful of its return, until it became a distant mote and finally disappeared. James drew in his first full breath since the episode began.

"What in hell was that all about?" one of the crew wondered aloud on the intercom, sounding blurry as though coming out of shock.

"Maybe he was saving ammo," the flight engineer offered. *"We're gonna crash anyhow."*

Stunned, even touched by the enemy's apparent act of mercy, James promised himself to return the gesture one day. It wasn't often the owl passed up a free meal.

Major Callahan's voice over the interphone brought him abruptly back to the moment.

"Ten minutes!"

James's hands were no longer shaking, although worms still writhed in his belly. He cinched down his helmet, secured the MP-40 automatic rifle to his shoulder and gave himself a jumpmaster's check. He was ready when the pilot leveled off at about 900 feet and began his run in to the drop zone. No ground fire was expected, as the selected DZ was located in a remote rural area.

Major Callahan lowered flaps about halfway through the run to slow the bulky aircraft to barely above stall speed. James heard the groaning of the three remaining Pratt & Whitney engines, the roar of wind past and into the ship from its ruptured side. He felt a momentary sadness for the inevitable fate of the crew. He was the lucky one to be abandoning this flying wreck.

"Action stations!"

Bomb bay doors slowly opened the Joe hole, admitting another gale of wind and revealing the grayish-green patchwork that defined the ground below. James shed his earphones to cut off communications with the crew. He sat down on the edge of the opening, with his feet dangling, and hooked the snap end of his static line to an eyebolt implanted in the deck for that purpose. The throbbing of the airplane filled his entire body. From farther up front, Lieutenant Myers lifted his head from the foldout stretcher where he was being attended by the medic. Both Myers and the medic watched him with expressions that said they never expected to see him again.

Somewhere down there, James thought, *are men who are going to kill me this time.*

"DZ markings coming up! Get ready!"

James shook out a Lucky Strike and clamped it firmly in his teeth. He waited for the white *X* on the field below to appear between his feet. The flight engineer bent over him.

"Keep a tight asshole!" he advised, shouting.

James looked at him, nodded, saw the *X*, and launched himself down through the hole, plummeting toward Earth and the dangers that awaited him.

The euphoria of an air-filled canopy followed sooner than expected after the unbelievable frenzy and disorientation of momentary freefall. Below his floating boots spread a small cleared field surrounded by forest that, even in the noonday sun, appeared as black and impenetrable as goblin-and-spook woods from the Brothers Grimm. A group of fifteen or twenty people burst out of the trees and ran toward the area where he would land. He hoped they were partisans—his reception party—and not Krauts.

He hit the ground with a bone-jarring impact that knocked the cigarette from his mouth and rolled him to one side as his parachute collapsed. He was mobbed before he could gain his feet. People were all over him, tugging and pulling, grasping at harness buckles until they freed him from the canopy. All the while they were laughing and shouting to one another in Polish, embracing him, opening bottles of wine and homemade beer, acting as though an Allied force consisting of one man was going to march down the road, give the Germans a quick thrashing and liberate Poland.

"*Jeszcze Polska nie Zginela!*" they shouted, laughing.

James, anxious to clear out but unable to make himself understood since he spoke no Polish, watched them with disbelief. They seemed to have no idea of the danger created by their racket. When he finally shouted to get their attention, a large, scar-faced man with cauliflower ears and the rough features of a prizefighter—apparently the leader of this herd—stepped forward and in surly, broken English explained that the nearest Germans were at least two kilometers away. Slightly more than a mile. A mile must seem a comfortable distance to Poles who had lived with Germans among them for the last five years.

No distance was comfortable if Jerries had seen the parachute.

After discharging its jumper, the black B-24 circled sharply in a pattern to head back in the direction from which it had come. The crowd cheered and waved and thrust weapons into the air as the plane flew over. James watched it depart, feeling a sudden sense of aloneness in spite of being surrounded by people. He saw the damage to its fuselage, the one still prop, and knew it would never make it back over the Alps, if it made it that far before crashing or being shot down. Crew members dared not even seek asylum in the Russian sector, since the Russkies were as apt as the Germans to torture and kill them in an effort to find out what special operations might be going on in Poland without their knowledge.

The Poles grew unexpectedly quiet and anxious when the plane kept going and they realized it wasn't going to make a second pass. It quickly diminished to a speck and vanished. That was when James realized the celebration wasn't because of *his* arrival. It was for the containers of weapons and equipment—Brens, Sten guns, battledress, and ammunition—the partisans had expected to receive in compensation for assisting the American.

The scar-faced boxer angrily whipped a German Luger from the belt of his baggy drawers and jabbed it against James's temple.

"We are not in needing *you*," he growled. "If airplane she is not returning, I will be in shooting you."

5

James was a bit piqued at having a gun stuck in his face right after having a Focke-Wulf stuck in his face. He half expected to be killed on this mission anyhow, considered himself fortunate to have survived German fighters and ack-ack over Budapest—but he never thought to go this way, at the hands of ostensible allies. Silent and threatening, Poles surrounded him in a circle as tight as a cell block. Most, including the several women, were armed with ancient hunting Jaegers, single-shot pistols, British Stens or captured German weapons. Someone relieved James of his MP-40; several men began arguing over who, rightfully, should take possession of it.

A minute ago these people had been full of wine and party. While they left him the .45 Colt and knife on his battle harness, to go for them against such odds would be like some ol' treed 'coon jumping out of a sycamore to take on a pack of snarling hounds. The 'coon wasn't apt to walk away from it.

He could almost understand their distress. As one of

the first nations to fall to Hitler, since 1939, Poland had suffered widespread destruction and death. Large portions of Warsaw and other cities had been bombed and burned down to charred soil. Millions of Poles, including most of the nation's Jews, were either killed or thrown into concentration or work camps. Others took to the forests and mountains to fight back with whatever weapons they could beg, borrow, steal or manufacture themselves.

They had cause to be suspicious of Nazis and Allies alike. Stalin, like Hitler before him, aimed to conquer and occupy Eastern Europe, thereby substituting Soviet rule for Nazi rule, letting the Nazis do the dirty work for him while he bided his time. Although Stalin had encouraged the Polish Resistance and the Polish Home Army to believe that the Russians were going to storm into Poland and assist them in expelling the Germans, he chose to keep the Poles unarmed and weak. The Home Army was crushed and the partisans minimized because Stalin refused to allow the Allies to assist the Poles by dropping arms and supplies.

Polish partisans were now as likely to resist the Soviets and the other Allies as they were the Nazi occupation. Sides for them were becoming less and less consequential. What they understood was that the Allies kept promising to deliver but never did. Once again—it must have seemed to them—they had been double-crossed and left holding the bag, which contained nothing but a short, freckled, redheaded American.

"You are in calling back the airplane," the prizefighter challenged James in butchered English.

He was at least a foot taller than the American and had to bend down to thrust his gnarled face into James's. His breath reeked of rotted onions, rotted teeth and rotted living. James had a feeling that anything he said would only exacerbate the situation. The last thing he wanted to do right now was piss off this monster by letting his bulldog mouth override his hummingbird ass.

Therefore, he kept his mouth shut. Gramps always said

a good bluff with deuces in the hole was better than aces and bluster.

Casually, deliberately, he took a C-ration pack of Lucky Strikes from his breast pocket, shook out a fag and lit it with a V-match. He inhaled, blew smoke to one side, and offered the pack to the prizefighter. The guy's thick brow lifted in astonishment. He glared. This American was one cool customer.

"The gun she is being loaded," he threatened.

"I doubt her not."

Scarface cocked the pistol. James continued to smoke while he held the big man's gaze. Not in an aggressive manner, but rather controlled and calm as one might face down an enraged dog until it returned to its senses. Self-possessed, almost detached, a rare quality even in the OSS, he once again offered the pack of cigarettes. Scarface's gun hand trembled with rage, the barrel of the weapon tapping against James's temple.

It had been one long day of one damned thing after another.

Just as it appeared Scarface was going to pull the trigger—*Damn everything and everyone!*—a voice sharply lashed out of the surrounding tension. *"Jurawski!"*

She hadn't been here before. She came striding out of the forest and across the field with purpose, small and striking, with short black hair and a single straight black eyebrow above eyes like points of anthracite coal. She was in her mid-twenties, with a childish face that hid an older, ruthlessly cool woman. She was dressed in a faded blue linen work shirt and navy canvas trousers far too long for her petite figure. She carried a stubby Sten sub-machine gun slung from one shoulder.

She had fire too. She marched right at Jurawski—for such must have been his name—like she was going to march up his spine and tramp his face into the earth. Small as she was, she got right in his ugly mug. She started wagging one finger in front of his nose and her black eyes flashed with fury. James failed to understand a word of the Polish tongue-lashing she ruthlessly administered, but, as Grams would have said, it was enough to blister paint.

Jurawski's defense was wholly inadequate. His heavy lips gaped, his wide shoulders slumped, and he actually seemed to shrink before her assault. No two ordinary men could have taken on the brute, but this slip of a girl totally dominated him. Clearly, she exercised some power over him. It wasn't difficult to guess what it might be, from the sullen mooncalf way he looked at her. Jurawski was pussy-whipped.

He eased down the hammer on the Luger and lowered the pistol to his side. He took a step back, glowering at James in an attempt to salvage at least some of his previous authority.

"Is it being true?" he demanded, in apparent reference to something the girl said.

"What is being true, Lawrence of Poland?"

Who wears a dirty burlap sack and rides a pig? Lawrence of Poland.

Jurawski frowned, as though trying to determine if he had been insulted. "The airplane, she is being sick?"

"You think it was flying on three engines because the pilot got cold from the hole in its side and turned off one of the fans?"

Jurawski's shoulders bunched. His eyes narrowed. The girl with eyes of coal murmured from the side of her mouth, in perfect English, "American, I would not push it if I were you."

"Good suggestion." James held up both palms. The cigarette pack was still in one of them. "What we've had here," he said, "is a failure to communicate. Let's try the next dance."

Briefly, speaking slowly to accommodate Jurawski's poor English, he explained how the B-24 crew had had to jettison everything not bolted down in order to keep the ship in the air. He concluded by promising to radio for replacement supplies. Jurawski's pistol disappeared somewhere underneath his dirty fatigues. He snatched the pack of Lucky Strikes from James's hand, shook out a cigarette and indicated James should light it for him. The rest of the pack disappeared where the pistol had gone.

"You will be calling America right away?" he asked, still suspicious.

James nodded. "Now that that's settled, don't you think we ought to move this party elsewhere before uninvited guests start showing up?"

"We don't want to get hammered," the girl said, looking directly at James.

James blinked. His contact, who had access to Professor Jahne, was supposed to meet him on the ground at some unspecified point and identify himself—*herself?*— with the code word *hammer*. James was to respond with *dog* to indicate he understood.

The girl turned to walk away before he had a chance to answer. James caught up with her after reclaiming his MP-40 from the partisan who ended up with it. He slung the weapon over his shoulder.

"For a little man," she said with an amused glance, "you have one big set of balls."

"You seem to have a pair yourself."

She laughed and walked off with Jurawski.

The mood of the gathering returned to one of conviviality. James shed his jump smock and stuffed it and his steel helmet into the parachute canopy. Underneath he wore faded Levis and a blue chambray shirt, over which he wore his battle harness. He took a Dodgers baseball cap from his pocket and pulled it down tight over his orange hair.

Someone hid the parachute and other air equipment in the Hansel-and-Gretel forest. Someone else took his kit bag to carry for him. Led by the hulking Jurawski and the girl, the band finally got lined out and took to trails through the dark forest. The summer sun was strong and the weather warm even in the deep shade. Bottles of wine passed up and down the file. These people were about as security conscious as a Girl Scout troop on its way to a picnic. James took a nip of bitter wine when the bottle reached him. *What the hell, when in Poland . . .*

After a while, they broke clear of the forest. Away went the wine. The partisans became suddenly serious. They went to knee at the edge of the woods where the blinding sun shone directly into their eyes. Jurawski scrutinized the way ahead for signs of danger.

On the other side of a wide field studded with old cornstalks and new green shoots arose a cluster of tin-roofed structures that looked to have been remodeled and added to piecemeal over the centuries. Windows and doors were of various sizes and heights, giving the appearance that materials had been thrown at the buildings and then attached wherever they landed. Nothing moved among them.

Satisfied, Jurawski continued the trek across the field, hurrying now. The dark-eyed girl dropped back to stride loose-jointed and easy by James's side. A thin line of sweat adorned her upper lip. She noted James's limp with a look but then ignored it.

"Do you still have the hammer?" James challenged.

"Not unless you brought the dog."

"That dog will hunt. I wasn't expecting . . . But now that we've settled bona fides, how do we get to him?"

She lowered her voice, even though few of the partisans apparently understood English. "Professor Jahne is in Grudwald under heavy guard. There is going to be another Jewish action. This time, even his former imminence in Germany and the work he is engaged in will not save him."

"When?"

The girl's expression turned pained, pinched. James couldn't help noticing.

"How well do you know Professor Jahne?" he asked.

They rushed along together in silence.

"My name," she said finally, "is Regina Jahne."

She stopped in the field. James stopped with her. They faced each other.

"He's your *father?*"

"Professor Erwein Jahne is my uncle. We must take him by tomorrow night." She pressed her lips into a tight line. "Otherwise, I am told by someone I trust, there will be another transport in which my uncle and the remaining Jews in Grudwald will be taken west to concentration camps, from which few ever return."

6

Hidden behind the ramshackle tin-roofed structures was a two-story farmhouse of stone with a steep gray-slate roof. A long, rutted drive led from a road that Regina said went to Grudwald. Parked next to the porch sat a gasogene-powered Citroen truck with a flat bed. Vehicles equipped with charcoal-burning engines had been around since the 19th century, but this was the first one James had seen since France. Civilians in German-occupied countries were prohibited from using rationed gasoline.

Most of the partisans continued past the farmhouse toward a rise of hilly forest beyond, in which their base camp was undoubtedly located. Jurawski indicated that James and Regina and a half dozen of his inner command were to remain at the farm with him.

Inside the house, some women were paring potatoes and beets to boil in the ancient fireplace. There were three of them, the older about sixty, the other two in their thirties. All were withered and worn, like most Polish farm people, and as battered-looking as their old table, which was thick and about the size of a farm wagon. Baskets left on it meant the women had probably brought the food from elsewhere. Women of whatever age typically enjoyed more freedom of movement under occupation than men, since they naturally seemed more innocent and didn't have to explain why they were not conscripted for labor.

The women were curious about James, casting shy glances at him while they worked, and James was curious about Regina. She appeared to enjoy a degree of status among the partisans that exempted her from normal women's duties.

They ladled potato-and-beet soup into wooden or clay bowls, adding a crust of hard bread on the side, and everyone ate at the table like farmhands, sitting side by side on long wooden benches. A place was made for James at one end. Regina took her place at the head of the table next to Jurawski. The conversation ranged good-naturedly back and forth, but it was in Polish and therefore excluded James.

Afterward, Jurawski got up, wiped his mouth with his sleeve and burped loudly. That was the signal for the start of business. The others rose, even Regina, and filed into another room. Before Jurawski joined them, he prodded James to make radio contact with the Allies.

"You are having a radio?" he asked, although he knew the answer, having already rummaged through James's kit bag.

"Why don't I just ring up Herr Hitler and tell him we're here?" James countered in astonishment.

German Intelligence and Security, including the *Abwehr* and the *Geheime Staatspolizei*, otherwise known as the gestapo, commonly prowled country roads in vans equipped with RDF (radio direction finding) equipment to ferret out clandestine radio signals.

"The Germans and the Russians she are being too busy one with the other to concern with us," Jurawski said.

"It could compromise my mission," James reminded him.

Jurawski dug in. "We are in talking about your mission when you are finish ordering more guns for my people." He shrugged. "Until then, well . . ." The implication being that no supplies for the partisans meant no cooperation from the partisans.

The pigheaded sonofabitch.

Jurawski joined the others in the separate room, closing the door behind him. James remained at the table, fuming with anger and frustration. What choice had the dumb Polack left him? He needed Regina, if not the others, and Regina brought along certain baggage.

The farm women grew bolder once they had James alone. The older woman, as wizened and wiry as a barnyard leghorn, reminded him of Grams. She rubbed James's ribs to indicate how skinny she thought he was and offered more soup. He declined. The younger women tittered and blushed. They sure couldn't cook like Grams—but then these poor people had very little to cook at all.

Still hungry, he remembered Grams' chicken and dumplings she used to make for Sunday dinners. Hot baking-powder biscuits and dumpling gravy, home-churned butter, black-eyed peas, corn on the cob, and blackberry cobbler for dessert. At planting time, Gramps dropped a few watermelon seeds in the hopper with the corn and cottonseed. It was always a delight to find a ripe watermelon growing in the middle of the patch during pickin' time. It could be eaten right there with one's fingers or carried to a shade tree to save for lunch.

He sighed deeply. He looked at the women, who tittered some more. From the table he could see out the front window down the long, rutted drive to the main road. Normally, you never transmitted radio signals from your safe house or base camp. On his own, he would never take such a chance.

Resigned to doing what must be done, and let the devil take the hindmost, he got up from the table and retrieved his kit bag. Someone had dropped it outside the room where Jurawski was meeting with his partisan leaders. Weapons were stacked along the wall outside the closed door.

He took the radio briefcase from his kit bag and set up at the table, where he could keep an eye on the road. It would be dark in another hour or so. The women watched him while he prepared the radio for message relay through Allied stations in France to London. Apparently, Jurawski trusted them.

The radio briefcase was divided into four separate compartments. The rear middle compartment contained the transmitter with the Morse key. The receiver with a socket for headphone connections occupied the front middle. The power supply was on the right side, while the left was crammed with a selection of accessories and spare parts.

He prepared his brief message using an encryption system known as the one-time pad. Employing the grids painted on a silk handkerchief and a pad of 8-inch squares with scrambled letters, he printed a brief message transposed over the letters on the pad. For the letters of ARRIVE, he wrote the first group from his one-time pad, which was BGSOHA. The first letter, G, told him which column to use from the grid on the silk handkerchief. G at the top of the column told him to replace the A in AR-RIVED with R, and so forth throughout the message.

His one-time pad was matched by an identical pad at the receiving station. Each sheet, different from all the rest, was used only once and then destroyed. Even if Nazi code breakers intercepted a message, they could not decode it, nor could they use it to break other messages, since different sheets from the pad were used each time.

"ARRIVED SAFELY W/O—REPEAT W/O— CONTAINERS AND EQUIPMENT. MADE CON-TACT LOCAL GROUP. SOME DIFFICULTIES. IM-PERATIVE EQUIPMENT REPLACED ASAP. AD-VISE SOONEST POSSIBLE DROPPING GROUND."

He transmitted the message, broke down his gear, put

it back in the kit bag and then went out on the wide front porch to smoke and keep an eye on the main road. He lit a Lucky Strike, touched the match flame to the one-time sheet and held it by the corner until it turned to ashes and smoldered in the slight late-afternoon breeze.

The sky beyond the main road was going red-and-purple bruised when Regina came out of the house. She closed the door behind her and stared pensively at the approaching sunset. Her young face looked surprisingly old and haggard in the reddening light. The dying sun seemed to have turned her melancholy.

"You can tell Jurawski it is done," he said. "There'll be a drop within a day or so."

"He should never have made you use the radio here," she said. "It was foolish and dangerous. We always hike into the hills before we radio, and always from a different location each time. This was his way of declaring dominance, I suppose."

"Like a dog marking his territory?"

"Are we so very different from other animals?"

She came over and perched on the edge of the porch next to him, but not close. He offered her a cigarette and lit it for her. They smoked in silence, watching the sunset. James thought of such times back in Oklahoma, when Gramps, Grams and he had sat on their porch after a day's work and chatted about crops, livestock and the weather. Sometimes his grandparents told stories about France and Germany, their "old countries."

"You must overlook Jurawski," Regina said. "He is very brave, but he is infected with the disease that is common in war. Nothing is more important than his own people."

"And you are one of his own people?"

She knew what he was getting at. "In war, there are two things you want most so you will not feel alone. One is sex. The other is God."

"For women as well?"

"There is no time for love, only for rutting when the need is great. You do not want to feel alone when death is always so imminent, for the next stage beyond is forever isolation in the grave."

She turned her head to look at him, her eyes forming slits against smoke curling up from the cigarette dangling from her lips. "Are you unfortunate enough to have some-one . . . ?" she asked. "I do not know your name."

"James. My name is James."

He thought of Gabrielle and the forty-plus hours they had had together in France before she vanished on D-day.

The dying sun was making them both melancholy.

"How long have you been doing this?" he asked her.

She looked away. "Since Warsaw," she said in a haunted tone. "I didn't know how war could be so terrible, how it could crowd out everything else in a person's life."

"You haven't been sleeping, Regina."

This time she looked at him. "I have nightmares. Do you have nightmares, James?"

"Each time you kill is worth a year of nightmares."

She nodded and he saw the ruthlessly cool woman behind the childish face.

"The war will end someday," he said, watching the red orb of the sun. "We will all have our lives back."

"Bah!" she scoffed. "You may believe that. You are an American. But for the Jews, there will always be war. We have been in Diaspora for two thousand years, since the destruction of the Second Temple. We have suffered mal-treatment from all countries during the centuries of our dispersion. Did you know that Jews were even blamed for the Black Death during the Dark Ages?" She made a little sound of disgust.

"Many times throughout history," she went on, "they have attempted to wipe us out. For a thousand years the oppression against Jews has never stopped. It has only varied in intensity from time to time. The Crusades under the flag of Holy Purification set out to kill every Jew in Europe. The Jesuits of Posen and Krakow triggered riots and pogroms. The Cossacks of the Ukraine became ob-

sessed with the idea of slaying every Jew in Poland, the
Ukraine and the Baltics. And now there is Adolf Hitler
and Josef Stalin." She spat out the names with contempt.
"Both Russia and Germany have pushed us around for
centuries. There is little to choose between them, for they
would both see us destroyed."

She seemed to want to talk, to let the bitterness out like
pus from a lanced boil. James needed to bring her around
to her uncle and how they should reach him and bring
him out, but he let her talk instead. Sooner or later they
would get around to Professor Jahne.

The land grew purple with the approach of nightfall.
Scents of summer grass and the black soil of distant culti-
vated fields wafted in on the evening breeze. Inside the
house, Jurawski's conference with his leaders continued.
Sometimes their voices carried outside to the porch. One
of the farm women lit a lamp and its pale illumination
squared out the window.

"Jews were welcomed at the beginning of the new
kingdom of Poland," Regina was saying, lost in the
troubled history of her people. "We were needed, for we
brought our arts, crafts, trades, professions and abilities
as merchants. We became the middle class that separated
peasants from the landed gentry. But it was short-lived.
Immigrant Germans managed to get us expelled from
competitive trades and professions. They levied a Jew's
tax against us. We were prohibited from owning farmland. And to Poland fell the disgrace of creating one of
the world's first ghettos where Jews were walled off from
other people and banned from participating in normal
life."

Gabrielle was half Jewish, but she lacked Regina's pain
and intensity of Jewish legacy.

"We Jews," Regina said, "are like birds without a home.
We fly and fly in circles, but whenever we try to land in a
tree to rest or build a nest, we are driven away again to fly
in aimless, endless circles."

It was almost fully dark by now and there was a night

coolness to the air. James traced with his eyes the profile of Regina's face against the lighter sky. She turned on the porch edge to front James directly. Her knee touched his. They had already smoked their cigarettes and discarded the butts.

"Your uncle," James said. "How does he feel about this? He was working for the Germans."

An even deeper sadness dulled the tone of her voice. "Uncle Erwein is in denial," she said. "He was considered a very important man at Strasbourg University. He believes that once the war is over, the Germans will restore him to his previous position and place of honor. He cannot accept that the only reason he and I have not been placed on the trains is because of his work in nuclear physics. I have tried to warn him that once he is no longer useful, we become merely Jews. He refuses to listen."

"Is that why you notified the Allies where he is being held?"

"Because I love my uncle," she cried in self-defense. "There is no one else in our family. He has been working in a laboratory inside an old wool mill for the past two years. But now the Russians are coming nearer and nearer. They will capture him and make him build an atomic bomb for them. Failing that, they will execute him to prevent his further work with the Germans. The Germans will either do likewise—or they will transport us right away. There is already a train waiting at Grudwald. Where does that leave my uncle? Either way, he has only one chance."

Even in the dark, James felt the power of her eyes locked on his.

"His only chance, James," she said, "is you."

7

The dying sun took the day's warmth with it. Regina shivered and hugged herself against the night's chill. James and she had not spoken for several minutes, when a boxy shadow nosed past on the main road to Grudwald, its engine humming. Regina stiffened and dropped her arms to grip the edge of the porch. It occurred to James that if they stood they would be silhouetted against light from the window.

The shadow stopped and backed up. It turned into the long drive, revealing blackout headlights, slitted and hunting like a cat's eyes. The eyes bore down upon the farmhouse.

"Damn you, Jurawski!" Regina hissed.

"Amen," James said.

The Polack was an empty beer bottle from the neck up—what with advertising himself during the parachute drop by all that hoopla with the wine, then insisting James send a radio message from the house. He had not even posted security. Were the Russians so close that it permitted the partisans to drop their guard against the Germans?

Regina would have sprung to her feet and dashed inside to sound a warning, except James grabbed her. Opening the door to let out more light would only expose them to the approaching vehicle. Regina understood. She snatched James's hand, and stooping low to hug the darkness nearest the house, led the way around to the back.

James glanced over his shoulder and saw that the approaching car was alone and traveling at a careful speed. If this was a raid, it would have been busting dust down the driveway, accompanied by a few truckloads of SS or paratroops. Basically cowardly, gestapo seldom left their compounds by themselves.

That awareness made James feel better, but still, any visit by the enemy, whatever its purpose, was nothing to trifle with.

James and Regina burst through the back door and initiated a flurry of frantic activity. Jurawski barked out orders and glared accusingly at James, as though *he* had brought this on. He and another fighter disappeared back into the conference room with their weapons. The door slammed. The remaining partisans gathered up weapons and any other equipment that might betray their presence and fled into the basement through a trapdoor in the kitchen floor. The older woman who reminded James of Grams concealed the trapdoor with a rag-woven rug. She and the younger women began clearing away dishes, shoving them, washed or not, into cupboards.

The car stopped outside. With no time to lose, James collected his kit bag and MP-40 and looked around.

"This way," Regina indicated. She had her Sten. She dared not stay with the other women since she was known in Grudwald and might be recognized by the Germans.

They hurried out the back door. Barely had it closed behind them when there was a loud knock from the front.

Damned polite for Krauts.

James and the girl crouched and stayed back from the kitchen window, where they could see inside but could not be seen. The older woman flung herself into a wooden rocker and began darning a pair of bloomers with needle and thread. She looked pale and frightened. Taking a deep breath to calm herself, she looked around the room one last time to make sure it was clear.

Her eyes bulged when she saw a Bren submachine gun that had been overlooked in haste and left propped against the wall. James thought she was going to faint. Regina's breath hitched in her throat.

Another knock at the door, more insistent this time.

From her rocker, the old woman directed the other two with desperate hand motions. The younger woman, who wore a full peasant's skirt, hurried to stand so that she concealed the weapon from view. The other answered the door and stepped to one side as two German officers politely but assertively pushed their way inside. Black uniforms with silver death's-heads on their caps and Nazi runes on their collars identified them as SS rather than *Wehrmacht*. They explained in German that they were new to Poland and on their way to Grudwald when they lost their way.

"Iche suche Grudwald, und wie kamme ich dahin?"

James and Regina listened from their vantage point outside the window. Clearly, the Polish women did not understand German. They stared uncomprehendingly. The young one propped in front of the Bren turned deathly white. She was trembling and trying to control her breathing. The SS looked at her curiously and repeated their request.

"Tochter," the old woman responded, with one of the few German words she knew. *"Tochter. Tochter."* Daughter. Daughter. She swept her hand toward the younger woman.

One SS made a face and looked at the other. "What else can we expect?" he said in German with a dismissive shrug. "They are Poles and little better than Jews. I had to set my watch back three hundred years when I crossed the border."

His companion chuckled. "Günter, how do you stop a Polish army on horseback?"

"How?"

"Turn off the carousel."

Günter chuckled and strode across the floor toward the rocker. He might make himself understood if he got near the old woman and shouted.

"Grudwald? Grudwald?" he repeated.

The elderly woman suddenly brightened. "Grudwald!" she exclaimed, relieved to understand that they were merely asking directions. She jumped up and started to the door, gesturing for the SS to follow so she could show them.

The young woman in the peasant's skirt shifted to keep the Bren covered. Günter, the blond major with eyes narrow and almost purple, paused to regard her with a speculative, suspicious air. She looked away guiltily and brushed at her hair with nervous hands.

"*Was stecht hinter Sie?*" What is behind you?

James held his breath.

"*Sich bewegan,*" the SS major ordered, advancing on the hapless farm girl with grim intent to shove her aside.

The old woman caught his arm. "Grudwald!" she said, almost pleading, pointing toward the door.

Günter pushed her aside. He took another step toward the cringing farm girl—and that was as far as he got.

He was completely unprepared for the two rough-looking Poles who banged open the door and jumped out from the conference room with weapons cackling. A burst of submachine-gun bullets ripped open his abdomen. He staggered back, containing his ruptured belly with one hand. He looked disbelieving.

Jurawski leaped into the middle of the room like a big cat and fired a burst from his Sten at the second German, wounding him but not stopping him before he slammed out the front door. Jurawski shoved Günter out of the way and chased the other SS. The three women and the other partisans sprang upon the wounded man like fierce dogs and brought him to the floor, where they finished him off with fists, nails, teeth and kitchen knives.

Outside, the other SS pulled out a hand grenade as he fled and threw it at the house, causing Jurawski to dive facedown off the porch. The German jumped into the car, whose driver had kept the engine running. The car roared off down the drive, bouncing in the ruts as it picked up speed, and skidded out onto the main road.

Racing from around the house, James heard the grenade bang, saw its flash and then heard the staff car speeding away. It was out of range and moving fast in the concealing darkness by the time he reached the porch. Smoke from the grenade bit his nostrils. He slammed his fist against his thigh.

"Damn!"

They'd be back. With reinforcements.

8

Fighters erupted from the basement. They stopped to take a look at the dead German on the floor in front of the fireplace, where the fire had turned to hot coals and the kettle of potato-and-beet soup was still bubbling. Jurawski nudged the body with one toe of his worn farmer's brogans, the movement causing the dead man's ruptured intestines to balloon out of the bullet holes in his belly. The younger women fled from the disgusting stench and could be heard outside retching on the grass. The older woman spat on the corpse and uttered a curse in Polish.

James was in as much of a hurry as the Poles to depart the scene of the crime, as it were. There was much at stake that required his survival. Whereas the partisans had only their own lives to lose, James's death and the failure of his mission might well doom hundreds of thousands and result in the Allies losing the war.

Prodded by Jurawski's growling, partisans rushed frenetically about gathering food, weapons, an ancient two-way radio, clothing, bedding and whatever other gear was readily available as they prepared to abandon the farmhouse. Regina wrapped some bread crusts and boiled potatoes in a patchwork quilt, made a roll of the quilt, and slung it across her back from a belt. That and her Sten gun, and she was ready to go. She looked at James. He had his kit bag, MP-40, combat harness, and the Dodgers baseball cap pulled tight to cover his red hair. He nodded.

Jurawski took Regina's arm. Flaring, she jerked free. He yelled at her, whereupon she delivered another tongue-lashing, which might well have peeled the skin off his face. James understood none of it, since it was in Polish, but body language told him the big leader was about to suffer a knockout. He fell silent, his lips thin and compressed, and turned a drilling look on James. James smelled potato-and-beet breath turned rancid.

"This old boy's swelled up like a dead toad," James said to Regina in German in order to exclude Jurawski from the conversation. "Maybe I should know what's going on?"

"He and his men have become a liability," Regina replied, also in German. "The Germans will give him no quarter. You and I shall go alone from here."

"Whew! No wonder he's sucking hind tit. Does he know why I'm here?"

"He knows nothing except what I tell him—and I have told him nothing."

The exchange infuriated Jurawski. "You are not in using that brutish tongue in mine own face!" he shouted in his quaint English.

Regina and he argued again in Polish. She recoiled when he tried to kiss her goodbye. That enraged him further. A jealous man was not easy to deal with. Jurawski glowered at James and thrust out his thick jaw, as though daring James to take a swing.

"It is being better that nothing is happen to my woman," he warned James. "I am in permanently kill you if hurt is coming to her."

"Permanently is the surest way," James agreed.

Jurawski finally left after hurling more threats. He and his men, along with the three farm women, hurried off toward the forested hills, where the main body of partisans had gone that afternoon. Lugging his kit bag, James trailed Regina away from the farmhouse and across the corn-stubbled field. He felt considerable disgust in having to depend on total strangers. Behind enemy lines, he had learned through experience, you trusted people at face value at your own peril. How much faith did he dare place in this girl who *said* she was Professor Jahne's niece?

Besides, how were one man and a slip-ass Jew girl going to thwart the ring of gestapo that presumably guarded the scientist, and then get him out of town in time to catch the Carpetbagger flight tomorrow night from a pasture north of Grudwald?

It was full dark and there would not be a moon until later. Regina paused once, out of consideration for James's permanent limp. His knee joint sometimes became stiff with exercise.

"It's an old injury," he reassured her.

He buried his radio and kit bag underneath a boulder at some distance from the house, keeping out only those things he might need: extra ammunition, the pistol silencer, chocolate, a couple of packs of Lucky Strikes, a deck of ordinary-looking playing cards that caused Regina to lift a brow, but which he did not explain. He stuffed a fistful of *zloty* and dollars into his pocket. If things turned to shit, he could always return later and dig up the radio.

"Okay, Kit Carson. Where are we going?" he asked.

"To Grudwald."

"I take it you have a plan?"

"A girl always has a plan."

He stopped her. "Do you care to share it?"

She looked back in the direction of the deserted farmhouse. "I am charged with taking care of my uncle's domestic needs," she explained with a sigh. "Each day I walk with him to work at the old wool mill and I return to walk him home in the afternoon. Therefore, his guards recognize me. It would have been a simple matter for several of you to conceal yourselves in the old gasogene Citroen, drive by, dispose of the guards, and whisk my uncle away whether he wanted to go or not."

"The best-laid plans of mice and men . . . So, what's the plan now?"

"You're the professional. It's still the same scenario. The only thing that has changed is that we do not have a vehicle and there is only you and me."

"Minor details."

"I thought so. We had better keep moving. The Germans will be coming."

They were soon sweating, even though it was a cool night. They traversed fields, keeping to streambeds and fence lines for cover, and passed close to several farmhouses whose lights were extinguished. A dog yapped, but they kept moving, stopping only long enough to drink from streams, and then climbing a low range of forested hills and crossing some roads.

Once they had to dive into a bed of gorse when three Kraut trucks loaded with troops sped past with blackout cat's-eye lights that could not be seen until the last moment, and only from the right angle. They were headed in the direction of the partisan safe house. In France, James had witnessed how the Germans operated against the underground in much the same way Amish farmers back in Oklahoma hunted coyotes, generally with great success. They began by surrounding a suspected site from miles out, then slowly closed the noose while shooting anything that tried to escape.

The little town of Grudwald lay in a bowl with low ridges of hills on three sides that protected it against winter winds. The Vistula River glimmered faintly as it twisted by beyond the town on the fourth side. James and

Regina halted when they reached the top of the hills and looked down into the shallow valley. Enveloping night all but hid the town. There were no lights shining from windows to delineate boundaries. From off in the distance, in the direction of Warsaw, came the faint thunder of dueling artillery.

"It has been going on for weeks now," Regina said. "The Germans and the Russians shell each other every night. Soon the Russians will be strong enough to resume their offensive."

They sat on the ground side by side and looked down into the darkness where the town was. They shared a C-ration chocolate bar. James craved a cigarette, but he couldn't take the chance of lighting one.

"When daylight comes," Regina said, "we can see from here where my uncle and I live and where we go to work at the laboratory in the old wool mill. I can show you, and then I must go quickly to walk Uncle Erwein to work before I am missed. James, we have to get him free before another night. We must!"

"Yes," James agreed.

She could get him to her uncle. Getting her uncle away from the gestapo and out of Grudwald to the aircraft pickup site by tomorrow night—well, that was where James came in.

James thought of entering Grudwald under cover of night and seizing the professor from the house he shared with Regina. Impossible. Far too risky, Regina cautioned. Germans were big on curfews. At night, partly because of the Russian threat, *Wehrmacht* patrolled the streets and surrounding countryside heavily and set up numerous checkpoints, stopping anyone who moved and shooting those who did not stop. A garrison east of town quartered nearly a division-sized element of *Wehrmacht,* SS, and combat support, sufficient troops to both secure the town and carry out operations against the Russians and any partisans who became a nuisance.

No, Regina said, the best chance for success was after

dawn, when civilians were allowed to move about more freely.

"My uncle is a good and decent man, James," she said, sounding sad and a little wistful. "It is just that, like many Germans, he is fooled by Hitler."

"You would think a Jew would have lost all illusions by now."

"Jew or not, my uncle is still a German. Loyalty dies hard in a man like Professor Jahne. Still, he realizes the horror and enormity of what he is asked to do in building a superweapon. He talks to me sometimes. He is very conflicted. No matter who builds the weapon first, he believes there will be a constant struggle in the rest of the world as other nations plot to get it too and unleash the threat of its power. If it exists, it will be deployed. There has never been a weapon invented, no matter how terrible, that has not been used. This one, my uncle says, could ignite the end of civilization."

"Yet, he is willing to build it for the Nazis."

"And you would have him build it for the Allies. If both sides have the weapon, what then?"

That was not for James to say. His mission was to bring Professor Jahne out. He also happened to believe in the moral superiority of the Allies' cause, *his* cause.

"We must convince my uncle," Regina said, "that he has been living a lie in Germany—and ultimately a fatal lie for the Jews."

"You convince him," James said. "But wait until after we are free of Poland. He mustn't know what is happening until we are on our way out."

"I have deceived him. I tell myself it is for his own good."

She fell silent, shivering from some inner chill. James looked back and nudged her. They both turned to watch the glow of a fire on the horizon. Flames licked at the black sky as the farmhouse went up like dried kindling. The Germans had arrived.

The blaze died down after a while. They ate some of

the bread and potatoes. Regina spread her blanket over the two of them and they dozed together in the deeper shadows beneath trees. The indistinct and distant sputtering of Stens and Bren guns from forests several miles to the southwest of Grudwald woke them. The moon was up and bright on the town and on the land. The peculiar belching of German Schmeissers and the jackhammer drill of MG-42 machine guns rose in volume to overpower the lesser weapons possessed by the partisans. Regina turned her back to the battle and hunched down into her shoulders.

"They are killing Jurawski," she said through dry tears.

9

There was one hell of a fight going on over there. It sounded as though Jurawski's men were giving a good account of themselves in spite of being outgunned and outnumbered. Rifles and automatic weapons bickered with each other, their muzzle flashes pecking the night. Volleys of rockets streaked across the darkness, resembling lethal supersonic fireflies. Illumination flares burst over the forest like miniature suns. James thought of the Normandy Invasion and how, from the cliffs above, he had watched soldiers of the American 29th being slaughtered on the sand below.

That had been the last day he saw Gabrielle.

Gabrielle had taught him something about himself—how it was in nearness to another being that one asserted his own humanness and struggled against aloneness when death lurked constantly in the next shadow. He also learned from her that hard lesson that man in war was truly an island and must not attach himself to any other island. Nonetheless, he still wondered sometimes how, if he ever found Gabrielle, she might fit into his ordinary, settled, postwar life. After all, he *had* promised to come back for her.

Gramps always said a man was judged by the promises he kept, that a man was not a man unless he lived up to his obligations.

Regina hunkered wordlessly down inside herself with her back toward the fighting and refused to look. Concealed with her inside a grove of pale-skinned larch, James sat with the MP-40 across his knees. After a while, she stirred and moved close again, their hips, thighs, and shoulders touching. She tucked the patchwork quilt tighter around them. Her need was plain. At such times nothing satisfied except physical human contact, transient and impermanent though it might be.

She went back to staring at the town in the valley below. James felt her flinch sometimes, when the savage noise of the distant fight rose in volume.

"Tell me about America," she requested in a voice far off, as if from the end of a tunnel where she was trying to distance herself from the present.

He hesitated a moment. "You mean, is it a land of milk and honey—or is King Kong still hanging from the Empire State Building?"

"Can it not be both?"

"Both, and many more besides. Depending on where you live."

"What is it for you, James. Where do you live?"

"Where *did* I live? Have you heard of Okies?"

"*Okies?*"

"Oklahoma."

"Of course!" she exclaimed. "Indians and cowboys. Which are you, James? Tell me about it so that we do not have to be here."

Sounded like a good idea. He didn't want to be here either.

"We lived so far back in the sticks that the sun set between our house and town and the hoot owls mixed with the chickens," he began in a low tone. She seemed to relax a little as he talked.

He told her about Gramps and Grams and the farm on Drake's Prairie beneath Wild Horse Mountain and not far from the Arkansas River. He told her about the one-room school at McKey, where each grade from first to eighth occupied a row of seats. Eighth grade had the last row of seats, next to the door leading out into the world. He told her stories of one-eyed mules and cotton fields, of 'coon hunting in the river brakes, of good, honest redbone and black-and-tan hounds who never gave up on you. He told her of how his parents had died when a team of mules ran away with their wagon, of how Gramps drank water from a Mason jar in the field and the water ran down his chin and dripped onto the ploughed furrows, of the sound corn made in the summer breezes when it was turning brown and the ears were almost ripe. Talking, he grew homesick, and longing for the ordinary, settled life, he trailed off into silence.

"It sounds as though you had your place in the world," Regina said. "Are there Jews in Oklahoma?"

"I suppose so. I knew a Jewish family when I was a cop in Oklahoma City."

She shuddered. "You were a *policeman*! Like the gestapo!"

"There are no gestapo in America."

She digested that.

"You think I do not want a place in the world too?" she said, her bitterness creeping back in. "You think I do not want a real life too and not merely to survive? You think I am not as weary of this war as everyone else?"

He hadn't meant to set her off. Presently, she said in a softer tone, "Jurawski does not smell like roses, true. He is jealous and has all the refinement of a bear let loose in a tearoom. But there is more to Jurawski than what you see."

"A light hidden under a bushel."

"You do not understand. Let me tell you," she said.

"My father was Professor Erwein's brother. I say *was*. When Warsaw rose against the Germans, my brothers and sisters were snatched from our parents' arms and promptly shot while we watched. My mother was raped and beaten to death. I learned later that my father succumbed to pneumonia or some plague in the camps. A similar fate awaited me if it were not for Jurawski."

James thought that was as far as she was going. A lull fell over the battle in the forest; the partisans were finally being subdued. Regina went on hurriedly, as though to stave off thoughts about it.

"Some of us who fought in Warsaw, all Jews," she said, "were herded into a group of about a hundred or so and marched into the woods by SS with machine guns. We were going to be executed. But on the way . . ."

She paused, overcome with emotion.

"On the way," she tried again, "Jurawski came. I owe Jurawski my life."

James said nothing for a long while. Neither did she. Distant gunfire spattered into silence, permitting once again the rumble of the Warsaw artillery duel to come through. Regina listened to the quiet coming from the place of Jurawski's last stand. Her chin dropped to her chest; her voice sounded choked when she resumed.

"Uncle Erwein, who had survived Warsaw because of his government work, was taken to Grudwald," she said.

In Grudwald, she explained, a former wool mill on the river was turned into a research laboratory. Before the last Russian offensive, the Germans had hauled in uranium and carbon from which at least a ton of "heavy water" had been manufactured. Her Uncle Erwein was "this close—*this close*"—to a breakthrough. All he needed was a little more time.

"We have managed to stay alive and avoid transport because of Uncle Erwein's work. Because I am family, he secured me a position as his domestic where I have been very useful to Jurawski and his band. But now it is all about to end with the advance of the Russians. I have been told that an SS officer has been sent from Berlin to blow up the lab and decide my uncle's fate."

"Is your uncle competent to continue his research if the Allies do bring him out?" James asked.

"He is sad and he is old," Regina snapped, annoyed. "But he is not senile. Besides, he still has all his research papers."

"Maybe I should have asked if he is *willing* to continue his research for the Allies?"

"He is horrified by the A-bomb project he helped initiate. Still, it is better that America have it rather than the Soviets. If it must be used, none deserve more to be destroyed than the Nazis. I would detonate it myself over Berlin."

They withdrew from each other then, into individual emotional and mental islands. There was the quiet from the southwest to remind them that Jurawski and his men were likely finished; and there was the artillery near Warsaw to remind them that the Russians were coming. The situation fit an old Okie maxim that said if you mixed a quart of ice cream with a quart of dog shit, the result would taste more like dog shit than ice cream. James didn't see how he was ever going to make ice cream out of this mess.

He was cut off from the partisans who might have assisted him, who in fact had probably been destroyed or scattered; and except for a slip of a girl, he was alone in "Indian country," where he was surrounded and being chased by the enemy. In spite of it all, he must somehow sweep Professor Jahne out of Grudwald and through a few thousand Krauts to an empty field for pickup in less than twenty-four hours.

Perhaps things would look brighter when daylight came and he could get a good look at the playing field.

There were stars, but still no moon. In slumber, Regina looked more childlike than ever. Her small, sharp face turned mobile in sleep. Her head dropped against James's shoulder. He tucked the quilt around her, then hesitated before he draped his arm over her shoulders. She nuzzled against his chest.

Even though weary after so eventful a day—one that had started on an airfield in Italy and ended on a hilltop in German-occupied Poland—James was surprised to find he could not sleep. Ghouls of war took control every time he closed his eyes. His heart raced, thumping so hard inside his chest that he was sure it would wake Regina. Panicked recollections of war attacked his senses: the women in the farmhouse savagely finishing off the SS officer, who had staggered back holding his intestines in his hands; the hideous, otherworldly screaming of the dying at Normandy; the reposed face of the blond German kid he had killed face to face; all the other lives he had destroyed, whose faces he could see, one by one, floating mockingly in front of his eyes every time he closed them.

War was a zone of chaos between living and dying, between existence and nonexistence. Truly, no soul was the same after war as it had been before. James was suddenly afraid Grams and Gramps might not recognize him when he returned to the farm.

Finally, from sheer exhaustion as the night wore on, he tugged the baseball cap over his eyes and drifted in and out of sleep.

In the blacker darkness before dawn, he opened his eyes and thought he heard partisan guns quibbling with German guns. It was only the breeze picking up and rattling the tree branches.

Night purple was fading into the more transparent haze of arriving daybreak the next time he woke. He tipped the bill of his cap back and saw the town in a single, dark, bloated entity in which individual structures were still indistinguishable. Regina slept curled up in a ball, using his lap for a pillow. He covered her feet with the quilt.

He realized suddenly that he hadn't awakened on his

own, that some sound had penetrated his slumber. He looked around, alert, his nerve endings electrified. A broad trail he hadn't noticed before wound down off the top of the hill through the trees toward Grudwald.

He heard the noise again. Then he caught fleeting glimpses of shadows moving on the trail below. Someone was coming. A German patrol!

10

James clamped his palm over Regina's mouth to keep her from crying out when she woke. Her eyes popped open, startled. He turned her head toward the approaching Germans. After a moment her eyes focused and she nodded.

Silently, they eased back into the deeper shadows of the larches. Weapons charged and ready, they lay on their bellies side by side as the enemy patrol climbed toward them.

There had been a dewfall. The ground felt damp through their clothing. Dawn's band of light in the east profiled about a dozen spade-helmeted *Wehrmacht* as they labored on up the hill and halted for a breather in the small clearing directly in front of the larch grove.

The soldiers conversed in low tones, grumbling and complaining about having been tossed out of their bunks so early for what seemed to them another senseless patrol. They broke out canteens and drank. One or two plopped down on the grass while the others leaned on their rifles to rest.

James considered making a break for it while their guard was down. Trying to sneak away in the darkness through unknown forest with all its underbrush and dead-falls would be as noisy as trying to drive a Brahma bull through a crystal store, however. It might be best to come out shooting first to drive the Germans to ground. Either way, they couldn't stay where they were without being discovered.

That about covered the choices, either of which made about as much sense as watching a piss ant bale hay. They were likely to be cut down no matter what they did.

"Take off your clothes," Regina whispered into James's ear.

James did a double take. "I can think of a better place and time."

"Don't be a fool."

She was already undressing. She rolled quietly to one side to slip out of her linen shirt. She was shucking her baggy canvas trousers before James understood. It was a long shot, but it just might work with a little *chutzpah* on her part and a lot of balls on his. Besides, they may as well be naked and caught in the two-backed act than to be shot in their two backs trying to run away.

He ripped off his battle harness, shirt and Levis. Regina piled their discarded clothing on top of their weapons to conceal them. James was still wearing his baseball cap. She snatched it off his head and shoved it underneath the pile of clothing. Both nude, they rolled into the quilt, skin melding against skin, just as the Germans prepared to move on up with a flurry of curses and rattling of weapons.

"Pretend!" Regina urged.

"I'm no good at pretending."

He ran his hand down her back and cupped it over her round, hard little buttocks. He pulled her into him.

"I don't think I can get it up," he whispered.

"Who cares?" Sounding exasperated.

"*I* care. What will it do to my reputation?"

"I do not *believe* this!" she hissed. "Get on top of me."

"Spread your legs."

"You do have a way with words. Hurry!"

To his surprise, he was suddenly ready. She wrapped her bare legs around his waist and, to his even greater surprise, he slipped into her, deep. They lay there like that, frozen in the moment, while the Germans busted their way in among the larches. Maybe they would go on by without seeing anything.

Small chance. The soldier on point halted not more than a dozen feet away, listening and peering about suspiciously. It was still almost dark in the trees—but they had undoubtedly been discovered.

Regina went into her act—moaning and emitting little kitten cries of make-believe passion. James began panting with her, working hard, and she was cooperating with him, helping him. It was an Oscar-winning performance if ever there was one, actors losing themselves in their characters and forgetting all about the eye of the camera.

A flashlight beam darted. A harsh voice demanded, "*Was ist das?*"

As though startled, compromised, Regina screamed and shoved James off, much harder than necessary. She jumped to her feet, taking the quilt with her to cover her nakedness. That left James clad only in gooseflesh standing in the blinding beams of flashlights—a wiry, freckled little man with clipped orange hair and a pug nose who looked about as threatening as a molting bantam rooster. One of the soldiers sniggered.

It was hard to maintain dignity in a situation like this, but James gave it his best shot, rising to the occasion as readily as he previously had underneath the quilt, if in a different manner.

"*Was wünschen Sie?*" he demanded, taking the offensive. "*Wer ist es?*"

That caught the soldiers off guard and placed them on the defensive.

"What are you doing here?" the patrol leader demanded

in German—but cautiously, taken aback by the audacity of the little red-headed man.

"What does it look like?" James shot back in his perfect German. "You fools! Have you forgotten what it is?" *Don't push it, James. You're the one standing here bare-ass naked.*

Light beams played up and down James's lean frame. Other lights flickered across the pile of clothing lying on the ground before lewdly caressing Regina's body. She drew the quilt tight to reveal her curves, and judiciously left a lot of cleavage showing. She hung her head demurely, as though embarrassed at having been caught.

"There is a curfew," the patrol leader admonished. James could not see him because of the bright light in his face.

"Avert your torches," James barked, not allowing the Germans to take the initiative.

The lights pooled on the ground in front of him, but others remained, fondling Regina.

"The curfew . . ." the patrol leader insisted. From reflected and silhouetting light, James saw he was rather tall and built square, like a blockhouse.

"Identify yourself," James commanded.

"I am Sergeant Wedekind. I must report this infraction to my superiors. Sir, what is your name?" He sounded uncertain.

"I would have it no other way but that you do your duty," James said, emboldened in the knowledge that he was dealing with an NCO, a *feldwebel,* and not an officer. It was in the German character to submit to authority. "Tell your commander that you have interrupted *Sturmbannführer* Gerhard Hoffman in the process of doing his duty." Senior gestapo men held SS ranks more prestigious than ordinary police or army ranks, an implication James hoped to convey.

He glanced from the corner of his eye at the pile of clothing, trying to determine if he had a chance of reaching a weapon to go down fighting if *Feldwebel* Wedekind refused to buy the story. There was a long pause before fresh respect entered the interrogation.

"*Heil Hitler!*" *Feldwebel* Wedekind said, snapping off a crisp salute.

"*Heil Hitler!*" James responded, returning a casual half salute as befitted his rank. How ridiculous he must look buck naked, paying tribute to the Führer, Germany's version of Charlie Chaplin.

The sergeant shifted his weight uncomfortably. He turned to Regina. "*Was ist ihr name?*"

"She speaks no German," James interceded quickly. "She is Polish and you know how the Poles are. They barely speak their own crude language."

He felt Regina glaring at him from beneath lowered eyelashes. *Feldwebel* Wedekind's flashlight spotlighted her face. "She looks familiar. I have seen her before."

"Highly likely. She is from the town. I must admit she is not overly attractive," James said man-to-man, drawing the sergeant into his confidence. "Nonetheless, there are things a loyal German must do for his country and his Führer. She knows the names and locations of criminals and partisans, which information I was in the process of extracting when you interrupted. May I suggest, *Feldwebel*, that you promptly continue your mission and leave me to mine? I will report that *Feldwebel* Wedekind is diligent and competent in exercising his duties."

"*Danke, Sturmbannführer.*"

The sergeant still hesitated, as if unsure that everything was really on the up and up. Here he had caught this man and woman in the act of violating curfew, if nothing else, and instead of being contrite and accommodating, this little fellow, as naked as the day he was born, had taken over. But then, the gestapo were an arrogant bunch. No wonder they were so thoroughly disliked by nearly everyone.

"*Sturmbannführer*, surely you know these woods are full of criminals and partisans," the sergeant said. "She may be seducing you into a trap. Is there not a bed for you somewhere in the town?"

"Have you no romance, Sergeant? These simple-minded Polish girls *like* to be under the stars. They are such animals. Most of them do not even wear underpants. Did you know that, Wedekind?"

He felt Regina doing a slow burn. He was enjoying this in a puckish way. Might as well get the most of it since he had to see it through anyhow.

Feldwebel Wedekind looked at Regina in a way that suggested he might be imagining her without underpants. The other soldiers, elbowing each other and giggling, had barely taken their eyes off her.

"We have been fighting the criminals in the forest to the southwest," Sergeant Wedekind said finally. "It is not safe to be outside the town."

"I will remember that. I am almost through with her anyhow."

Sergeant Wedekind nodded in understanding. "Then, sir, I shall leave you to your . . . duties."

"And I you to yours, *Feldwebel* Wedekind."

It was light enough by now that James watched the patrol drift into the trees like ghosts. The sergeant turned once in afterthought and snapped up a palm. "*Heil Hitler!*"

"*Heil Hitler!*" But under his breath, James murmured, "Heil all hell to Hitler."

Regina released a long sigh of relief mixed with disbelief. "You cocky . . ." she finally sputtered. "'Animals,' are we? 'Not overly attractive'? I thought you said you could not pretend."

James looked her up and down. He grinned innocently. "Where were we when we were interrupted?"

"Wherever we were, you are now nowhere. Get your clothes on."

"I was thinking—"

"Pretend," she said, quickly dressing. She was giggling with excitement that they had pulled it off.

11

James and Regina quickly ate the rest of the bread and potatoes for breakfast before beating a hasty path down-hill toward the town and away from their close encounter with the patrol. Both had decided that since the snatch had to take place this morning in Grudwald, they should start out right away and get prepared. All the best plans followed the KISS principle: *Keep It Simple Stupid*. James thought of it as taking the dog shit out of the ice cream. Things *were* starting to look brighter in the daylight; it might be doable even without partisan assistance.

The forest ended at the edge of town near a railroad sidetrack and a trestle spanning a stream. A line of battered transport cars was strung out on the track, but it didn't appear to be hooked to a locomotive. Some wag had scrawled in large red letters, in German, on the side of one of the cars: WE ARE OFF TO POLAND TO THRASH THE JEWS.

It was dark underneath the narrow bridge, but to the east the sky was opening and starting to paint the Polish countryside in a spectrum of yellow and gold. James hunkered down with Regina in the shadows beneath the trestle, out of sight from any but the most inquisitive of the guards walking sentry on the train cars.

"It is waiting to transport the rest of the Grudwald Jews," Regina said.

James's mind was on business, working on a plan. He felt good this morning, solid, as he generally did once the game started. Any residue of nerves from their run-in with the patrol had dissipated.

"How many Krauts escort your uncle and you to work?" he whispered.

"Normally, two."

"Your uncle *is* going to work this morning?"

"I will make sure of it."

"I'll be waiting somewhere along the route." KISS. Snatch the old man, disappear with him, hide out until nightfall and the extraction.

She looked at him. "You will never get past the check-points. You are too young and—"

"Good-looking?"

"I was thinking *brash*. They will think you should be in a labor camp—which is exactly where you will end up, without getting anywhere near my uncle. Or you'll be shot."

"Will you miss me after all we've been to each other?"

"No."

He pondered. "I'll need a disguise. You can move about town freely, right? Get me an old overcoat, a hat, a walking cane, and some flour. The rattier the clothes, the better."

"Jews have nothing left but rags. You'll have to wait here."

"Too risky. It's about to get light."

"Follow me—but get rid of that damned baseball cap." As if the Dodgers cap would give them away, when they were already walking around armed like a couple of Poncho Villa bandits.

Nonetheless, James shrugged and wadded the cap into a washout in the bank of the little stream. She nodded approval and led the way cautiously along a faint walking trail that twisted away from the trestle through a willow brake. On higher ground, they broke free of the willows into an even thicker grove of poplar. She had plainly used this route before in getting in and out of town past guards and checkpoints. She stopped and knelt within sight of a street with a few houses lining its opposite side.

James looked back through the trees and down upon the twin ribbons of the railroad track gleaming in the morning light and the long line of dark transport cars. A helmeted sentry carrying a Mauser lit a cigarette and gazed pensively off in the direction of the Fatherland. James recalled similar postures in homesick GIs.

Regina handed James her Sten. "Wait here."

Those eyes of hers, as hard and dark as anthracite, raked over the silent hills where Jurawski had presumably made his last stand. Jews had no home, she had said, and she had no one left except her uncle. She didn't even have Jurawski anymore.

After checking the street to make sure no one was watching, she stepped casually from cover and walked away without looking back, swinging her arms and her hips. From his hiding place in the bushes, James watched as she turned and ambled onto a narrow side street lined with ochre-colored houses with slate roofs. There had been fighting even in this small town, as throughout most of Hitler's Europe. All that was left of some houses were jagged walls of stone sticking up like dragon's teeth.

She disappeared. Her being out of sight made James uncomfortable. It meant he had to trust her; a man in his position learned to trust no one. He was also dealing with his guilt over what had *started* to happen between them this morning—even while Gabrielle was languishing somewhere in a concentration camp in Germany or Poland. He would deal with that, however, in the same way he intended to deal with an entire range of issues spawned by the war: *later.*

She wasn't gone long enough to give his anxiety a good feed. She had changed clothing and freshened up, which meant she must have gone home to see Uncle Erwein. A black peasant's skirt swirled full around her ankles, and she wore a tan short-sleeved blouse bunched at the shoulders. Her black hair, freshly combed, shone in the morning sunshine. A plain blue barrette held it back on one side. On her blouse was sewn a crude yellow Star of David. German law required all Jews wear them so they could be readily identified. Failure to do so could lead to execution on the spot.

She carried a bundle underneath her arm. She stopped as though to remove a pebble from her shoe, but what she was really doing was making sure no one was watching. Satisfied, she slipped into the bushes where James waited. He looked her over appreciatively.

"You clean up real good," he complimented her.

She tossed him the bundle. "I am afraid you will not do so well."

The package contained a battered fedora, a tattered black overcoat fashionable along about 1925 and a small pack of flour tied with a string. The overcoat also bore a yellow star. Regina smiled wryly and quoted:

> *If you want to be in movies,*
> *You don't have to travel far.*
> *We Jews are like Hollywood;*
> *All here have a star.*

"Now, get in disguise," she added. "Uncle Erwein will soon be ready to go. I told his guard I was coming out for bagels. Good thing they didn't see me sneaking in a back window. The job has been too easy for them."

"Let's see if we can add a few complications."

He quickly transformed himself into a wizened old

man with the ragged overcoat, slouch hat, and some flour skillfully worked into his red hair and two-day-old whiskers to turn them gray. Only close inspection would betray him; he didn't intend letting anyone get that close. His natural limp and the way he hunched his back and shuffled along added miracles to the disguise. Regina clapped her hands silently in approval.

"You are simply full of pretend," she exclaimed.

"What I might be full of my Gramps didn't call 'pretend.'"

Regina had been unable to acquire a walking cane. James selected a staff from among the deadwood and rubbed it thoroughly to make it look worn. That done, he took out what appeared to be the plain deck of used playing cards saved from his buried kit bag. Peeling off their backs, he arranged them in a pattern on the ground to display a street map of Grudwald and the surrounding countryside. James had previously memorized grid coordinates for tonight's aircraft pickup, but saw no need to let Regina in on where it would be.

They hovered over the map on their knees while Regina traced the route Professor Jahne, she, and their gestapo escort would take from his home prison to the laboratory in the old wool mill. She suggested an ambush site along a street that had been heavily damaged during fighting between Germans and Polish partisans following Warsaw. Few residents remained in that sector of town. Nonetheless, she warned, the ambush would have to be conducted swiftly, violently, and, most of all, silently.

James stood up, and without a word took the noise suppressor from his pocket and screwed it onto the muzzle of his .45 Colt.

"Will your uncle resist?" he asked.

She looked at the silenced pistol. "You take care of the guards. I will take care of my uncle."

12

The town lay silent this early in the morning. Most of the houses were shuttered. Even the dueling cannon off in the direction of Warsaw were quiet. A few Poles—older men mostly, along with some women and a few children too young for labor conscription—were out and about, on their way to work at the shops downtown.

Most of the remaining Jews in Grudwald, as Regina had discovered only this morning on her sojourn, were to be rounded up and driven to a fenced compound down near the railroad tracks to await transport. The elderly and infirm, as James pretended to be, and special cases such as Regina and her uncle would be the last arrested.

James gave Regina a few minutes' head start before, hearing or seeing nothing to indicate their ruse had been discovered, he also ventured into the town. Hunched over in the overcoat so big on his frame that it easily concealed his battle harness, MP-40, and Regina's Sten, he leaned heavily on his walking staff as he proceeded toward the selected ambush site in his crippled old-man's gait, tap-tapping cautiously with the stick to suggest near blindness.

Twice, he made his way past German checkpoints. To be spotted attempting to avoid them would be more suspicious than bluffing his way through. *Wehrmacht* stared long and hard at him as he tottered by, but they apparently considered him harmless. Near one checkpoint, a convoy of loaded trucks appeared to be ready to pull out and evacuate the town should the Russians push through at Warsaw. A soldier whose team had sandbagged in a machine gun at the intersection was more wary than the others had been.

"Warten Sie bitte!"

James's heart hammered. It was all over if he were to be discovered now. About the most he could hope to accomplish was to take a few of them with him.

He paused and peered blindly about, as though unable to locate the source of the unexpected annoyance. Then, tapping his staff, ignoring the soldier's brisk approach, he resumed his laborious journey. A crazy, deaf, nearly blind old Jew wearing a yellow star. The soldier was closing in on him and James's muscles were beginning to bunch up, when one of the other *Wehrmacht* called out, "Watch him, Otto. He might gum you to death."

The others laughed and hooted.

"Leave the old *Jude* crawling," someone else suggested. "He will be dealt with soon enough, I wager, pests and lice that they are."

James slowly continued. He turned a corner and was out of their sight before he allowed himself to breath normally.

Soon enough, relying on Regina's direction and his memory of the playing-cards map, he reached the abandoned part of town through which Regina, the professor and their gestapo guard must pass on their way to the laboratory. Walls and parts of chimneys stuck up out of encroaching weed beds, stark monuments to an age of violence brought out in high contrast by the rising red sun.

He crawled into the ruins of a little cottage on the street and found a hiding spot where he would have quick and easy access to the professor and his guards when they passed. He placed the silenced .45 near at hand but kept the two long guns concealed beneath his overcoat. By tomorrow morning at this time, he thought, he should be back in Italy having breakfast, a hot cup of java and a Lucky Strike.

Now all he had to do was wait.

He thought he heard sounds, perhaps even the crunch of a footfall, coming from another ruin farther up the street. Ducking low, he scrutinized the entire area sector by sector as a trained soldier does. Spotting nothing untoward or out of place, he ordered himself to relax and prepare for action.

He was almost certain it was a footfall the second time he heard it. He squinted against the sunrise, .45 in hand. A lanky, half-starved yellow dog slunk out of the ruin and trotted off up the street. It had big feet and one crippled leg. It stopped at the corner and looked back. Then it tucked in its tail and disappeared.

It must have been the dog making all the noise as he scratched around in the rubble hunting for rats. Nonetheless, James couldn't shake the uneasy feeling that he was not alone on this deserted street. *Damn his nerves.*

Regina, in her tan blouse and black peasant's skirt, looked almost frail in contrast to her uncle and the two burly gestapo agents wearing trench coats. The gestapo led the way along the street, marching side by side a few paces ahead of uncle and niece. It was a cool, pleasant morning, and they were chatting each other up and giggling like a couple of German *frauleins* on their way to work at a factory. Their machine pistols were slung over their shoulders. They couldn't have made it any easier for the American agent who lay in wait for them.

The stocky old man at Regina's side plodded along

with pronounced dignity despite the yellow star branded on his long walking coat. He appeared the perfect example of the self-absorbed academic, with his mop of white hair, full silver beard and bright, inquisitive eyes almost as dark as Regina's. A thin nose with nostrils slightly flaring lent him the appearance of an aged raptor. He swung his legs out at the knees, his long coat flaring open with each step to reveal a white shirt with tie and dark slacks worn shiny with use.

They reached the ruin in which the yellow dog had been hunting. James gripped his .45 and supported it with his other hand, aiming at the gestapo on the right. This man had a pencil-line mustache.

James took up trigger slack.

An instant before the sear broke to drop the hammer, a pair of men armed with Russian submachine guns sprang out of hiding and directly into the path of the oncoming gestapo. Barely had the Germans expressed surprise and shock when muzzle flames spewed from the attackers' weapons and mowed them down in their tracks. Blood splashed. The chattering of the weapons reverberated through the town as Regina shoved her uncle to the street and flung herself on top of him to shield him with her own body. James's first concern was that the noise would bring every Kraut in town running. His second concern was for the professor and his niece.

The bushwhackers rushed toward Professor Jahne and Regina, jumping over the twitching corpses of the fallen Germans. Their intentions were clear. Russia also wanted the A-bomb—and this was the scientist who knew how to build it. James couldn't let them have him.

13

There was no longer any need for stealth. James flung off his long coat and at the same time holstered the less-efficient pistol. He charged into the street like a madman, Sten still slung to his combat harness, finger on the trigger of the MP-40. It was his turn at surprise.

The Russians hardly knew what hit them. James sprayed both with a lethal burst of fire from the automatic rifle even as their befuddled brains registered the threat and they spun about to meet it. The first man dropped hard to the street, spurting blood from a wound in his neck. He writhed in fear and pain, his eyes staring in horror at the wiry demon bounding toward him.

A bullet from the MP-40 finished him off.

Although down and wounded, the second man remained in the fight. He rolled to one side and brought his weapon up. James whirled just in time to see Regina pounce on the Russian, deflecting the shot meant for him. That was the man's last chance. In two long strides, James was by Regina's side. He grabbed her by the arm with one hand and flung her aside while with the other he swung the MP-40 and blasted a hole in the Russian's face.

Both were done for, their torn remains sprawled in the street with those of the Germans. Their blood mixed in the gutter.

The Russians had Slavic features. One of them wore a fur cap with a red star on it.

James knelt next to Regina where he had thrown her off her feet. "Thanks," he said. "You saved my humming-bird ass."

Frozen in place from shock, Regina looked pale, her eyes wide and staring and horrified. She wasn't as hard-boiled as she sometimes liked to pretend. Her uncle still lay huddled on the street, with his head buried beneath his arms.

"What happened?" she stammered. "Who are these men?"

"Get the old fellow on his feet," James rasped.

Regina snapped herself out of her shock. Together, they pulled the professor to his feet. He was trembling and his legs were unsteady.

"Professor Jahne! I've come to rescue you," James said in German.

Jahne looked at him from hollow, frightened eyes. "Rescue? You're from the Führer?"

"Yes!" Regina interrupted. "From the Führer." She cast a meaningful look at James that told him to keep his mouth shut and play along.

"Who . . . are they?" the scientist muttered, overwhelmed by the unexpected violence. "What is going on?"

"We have to go, Uncle," Regina urged, not looking at the mess of the four dead men in the street.

"Where? Am I being summoned to return to Stras-bourg?"

"Uncle—"

"There's no time for explanations," James barked. His eyes darted. So far, the street had remained vacant. "This town's not big enough for all of us."

He and Regina half-dragged the dazed old man toward the nearest side street, which led deeper into the town's demolished zone. Somewhere not far away the wailing up-and-down blare of a klaxon siren sounded, spurring them on.

It was slow going at best. The old man proved to be not nearly as strong as he looked. He seemed disoriented, uncertain, as he might well be after such a brutal experience.

James directed the way through the ruined and abandoned streets to an occupied neighborhood of rundown cottages and rooms for let near the outskirts. He felt unseen eyes staring out at them from behind shuttered windows, but no one came out to offer assistance or to block their way. Regina and her uncle still wore yellow stars; what happened between the occupiers and the Jews was their business.

Klaxon sirens trailed off as the authorities arrived at the scene of the carnage. Roaring engines announced the passage of large military vehicles, each doubtlessly packed with troops and security personnel. Shouts and whistles accented the growing bedlam. Once the Germans determined what might have happened, it wouldn't take them long to seal off the town and organize a block-by-block search. James calculated he had at most a half to three quarters of an hour to get Dr. Jahne and Regina out of Grudwald.

"Where are we going?" Dr. Jahne protested. "I cannot leave without my research papers."

Regina hurried him along. "Can you not hear, Uncle Erwein? There is no time."

"We can explain to them what happened," the professor protested.

"They are not our people," she lied. "The Russians are taking the town."

"That is all the more reason why I must return to my laboratory. The Russians must not be allowed the fruit of German research. Do either of you understand?"

They were hurrying across the narrow yard of a vacant house to an empty back street when Dr. Jahne's resistance turned to outright rebellion. He jerked away and took off in a shambling gait in the direction of his laboratory. *The damned old fool.* James easily overtook him, whereupon the old man plopped down on his butt in the middle of the street. He folded his arms stubbornly across his chest and thrust out his white-bearded chin. No amount of coaxing or threats could get him back on his feet. Tears pooled in Regina's eyes as she begged him to get up and cooperate.

"I cannot leave my papers to barbarians," he insisted.

The scientist weighed nearly two hundred pounds, far too much weight to be thrown over a shoulder and carried very far. James tried to control his frustration and anger. Time was running out. Closer now came the howl of pursuers as the Germans spread out to search for the missing scientist and whoever may have kidnapped him.

Kneeling, James locked his eyes onto the old man's. "A word to the wise is not necessary," he said. "It's the stupid who need advice. Get up."

"No."

"Please, Uncle? Don't be difficult," Regina pleaded.

"No."

James lurched to his feet in frustration, swiping the fedora off his head and slamming it on the ground. He wheeled in a circle, clutching his head. "Damn you!" he raged. "Damn both of you!"

He charged back, trembling with fierce impatience, and jabbed the barrel of his MP-40 in the direction of the railroad tracks on the other side of town.

"You crazy old sonofabitch!" he shouted beneath his breath. "Don't *you* understand? There's a train down there. You're a Jew. That's the only thing the Krauts care about. You are going to be on that train when it leaves— and you won't be coming back to Strasbourg or anywhere else. Now get off your ass and on your feet."

Searchers were shouting to each other only a few blocks away. Clearly, the old man was having difficulty comprehending what was going on. His eyes darted uncertainly toward the sounds of pursuit, then back to his niece and the old-young man with the graying-red hair and weapons slung all over his body.

James switched to English and turned on Regina. "You said you would take care of him," he snapped. "The old fool's a Nazi sympathizer."

"He is a Jew, James, and a German. He is confused."

"Regina, talk to him. Make it quick."

On her knees, she clasped her uncle's bearded face between her small hands. Earnestly, hurriedly, she explained how he *had* to get up and go. He dug in. Whether out of sheer cussedness or from stress and confusion, he refused to budge. Defeated, Regina looked up at James. Her hair had fallen loose and the blue barrette was hanging on for dear life.

James got down in the old man's face and blistered him in German. "Listen, will you? They are coming to toast your sorry old ass."

Dr. Jahne turned his head away, unconvinced. Regina tried to reason with him some more. As for James, Uncle Henry had given him a second option: The scientist must either be brought out or . . . No matter what, he must not be allowed to stay with the Germans or to fall into Russian hands. OSS training taught that an agent must sometimes do abominable things for the good of the war effort. Wild Bill Donovan once explained that the only way America could defeat the Germans was to "play a bush-league game, stealing the ball and killing the umpire." What he meant was that mission came first, above all else. No matter what it took. Above any individual's life, including one's own.

The old man meant shit to James. His mission was accomplished if he shot the old bastard right now. He would be on that lift and out of here tonight, with or without Dr. Jahne and his niece.

He drew the .45 from its holster, stepped forward, pressed the silenced muzzle against Doctor Jahne's forehead and cocked the hammer. He wasn't bluffing. Regina's eyes widened in disbelief.

"On your feet," James ordered in the cold, flat voice that accompanied his emotional disassociation from what must be done.

"*What are you doing?*" Regina screeched.

She deflected the .45 and threw herself between the two men. James swung the pistol back and pointed it at her head. She glared past the gaping muzzle defiantly, daring him, her straight black brow scowling over her dark eyes. There was no longer anything childish about her ruthless face.

"Are you like the Russians and Germans—with orders to kill him if nothing else?" she challenged in English. "Kill me then also."

He had already reckoned on that. He continued to aim the gun. Regina's eyes gazed directly back at him up the Colt's barrel. They were calm now, resigned, almost as though she felt relieved that the pain and sorrow of the war years would soon be over.

James hesitated. He was afraid she would see his hand shaking.

Regina said, "James, he is getting old and forgetful. Without his research notes, he is of much less value to the Allies. Those papers are his life's work. We must retrieve them from the laboratory."

James narrowed his eyes. *Damn it.* They would be lucky enough to get out of town alive, much less to the laboratory and then out of town.

Regina said, "There will be no bomb without his research papers. Which is more important? To complete your mission to the letter—or to accomplish the larger goal?"

The .45 remained pointed.

"James, the Germans do not yet understand what has happened. They are running around not knowing exactly what they are looking for. The laboratory is only twenty minutes away, and it is that way." She pointed. "That is the fastest way out of town, plus they will never think to look for us at the lab. We can be there and gone before they know."

James thought of the Irving Berlin recording *They Were All out of Step but Jim*. But what she said did make sense. Maybe *he* needed to get in step.

"My uncle will cooperate and go willingly if we get his papers first," she promised.

James took a deep breath. "What's to keep him from betraying us?"

"You can still shoot us then."

He lowered the gun. "I have got to see a shrink to get my head examined if we ever get out of this."

"I will go with you."

14

Common sense told James to take what he had and run with it, even if he had to drag the old man or kill him. Yet, Uncle Henry had stressed how vital it was for the Allies to build the A-bomb while depriving Hitler of it. That meant Professor Jahne and his papers were a single package.

Although reason said the professor's lab would be the last place the Germans would look for fugitives, it didn't make James feel much better. First of all, he didn't trust the elderly scientist not to give him away at the first opportunity. It confounded him how a Jew could have been deported because of his race, gone through the Warsaw uprising, witnessed subsequent mass executions, and still retain even the slightest allegiance to his persecutors. But, as Gramps sometimes said, the more you beat and abused some dogs, the more they submitted to the boot that kicked them.

Also, Regina's loyalty was to her uncle. That made James odd man out in the event he got his nuts caught in another crack.

Nonetheless, against his better judgment, he set out at a fast pace with the Jahnes toward the Vistula River and the old wool mill turned nuclear laboratory. Professor Jahne seemed more afraid of the American who came to rescue him than he did of the Germans pursuing them. Regina reclaimed her Sten. There was something incongruous about a peasant girl in blouse and skirt toting a submachine gun rather than a milk pail.

They kept to side streets and avoided areas where there might be activity. Most of the town's residents seemed to have gone to cover at the first indication of trouble. The artillery duel near Warsaw resumed, all combatants apparently having returned from breakfast and their morning ablutions. It sounded closer than last night; the Russians might be advancing again. At this rate, it wouldn't be long, perhaps only days, before the Soviets built up enough momentum to resume their march toward Berlin. According to Uncle Henry, the Germans needed a superweapon such as the A-bomb to enable a *blitzkrieg* that would conquer the world and put their "master race" program back on track.

They reached the edge of town fairly quickly without being discovered. From the top of a wooded hill beyond the last dwellings of Grudwald, James looked out over the farm flats through which ran the Vistula River, studying the lay of the land with a professional's eye toward avenues of approach and withdrawal, defensive strengths and weaknesses, blind spots and other terrain features that might prove important. There was something lulling and falsely soothing about the pastoral scene, with its little slate-roofed farmhouses set like jewels among square fields of growing grain.

"If you forget about the war," Regina commented wistfully, "it looks like the old Poland before Hitler invaded."

James mentioned nothing about the house here and there that had been burned down or blown up.

Morning sunlight glinted off the brown river. The

river flowed southwest in a slow but strong current past the plant located directly in front of them on its near bank. The plant was not large—about the size of two or three Midwestern U.S. stock barns joined together. No self-respecting American farmer would have let his barn deteriorate to such a degree, however. The metal sides and roof had rusted through in places. Willows and cane brakes and other wild growth crept up from the river to the very back of the building.

From the right, a road twisted out of the town and continued past the mill and toward a distant bridge. A long drive met the road and dissected a grassy field of perhaps twenty acres in size to end in front of the laboratory. A single vehicle was parked there, a black, boxy machine known as a Volkswagen. The "People's Car."

Everything looked quiet and normal.

At James's request, Regina described Professor Jahne's office on the second floor, where he kept most of his research notes and papers. She pointed out entrances where guards were stationed. Generally, she said, only three sentries kept watch over the plant: a soldier at the front door, one at the rear by the river, and a third who acted as a roving patrol. A Waffen-SS detachment at the edge of town was always on alert as a ready reaction force and could respond to an alarm in less than three minutes.

Inside the plant, an SS captain was in charge with his German female clerk. Six civilian laborers and lab technicians, not including Regina, assisted Professor Jahne in his research. Clearly, Regina had done her homework as a spy for Jurawski and his band.

As far as James could determine, there was no way to sneak inside the lab without being spotted. Now that he had actually seen the plant, every fiber of his being screamed out in protest: The plant was so exposed and accessible to quick reinforcement that to go down there was tantamount to suicide.

"I suppose," James observed with dripping sarcasm,

"that we are going to walk in there as bold as crows, then walk out again with your uncle's papers without so much as a by-your-leave from the guards and the plant commander?"

"Uncle Erwein and I will report in as we do on any normal day," Regina explained. "I doubt they will have heard about what has happened in town yet. We collect Uncle Erwein's papers, after which he unexpectedly comes down ill. Naturally, I will have to take him home. You, James, will wait for us on this side of the road in the forest."

"I was afraid of that."

"Do you have a better plan?" she asked, sounding cross and impatient.

"What about your gestapo escort?"

"This will not be the first morning they haven't come with us."

James still hesitated. His glance lingered on Professor Jahne. He felt like a dupe to trust them. Regina read his mind. So did Professor Jahne.

"I have always been apolitical," the old man said, "in that I prefer to remain the scientist even under political complications."

James chose not to remind him that building a weapon was itself a political act.

"I am not totally oblivious to my situation and that of my niece," the professor continued. "I will go with you, young man, once we secure my research. Not because of your threats, not because of the war. I accompany you only because I love my niece and I can see that, because of her association with you, she will be in dire danger if we remain in Grudwald. I will do whatever 'Gina wants because I trust her practical judgment over mine."

Regina's eyes teared. "Uncle Erwein . . ."

Professor Jahne held up a palm. "Shush, child. I understand. We have been compromised. Even if we tell the police we were kidnapped and escaped, they will not believe us. After all, we are Jews."

Maybe the old buzzard was starting to come down to reality.

"You have my word," the professor promised, extending his hand. James shook it, though he couldn't still that nagging little feeling that accepting the word of a Nazi— even a Nazi Jew—was like expecting a turkey buzzard to give up road kill.

It was a brisk walk down the hill through the woods to the road across from the old mill. Regina secured her hair with the blue barrette and handed her Sten to James with a shrug. "Wish us luck," she said.

"Don't stop to smell the roses."

Uncle and niece stepped onto the road in full view of the door guard at the laboratory. This was their normal shortcut to work and should arouse no suspicion. From hiding, James watched them walk down the drive across the short-grass meadow, Regina's hand tucked comfortably into the crook of her uncle's elbow. Her long skirt swirled, caressing her hips. James watched, thinking of that morning under the quilt. Gramps was right—a penis was a leash in the pretty hands of a sexy lady.

When the pair reached the guard at the mill's front door, Regina patted his arm and laughed with him over some comment, whereupon the guard opened the door and they went inside. He closed the door behind them. Alone again, the guard yawned, stretched and leaned his rifle against the wall next to the door while he lit a cigarette. He smoked it slowly, looking bored. The excitement in Grudwald had not yet spread this far.

James craved a cigarette himself, but it would have to wait.

Soon thereafter, a black German staff car sped around a blind curve in the road coming from town, trailing a rooster tail of dust. James flattened himself in the bushes as it roared past and slid into the long drive that led to the mill. It was in a hell of a hurry. He glimpsed in the rear passenger-side window the tanned face of an SS officer wearing a black bill cap pulled low over his eyes.

The vehicle braked to a dusty stop at the front door. The guard almost swallowed his cigarette in his haste to assume the proper posture. The officer in SS black and two spade-helmeted *Wehrmacht*, both heavily armed, jumped out of the car and rushed past the flustered sentry into the mill. A minute later, one of the *Wehrmacht* returned to double the guard at the door. Regina and Professor Jahne had been located. The Krauts weren't about to twice make the mistake of inadequate security.

James saw his mission floating down the river in failure.

15

James had had the professor in his hands, a bird in the hand being preferable to one in the bush, and had let him go. Now he was right back at the beginning. Worse than the beginning, in fact, since the Germans were on the lookout for infiltrators and prowlers and had Regina and the professor in custody. His mind cast about frantically for some way he might salvage this mess. Whatever he did, he had to hurry before other reinforcements arrived or the SS officer loaded up the missing Jahnes and hauled them back to town, where his chances of getting to them again were about the same as a snowflake falling on an August afternoon in Oklahoma.

He considered and promptly dismissed any effort directed at the front door. He couldn't get within two hundred yards of it across that open field without being spotted. That left the rear door next to the river.

From above on the hill at the edge of town, he had observed how the Vistula curled back on itself to the east and snaked underneath the road at a bridge only a short distance away. Insane as it seemed, it might be doable to reach the back door by that route. He examined that option carefully, discarded it as foolhardy, looked for other options, found none and returned his consideration to the river. It would be so easy to talk himself out of it.

Once when he was a kid, he had attempted to swim the Arkansas River. The Arkansas was about the size of the Vistula, the same ominous color of soil and erosion. Like its Polish counterpart, it was also mined with snags, deadheads, and the corpses of floating trees. He had made it about halfway across when a loose tree trunk administered him a bang on the head that was almost his undoing. Addled, half-drowned, he clung desperately to the tree trunk for hours before it finally washed ashore after dark. Until now, he had never even contemplated another stunt like that.

He rose and set out in the direction of the river bridge before he had a chance to talk himself out of it. The B-24 Carpetbaggers had risked their lives—maybe even sacrificed them—for the success of this mission. Could James expect any less from himself?

Wearing his combat harness, pistol and knife, carrying the two long guns, he trotted east in his limping gait, paralleling the road while keeping trees and undergrowth between it and himself. There was no traffic since the road was likely blocked off somewhere between here and Warsaw. Sweat soaked his clothing by the time he reached the bridge.

He stopped short of it to get his bearings and make sure it wasn't guarded. After watching and listening for a minute, he ventured down to the water's edge through a swamplike morass of stumps, fallen rotted logs, stagnant sump holes, new growths of cane and willows, and mosquitoes. The river gurgled and lapped at the muddy bank as it flowed brown and forceful underneath the single-lane bridge and on around to pass by the old wool mill.

Simple enough, he thought. *All I have to do is grab a log and float with the current until I reach the laboratory.*

Girding himself for the challenge, he pulled a dried-out timber from the top of a flood drift and dragged it to the river's edge. It floated well enough. He cached the Sten where it could be retrieved on his way to tonight's pickup point, the river offering the most secure route, but kept the other weapons, his clothing and boots. He wasn't about to corner a batch of pissed-off Nazis wearing only his underdrawers, even though the sight would probably kill them of laughter.

He tarried long enough to smoke a Lucky Strike. A condemned man deserved a last cigarette before he donned the blindfold. Then, as ready as he was ever going to be, he shoved the log the rest of the way into the current and waded in after it up to his waist. *Damn, the water is cold.* He wondered if snow melt-off fed the stream from distant mountains. Regina wouldn't be impressed with his "big set of balls" if she could see him now. They had shriveled to the size of BBs.

He had barely pushed off to consign himself to the river's muscle, MP-40 balanced on top of the log, when he heard the sound of some kind of vehicle racing toward the bridge from the direction of Warsaw. He quickly determined it was a motorcycle, and that it and he should reach the bridge at about the same time. Literally, he was up the creek without a paddle. Sometimes it seemed to him that his life was one damned thing after another.

It was too late to go back or try to reach shore. He would be seen for certain. All he could do was ride it out and try to look like driftwood. He dragged the automatic rifle off the log and into the water while he got as low as he could behind the log.

The rattle of loose planks on the bridge announced the bike's arrival. A motorcycle and sidecar. Its moving shadow cast onto the river's surface created an intricate pattern interwoven with the straight lines of the bridge.

Keep on going, assholes . . .

Halfway across, the bike slowed and then stopped. James's log swirled past the rock riprap that anchored the near end of the bridge. It got caught in an eddy underneath the span and began to slowly spin in place. The bike's engine died. Boot steps echoed above his head.

Frantic with sudden dread, he sucked in a deep breath and ducked his head underneath the brown water. He clutched a snag on the log with one hand, the MP-40 in the other, and kicked hard once to break free of the eddy and allow the log to carry him on downriver. In his haste and desperation, he fumbled his grip on the automatic rifle. He grabbed for it and almost lost his hold on the log. His heart raced as the weapon sank into the stream's cold depths. He retrieved his log, but he was left with only his pistol and a knife to take on the Krauts at the laboratory.

If he ever reached the laboratory.

He felt like cussing a blue streak upon which old Preacher Seabolt back at his little Drake's Prairie country church might build an entire month's sermons. Instead, all he could do was hold his breath, duck beneath the surface, and clutch the snag on the log with both hands. He went limp to avoid leaving any swirl or sign that the piece of driftwood was anything other than what it appeared to be.

It occurred to him that he must have already been spotted. Why else would the motorcycle have stopped? The muscles in his stomach tightened. He squeezed his eyes against the pressure of the water. His lungs burned. It was a hell of a way to die—like a big carp or gar about to be gigged in a shallow backwater.

16

Caught by the strong current, the log bobbed downstream away from the bridge. Underwater, James clung to it out of sheer desperation and wondered why no bullets were slashing the water. Finally, when he had to either surface for air or drown, he allowed his face to break water next to the log where, hopefully, he wouldn't be observed. He gulped air. Still no gunfire.

Blinking away river water, he spotted the gray-green military motorcycle and attached sidecar blocking the bridge's single lane. Next to it, two German soldiers were leaning on the side railing while they smoked, joked and deprived a village somewhere of its idiots. James's first thought was that they had been alerted to the goings-on in Grudwald and dispatched to cut off this escape route, a task they were apparently taking none too seriously.

Encouraged by their lack of interest in their duties, James stayed low in the water and let the current pull him and his log further downstream. He soon rounded a bend out of sight of the bridge and breathed a little easier.

He shivered from exposure to the cold water—or from nerves.

Uncle Henry had expressed reservations about sending James out again so soon after Normandy. Close brushes with death over time did something to soldiers, leeched them of their confidence, made them cautious and less prone to take future risks. But, James countered, if you got bucked off a horse, you had to get right back on or you never would again. Besides, hadn't the OSS recruiter promised him a life of travel and adventure?

Ahead of him on the riverbank, the rust-red roof of the old wool mill slowly took shape. Willows and cane brakes growing in profusion masked the back wall. Things seemed quiet and peaceful. He paddled with one hand while he held onto the log with the other, guiding close to the overgrown shore where he was least likely to be spotted. Sunshine on the greenery reminded him of how cold he was in the water and how pleasant it would be to crawl out on shore, take off his wet clothes, and let the sun bake revitalizing warmth back into his stiffening body.

As the log floated past the back of the building, he paddled it into a patch of water weeds clogging a tiny inlet. Clothing, boots and combat harness made swimming out of the question. As soon as his feet touched bottom, he gave the log a shove and slithered up the sloping bank as deadly and silently as a swamp cottonmouth. Thick growth screened his view of the mill; it also hid him from sight of the door guard.

He lay on dry ground for a minute, letting water drain out of his boots while he listened for movement. He took his .45 from its holster and shook it dry before replacing it. He listened some more. The river gurgled, a crow cawed. Much as he would have liked to bask in the sunshine, he tarried only long enough for some of the chill to dissipate. As soon as he stopped shaking, he crawled up the bank through bulrush and willow sprouts until he came to the mowed clearing behind the building. The sound of the river covered any noise he might make.

The opening between the river growth and the back of the mill was only a few long steps across at most, dominated by the corroded rise of the building and a giant waterwheel left to decay. In the shade next to the single door stood a Kraut who might have spotted James had he not been half asleep from boredom. *Send these guys up to the Russian front and they wouldn't look so bored.*

Time to go to work.

The first order of business was to get inside the plant to assess the situation and form a plan of rescue. The trick was to do so without announcing his presence. Everything depended on stealth, surprise and pure raw luck.

He tossed a pebble to draw the guard's attention elsewhere. He had to toss a second pebble before the guy reacted. As soon as the guard took a step forward and turned to look toward the waterwheel, James sprang to his feet, knife in hand, and rushed him in that old side-to-side crouch that helped cushion his footfalls. By the time the victim knew what was going on, it was too late.

James caught him from behind, clamping one hand over his mouth to keep him from crying out while the razor-sharp stiletto glittered toward his jugulars. He dumped the soldier on his butt and braced a knee in his back as he sliced the knife across his throat deep and finished him off. The thought flashed through his mind that he had promised to spare a German in repayment for the Focke-Wulf pilot's magnanimity.

But not this one.

The German's heavy boots thumped on the ground. His helmet rolled to one side, the chin strap slashed along with his throat. James held him until he went still. Hot blood washed over his hands, along with a peculiar, nauseating, copper-like odor so strong that it penetrated taste buds. James spat to one side in disgust. His hands were shaking. The soldier was a brown-eyed kid of no more than nineteen or twenty.

This was definitely worth a year of nightmares. Someday.

He dragged the body to the river's edge and hid it in the foliage after stuffing a handful of leaves into the kid's mouth, just in case he wasn't quite dead and tried to call out. He washed the blood off his hands in the river. On his way to the back door, he snatched up the guard's discarded Mauser and made sure a round was chambered.

There were no windows on this side of the building. The back door was unlocked. He cracked it cautiously and peered inside. According to his calculations, based on information he received from Regina, there should be six Krauts left—two remaining regular guards, the officer in charge, and the recently arrived SS major and his two goons. Civilians didn't count, since they were unarmed and unlikely to intervene.

He saw no human activity. Large vats and contraptions that resembled locomotive boilers studded the concrete floor. He knew nothing about the harnessing of atomic energy other than what Uncle Henry had explained to him, but he assumed all this had something to do with building an A-bomb. He shuddered at the thought of the energy this lab might be capable of releasing.

Steeling himself for action, the stiletto in his fist replaced by the Mauser, James slipped inside, closed the door softly and crouched next to it to let his eyes adjust from the strong sunshine outside. Crates, boxes and barrels scattered about offered some cover and concealment. A narrow platform of sorts that served as a loft catwalk circled the open edges of a second floor, off which doors opened into offices or rooms. From somewhere up there came the murmur of voices, but James couldn't discern what they were saying or to whom they might belong. He knew only that Professor Jahne's office was on the second floor; he assumed that was where he and Regina were.

So, he was inside. Now, how did he get to Regina and the old man and get them out of there?

A direct assault was out of the question. He was outnumbered and outgunned six to one. His eyes darted about. What he needed was some sort of diversion. What he *really* needed was a company of U.S. Army Rangers.

Water dripping from his clothing made little plopping sounds on the concrete. His socks squished in his boots as he slipped forward and ducked down behind a stack of empty wooden crates. He peered around its edge and saw near the front door one of the *Wehrmacht* who had arrived in the staff car with the SS officer. He and the roving patrolman were discussing something in quiet tones, their backs toward James.

Two Krauts there, two on guard outside the front door. That left the SS major and the other officer—probably the source of the conversation upstairs.

To James's right, a set of wooden stairs descended from the catwalk. He heard footsteps clacking on the catwalk, then watched as two civilians in dirty green coveralls took the stairs to the lower floor. They appeared nervous and were not speaking to each other. Yellow stars on their coveralls explained why they might be upset over a visit by the SS. James wondered how they had been recruited for this job and why they had not been herded with other Jews into the transportation compound down by the railroad tracks. It probably had something to do with Professor Jahne's initially having been permitted to choose his own assistants and lab workers.

Both men were well past middle age and looked malnourished. They strode out into the middle of the floor among the boilers and vats and began tinkering with gauges and valves. While engaged in this activity, all the while keeping their eyes on the *Wehrmacht* at the front door, one of them carelessly released a gush of water that soaked his trousers and shoes. He jumped back. The other worker rushed over. They seemed excited at the mishap, as though the water might be radioactive and would make them start to glow at any moment.

They secured their machines and hurried in James's direction. James crouched in the shadows next to the floor behind his crates. The *Wehrmacht* on the opposite side of the building turned their heads to look, but then returned to their conversation, backs to the room. The two workers slammed into a room below the stairway.

Only a minute or two passed before the workers re-emerged, the contaminated one having changed into dry coveralls. Perhaps Lady Luck had just smiled on James. He waited until the two Jews returned upstairs before, keeping to the shadows beneath the stairway where it would be difficult to be seen, he slipped into the little side room and closed the door behind him.

He listened at the door for a moment to make sure he hadn't been observed, then felt around in the darkness for the light switch. The room brightened with a click.

It was too much to hope for. Shelves on one side were stocked with towels and clean green coveralls. They renewed his confidence. He stripped off his wet Levis and chambray shirt and stuffed them into a box of rags in one corner. After toweling dry, he pulled on the smallest pair of coveralls he could find; they were still baggy on him. All came with yellow stars. He even discovered a bin of dry woolen socks. God was good to him. Amazing what a change of clothing could do for a man's morale. He was ready again to go out and beard the lion in its den, slay dragons and rescue damsels in distress.

The plan forming in his mind required him to leave the Mauser and his combat harness behind, at least for the moment. His .45 pistol stuck in one pocket, knife in the other alongside his leg, he ventured out onto the main floor and into full view of the *Wehrmacht*. Looking businesslike, as brazen as a whore on her favorite street corner, he climbed the stairs toward the voices. A man who *looked* like he belonged was seldom challenged. That was why a private with a clipboard could go almost anywhere he wanted in the army.

He had almost reached the catwalk when a command in German rapped him on the back of his neck.

"*Warten Sie bitte!*" Wait a moment.

Damn! James should have thought of a clipboard.

17

The command was repeated in a louder, harsher tone. James's red hair must have given him away. The guards would know if there was orange hair among the usual workers. James ignored the command, pretending not to hear, and kept going up the stairs. He was only a few steps away from the door behind which he heard voices, Regina's sharp tongue among them. She was giving somebody hell.

From the corner of his eye, he saw the two soldiers start across the lower floor toward the stairway. He opened the door and stepped quickly inside, closing the door and at the same time whipping the concealed .45 from his pocket.

Sudden, startled silence greeted him. James took in the scene at a glance: the tall, blond SS officer with his black bill cap pulled low over piercing blue eyes; Regina, whose dark eyes widened with disbelief at seeing James; Professor Jahne, stocky and bushy-bearded, looking exasperated and compressed in his long black coat. They were standing facing each other in the middle of a small office that contained a desk piled with papers.

Pointing the Colt at the Nazi's head, James moved behind him and expertly relieved him of his holstered Luger. He looked at it and tossed it to Regina. She caught it deftly and turned it on the officer, whose eyes narrowed dangerously. Professor Jahne looked conflicted, his startled gaze switching back and forth between the German and the American. Heavy boots pounding on the catwalk announced the rapid approach of the soldier guards.

"*Verzei hung!*" James barked in German, jabbing his .45 hard against the back of the SS major's head. "Whether you live or die within the next minute depends on you. Understand?"

"*Nein,*" the officer countered. "Whether *you* live or die depends on me."

"I don't think you understand, Herr Superman. There's going to be a knock on the door. Get rid of them, else I shoot you in the head and you die first in the name of the Führer. After that, it won't matter to you what happens."

Everyone inside the room stiffened when the knock came. No one moved for what seemed an hour or so.

"Major Fischer?" rose an inquiry from the catwalk outside.

"Tell them everything is okay," James hissed. "Tell them to go away."

Major Fischer remained frozen in place, his lips compressed in a stubborn line; James could almost hear the wheels in his brain grinding.

"Major Fischer?" The inquiry more insistent this time.

Professor Jahne broke the impasse. Glancing once at his niece, as if for confirmation, he squared his shoulders and stepped toward the door. James moved behind Major Fischer in case the soldiers insisted on entering. He didn't intend to blast Fischer first. He would use him for cover while he knocked off the two soldiers. *Then* he would kill the officer, narrowing the odds in the mill down to three surviving Germans. He would also shoot the scientist if the old fool attempted to betray him.

The professor spoke in a surprisingly calm voice to the closed door. "Yes, yes. What is it you want?" He sounded impatient, as though disturbed in the middle of something important.

"Is Major Fischer in there?"

"He is in the back office. What is it, man?"

"We saw someone strange come in here. He limps."

The professor shot a sour look at James. "He is indeed a strange man," he said, "but he is an associate."

James gestured with his free hand: *Get rid of him.*

Professor Jahne nodded. To the door, he said in a commanding voice, "Major Fischer is momentarily indisposed. He will be out shortly. In the meantime, there are some boxes in Captain Kauffmann's office downstairs in the west wing. Major Fischer desires you transfer the boxes to his car once you secure them. Captain Kaufmann will know where there is packing tape. Now, be off with you, and curtail your infernal caterwauling."

The old man was doing great.

There was a moment's hesitation on the other side of the door. Major Fischer shifted his weight. James pressed the muzzle of his .45 harder against the back of the man's head. "Don't," he whispered.

Boot heels snapped together beyond the door. "*Jawohl! Gerade jetzt.*"

The soldiers stamped away, their boot heels clacking on the catwalk. James relaxed.

"Thanks," he said.

"I gave my word to cooperate," the stubborn old man said.

"A simple 'You are welcome' would have sufficed." James turned to Regina. Her expression reflected how thankful she was to see him. "Where's the other officer, the one in charge of the laboratory?" he asked her.

"That would be Kaufmann," she said. "He is the one

downstairs in his office packing his stuff. This man"
—she indicated Major Fischer— "came to blow up the
laboratory to keep the Russians from getting it. Whatever
you are planning, we had better be quick. Major Fischer
called for more men when he saw Uncle Erwein was here.
Everyone is looking all over Grudwald for us."

It was still a long time until tonight and a long way to
the pickup spot. Perhaps the longest distance of all lay
between here and the front door.

"What about those damnable papers?" James asked
the Jahnes.

"We were gathering the most important ones when the
SS got here," Regina explained. "That was what the fuss
was about. We are almost ready."

"Let's go then." They had to hurry before the guards
completed their fool's errand downstairs or more troops
arrived from Grudwald.

Professor Jahne took a large tin box off the desk. He
almost staggered under the weight. James frowned.

"I can do with no less," Jahne protested.

"It's your back."

James tapped Major Fischer with his gun barrel to get
his attention. "I misjudged you, Herr Major. You don't
seem so eager to die after all. That's good, because we're
now all going to walk right out of here together like old
chums."

"I'll grant you one thing," Major Fischer said. "You
have a set of them."

Regina half smiled. "You do not know the half of it."

James and Regina concealed their pistols, and after
cautioning the SS major that failure to cooperate meant
his immediate and certain demise, forced him to walk
out ahead of them. The two Jewish workers from earlier
were packing something in boxes further around on the
catwalk. They glanced up and went back to work. There
was no one else in sight. Regina whispered to James
that most of the lab techs and assistants were in various

rooms gathering up materials to save from the pending explosion.

"Who are you?" Major Fischer asked James. He eyed Professor Jahne's tin box. "Are you under Russian orders? Give us the papers and the old man. You and the woman may go. You can't get away otherwise, you know."

"We must have a failure to communicate here, Herr Superman," James snapped. "Get going."

They descended the stairs in a tight group, Professor Jahne struggling with the weight of his tin box. Boilers on the main floor hissed and clanged. They wended their way through them toward the front door and made it without being challenged.

Outside, the sun was still shining and the artillery duel beyond Warsaw sounded like a gathering thunder boomer getting set to blow up a real storm. The guard and Major Fisher's *Wehrmacht* escort snapped to attention and heiled Hitler. James elbowed the major, who heiled back. They walked to the staff car while the soldiers watched. The ignition keys were missing. Major Fischer smiled slyly.

"We can wait for my driver," he suggested smugly.

"Take a look in the Volkswagen," James told Regina.

She walked around to the VW while, for the benefit of the guard, James laughed at something Major Fischer supposedly said and pretended to be in an ongoing conversation with an old associate. Regina caught his eye and nodded. She also smiled. The People's Car had keys.

At James's direction, Professor Jahne climbed into the back seat with his box while Regina eased into the front passenger's seat. She drew her Luger and pointed it at the Nazi, keeping it low and out of sight of the guards.

"What about him?" she asked.

"What about me?" Major Fischer mimicked, a demented grin sweeping across his face and his blue eyes narrowing as they focused on the road from Grudwald. The grin turned to a triumphant laugh.

James and Regina saw it at the same time. A German troop truck bristling with soldiers and weapons turned off the main road and headed down the long drive across the meadow directly toward them. Dust swirled. Their getaway hadn't been fast enough.

He was going to have to get into another line of work.

Major Fischer held out his hand. "I will take your weapons," he offered. "I think we might say your goose has been cooked."

18

No goose was cooked until it was in the oven and the fire turned up. James reacted with a single deft movement that dropped Major Fischer on his butt on the ground. The sentries at the door made as though to rush to the officer's aid. James drew his .45 and winged a shot at them. The bullet *pinged* as it pierced the metal siding. The startled soldiers ducked into the mill.

The pistol swung on through and settled on Fischer, who was about to regain his feet.

"Bleiben!" James warned.

Major Fischer glared up at his executioner. James heard Regina shouting from the VW for him to come on. The truckload of troops was almost halfway down the drive barreling toward them like a train on a track. James jammed his boot into the SS officer's face and shoved him sprawling onto his back.

"You owe your life to a Focke-Wulf pilot," he said. It was done. He had kept his promise to spare a Kraut.

He slid behind the wheel of the little black car. The

engine fired right away. It had limited power, but James twisted the wheel sharply and jammed the gas pedal to the floor. It spun a slow donut, throwing Regina into him and jolting Professor Jahne across the backseat.

"Stay down!" James ordered. The old man ducked below the level of the doors and windows.

Gradually, slower than a team of tired mules, it seemed, the underpowered little car revved up and trundled up the drive on a head-on collision course with the oncoming troop truck. Spewing smoke, the gray-green monster loomed in the windshield. Regina braced herself in her seat with both hands, her eyes riveted ahead. James pumped the gas feed to elicit more power.

A glance in the rearview mirror displayed Major Fischer running in the road waving his arms and shouting. Beyond, in the mill's open door, the sentries were trying to get a clean shot at the escaping fugitives without hitting either the major or the truck. Troops in the truck, utterly confused by the goings-on, dared not open fire either, for the same reason of avoiding shooting up their own people.

James pointed the little car at the truck. Deep drainage ditches on either side of the drive flashed by like unraveling string. The gap between the two vehicles narrowed. Regina's eyes bulged.

"What are you doing?" she cried.

"Playing chicken."

"*Chicken!* Oh, my God!"

She tucked her head between her knees. This she didn't want to see.

The unnerved truck driver slammed on his brakes, fishtailing his big machine. Boiling dust engulfed it. The VW kept coming, whereupon the German "chickened out" and twisted his truck off the road. It swerved sharply and bounced over the left drainage ditch with such violence that several soldiers in the open bed went flying.

James sped on by, missing the truck's rear tires by the width of a sigh. Half wild with excitement, relief and triumph, he thrust his head out his open window and vented a loud, taunting hen's cackle that seemed to echo through the dust.

The road at the end of the drive led two ways—either toward Grudwald or Warsaw. Another of those cross-roads in life. James skidded the Volks through a sharp right turn toward the bridge to Warsaw. Better to face the village idiots at the bridge than an alerted Grudwald.

Astonished at still being alive—peeved, too—Regina peeped up over the dash. "I think you must be mad."

"We all are. Haven't you noticed?"

"Some more than others," she said.

She craned her neck out the window toward the rear.

"Now is the time to use them if you have any more tricks," she exclaimed. "You have really pissed them off this time. They are coming fast."

The back window and a rear side window exploded from an angled rifle shot, showering broken glass. Professor Jahne cried out and curled up on the backseat around his precious box of papers. He sounded like he might be praying.

"Can you not go any faster?" Regina pleaded.

"The squirrel in the cage is running as fast as it can."

"It's not fast enough. They will catch us."

"Maybe if one of us got out and pushed."

She glanced at him. "You *are* mad."

"Certifiably," he agreed.

Rifles popped like strings of firecrackers as the truck full of soldiers gained on the slower VW. The little car's engine was mounted in the rear. A lucky round would pulverize the squirrel. Fortunately, the Krauts were shooting from an unstable platform. Dust churning from the Volkswagen's tires helped mask it.

Ahead appeared the bridge from which James had launched his river journey less than an hour ago. Idiots or not, the bridge sentries were bound to catch on and decide they had to do *something*. At the moment, however, lacking an officer to tell them what to do, they stood at the approach end of the bridge, gawking at the black car charging down on them at top speed. The motorcycle's sidecar, parked behind them, effectively blocked passage cross the single lane.

"You take the one on the right," James told Regina. "I'll take the other one. Can you do it?"

"What do you take me for—a lily?"

James didn't think that at all. He had already seen she could be one hard-edged dame.

Regina stuck her head and shoulders out her open window and used both hands to grip and steady her purloined Luger. She began firing, squinting as she aimed into the wind at her assigned target on the bridge, black hair flying. The spiteful *Crack! Crack! Crack!* of her German handgun whipped through the car from wind wash.

James kept the gas pedal crammed against the floorboard. The engine whined tight. A speeding car on a rough gravel road wasn't the best platform for accurate shooting.

Regina's German returned fire with his Mauser. The other lost his nerve and fled, leaping over the motorcycle like a deer and hauling ass for the neutral opposite end of the bridge. James hen-cackled, unable to resist. Regina even laughed this time, inappropriate though it might be, unable to suppress the exhilaration of speed and danger.

James opened up with the .45 in his left hand stuck out his window. The Colt went *Pftt! Pftt!* because of its silencer. The duel between the remaining sentry and the attacking VW continued as the distance between them narrowed. The Volks's windshield shattered, spraying James's face with flying broken glass. The fight ended abruptly when the Kraut dropped, felled by bullets from either Regina's Luger or James's .45.

"Hold on!" James yelled.

He braked hard to avoid crashing headlong into the motorcycle. There was no way to avoid the body lying in the road. The Volks bounced over the squishy speed bump. James downshifted and rammed the motorcycle at low speed, intending to either shove it over the railing into the river or push it across the bridge ahead of them.

Instead, the motorcycle broke free of the sidecar. Both parts jammed into the sides of the bridge and stuck there. The VW came to a dead stop against the wreckage, its rear tires spinning and smoking and burning rubber. Bullets from the approaching truck *spanged* and whizzed and ricocheted off the bridge. Near rounds made sinister little sizzles, like bees farting.

Regina looked back with wide eyes at the truck closing the gap on them. She pounded the dash with her palm. "Hurry! Hurry!" she chanted.

Too late. A bullet penetrated the engine, bursting it with the sounds of gears and shafts and pistons grinding and flying apart. The squirrel died with a final whimper.

"Damn!"

James sprang from the dead vehicle and knelt on one knee next to it while he threw .45 rounds at the attacking troop truck. It loomed large and ominous and was rapidly growing larger as it charged through the cloud of dust like a fire-breathing dragon. James's bullets shrieking off its hood and spidering its windshield slowed it somewhat.

"Get your uncle out!" he shouted at Regina.

In an instant, she had the old man out of the Volkswagen, he clutching his heavy box of research papers, she looking around in desperation. James grabbed the professor's other arm and motioned for Regina to follow him.

Cornered, with nowhere else to go, holding onto each other, the three of them sailed over the railing of the bridge into the swamp below. Professor Jahne's scream of terror and surprise hung in air shredded by gunfire.

19

They plunged downward into a willow canopy of greenery. The soil beneath was soft and marshy and slanted toward the river. James landed lightly on his feet, favoring his right knee only a little. Regina hit and rolled, then sprang to her feet. A dab of mud smeared her cheek; the blue barrette had shaken loose. Her uncle was not so fortunate. There was a singular *snap!* He cried out in pain, then collapsed when he tried to gather his feet beneath him. He dropped the tin box in favor of his foot.

"My ankle!" he lamented. "I have broken it."

James examined it. The entire foot was already swelling, but at least no bones protruded through the skin.

"You have got to get up," James said. "We'll look after it later." *Later in hell*, he thought, *because that's where we'll be if we don't move.*

"I cannot walk. Leave me," the old man objected.

Regina cast a wary look at James. "We are not leaving him," she said.

Without a word, James bodily wrenched the scientist

to his feet and pulled the old man's arm around his own shoulders in a modified fireman's carry. Professor Jahne groaned in agony, but bit his lip to keep from crying out. Regina slipped her uncle's other arm around her neck. James hoisted the tin box under his free elbow and they set off upstream, half dragging, half carrying Professor Jahne between them.

Regina still clutched the Luger. She had one cartridge left. James had three left for his .45. *So, with four bullets they were going to take on the German army?* he thought. Nursing a crippled, old man. They were all the same as dead.

Behind them at the bridgehead rose a cloud of dust as the German truck braked and its rooster tail caught up and enveloped it. Men shouted and weapons clattered as troops unassed it. Momentary confusion reigned. Apparently, no one had seen in which direction the prey escaped because of the dust. It wouldn't take them long to sort it out, however.

James left Regina and her uncle long enough to take the professor's tin box out of sight and bury it. No use giving the Krauts any more than necessary; besides, it was too heavy to carry much farther. Then he looked for and found the place where he had cached Regina's Sten gun earlier and retrieved it. Although the Sten was the cheapest, simplest weapon of its kind ever made, it was nonetheless an engineering marvel. It resembled a mechanic's grease gun, ugly and uncomplicated. Its thirty-two rounds added to James's four-round arsenal made it even more appreciated.

Regina glanced at the weapon when he returned, suddenly comprehending how he must have used the river to sneak into the wool mill, and why he was wearing baggy green coveralls.

"Your other clothes were undoubtedly wet," she commented.

"Sorry I couldn't make it to the tailor's."

"You continue to amaze me, James."

"Sometimes I amaze myself."

Professor Jahne looked resentful about his missing papers, failing to realize that their disposal was a final act of desperation.

"If *he* had not come," the professor complained, his rheumy old eyes boring holes into James, "I might have continued my work undisturbed."

And given Hitler the A-bomb, James thought, feeling resentment of his own.

"Uncle, the Germans were going to transport both of us," Regina argued.

"I am far too valuable to them, 'Gina."

She sighed. "You are a Jew, Uncle Erwein."

"I am a German as well."

From the rear, more quickly than James had anticipated, came sounds of pursuit. Men crashing through thickets. Low shouts. Hounds baying after 'coons they intended to catch and kill.

"I don't think they give a big rat's ass back there what you are or are not," James snapped. "Move out!"

The older, ruthlessly cool woman came through in Regina's dark eyes. She accepted, along with James, the inevitable outcome of this race. What James did not want her to know was the decision that again faced him on how far he would allow this to go before he made sure, once and for all, that the Germans never got their hands on Professor Jahne again.

They struggled on together with the professor between them, wading through mud and knee-deep sump holes, clambering over deadfalls, punching their way through cane brakes and willows growing so thickly they could barely penetrate them. All three were soon caked in mud and grime—swamp monsters from the bog. James had been chased out of Grudwald, out of the wool mill laboratory, and now out of the swamp. He was damned fed up with being chased.

Professor Jahne was in a great deal of pain. Beneath the mud-splattered beard, his face turned pale and pinched. He begged for a minute's rest. James and Regina urged him on.

The Germans were coming. James threw a spray of bullets through the thickets in the direction of the sounds of pursuit to try to slow them down. A few blind rounds responded, but none came near. It got quieter back there after that. As far as the Krauts knew, the swamp might be full of Polish partisans or Russian troops setting up ambushes. The ongoing artillery duel near Warsaw and the Russian invaders in Grudwald were enough to convince them that Soviets were infiltrating German lines and could be almost anywhere.

"I'm sorry you had to get mixed up in all this, Regina," James said.

She looked calmly toward their back trail, as though having already accepted the tragedy overtaking them.

"It was I who got you mixed up in it," she said.

"Pretty girls have always been my downfall. Jurawski is going to have to hurry if he wants to beat the Germans in killing me."

It wasn't very funny. Regina blinked back sudden tears.

"If Jurawski is still alive," she declared, "he will come for me."

That was some kind of faith. James wondered if Gabrielle had that same faith that he would come back for her.

The Germans were closing in. James expected at any moment to see point men bursting out of the bushes to consume them like an Oklahoma tornado. Even by the most optimistic measure, things were becoming increasingly hopeless for the prey and more promising for the predator. Professor Jahne was about to collapse. He placed more and more of his considerable weight upon the shoulders of his niece and James. They were almost carrying him. His feet left drag marks that a blind man could follow.

James kept the river close to their right because he knew the swamp was their only chance, what slim chance remained. Fatigue and nerves caused time to merge into a single continuum of *now* as they fought their way on. Postponing fate was about the best James could hope for. Tears of pain and exhaustion dribbled with sweat and mud into Professor Jahne's beard. Regina was breathing hard. Sweat plastered strands of short black hair to her forehead. She stripped the blue barrette from her hair, where it was barely clinging, and asked James to keep it for her, since she didn't have a pocket in her skirt.

Open farmland adjoined the swamp. Regina said there was another road about a mile ahead. It might increase their chances of survival and escape if they could get across it and into a range of foothill woodlands, through which they could circle back to the northwest to be picked up by the Carpetbagger plane at midnight.

At some point, a tremendous explosion from the direction of the wool mill jarred the air. A mushroom cloud of black smoke boiled into the distant sky. Major Fischer and the Krauts must have touched off the lab. Professor Jahne grimaced and refused to look back.

"I hope you do have another trick in that bag of yours," Regina gasped. "It had better be a good one."

Mission came first. That was the message drilled into James, into all OSS recruits, during training and afterwards. The professor *was* the mission. He had to be either gotten out or disposed of, no matter what happened to James.

James's nerve endings were playing *I Cried for You* by the Glenn Miller Band when he stopped Regina. He might have one more trick. It was their only choice, other than to simply give up. He had reached rock bottom and was starting to dig.

Regina's eyes filled with tears after she heard him out. "They will kill you!"

Need he explain that they were going to be killed anyhow? "It's the only chance you and your uncle have," he said. "Get him out, Regina. That's what's important. Listen carefully now . . ."

He described the location where she would meet the plane tonight and the signal she must use to guide in the Carpetbagger aircraft. He finished by describing a giant sweet gum tree at the foot of which he had buried the professor's tin box of research papers. "Memorize this telephone number. If I don't make it, call the number once you reach London and tell the man at the other end where the box is hidden. Got that?"

"James . . . ?"

"Damn it, do you have it?"

"Yes. *Yes.*"

"Can you manage your uncle alone if I buy you the time?"

She was so choked up that all she could do was nod. He kept the Sten and gave her his .45 along with its three bullets.

"One more thing. There's a Jewish girl named Gabrielle Amandine Arneau. The Germans took her from France in June. I think she's in a concentration camp somewhere in Germany or Poland. Will you look for her if you get the chance? After the war is over, I mean. If you find her, tell her . . . tell her . . ."

What *could* he tell her?

"I will tell her, James," Regina whispered.

She bent forward and kissed him softly on the cheek. "I choose to believe that you will meet us at the pickup point tonight."

He grinned wryly. "I choose to believe it myself."

He would have liked to leave her with something memorable, something Churchillian, like *I have nothing to offer but blood, toil, tears and sweat.* Instead, all he could come up with was Humphrey Bogart. "Be seeing you, kid. Now get out of here."

With that, looking jaunty and confident in spite of his pounding heart, he turned away and, limping from his old wound, trotted back toward the German soldiers closing in on them.

20

Getting down on his belly, he wriggled into a briar thicket
across which a fallen tree provided cover. A small glade
opened in front of him. It was overgrown with saw grass
or wire grass—whatever it was called in Europe—and
littered with dead logs that reminded him of corpses.
The sun, almost full overhead now, shone down brightly
into it. Knowing soldiers the way he did, he expected the
Krauts to approach it cautiously and pause on the other
side to look things over.

It was shady and humid in the thicket. Mosquitoes
buzzed around his ears. The black column of smoke
from the burning wool mill rose as straight as a chimney
above the treetops. He saw how the summer sun gilded
the edges of leaves and made golden halos of dragonfly
wings. He touched the dead bark on the fallen tree with
his fingertips. A column of ants carrying booty marched
along a rotted limb. One enterprising fellow lugged along
a dried-up grasshopper fully five times his size.

How delightful summer days had been when he was a boy back on the farm and could fantasize of adventure and romance. That was before he became a cop and grew jaded from experiencing humanity's underbelly, before war set the world ablaze.

He took Regina's blue barrette from the pocket of his coveralls and looked at it. He had nothing like it to remind him of Gabrielle. He put the barrette back into his pocket.

God, how he wanted to live.

The more a man had to live for, the greater his dread of dying. Winston Churchill once said that the brave man was not the man who felt no fear; the brave man was one who overcame his fear. James concentrated on overcoming his fear. Dismissing all thoughts, he pulled himself into his combat cocoon. Duty and mission were the only things that counted. He felt chilled to the bone and surprisingly hungry.

The first indication he received that the Germans were coming was the *thuck-thuck* of heavy boots in mud and soft earth. Foliage shook. He supported the barrel of his submachine gun on the fallen tree trunk, using the box magazine as a forward grip. He inhaled deeply; his hands were not shaking. He lay belly down with his cheek against the wire stock, sighting down the stubby barrel to where he expected the first enemy to emerge into the little glade.

Trees shuddered. The patrol's point man, a kid with his Dutch Boy helmet pulled low over his eyes and mud smeared on his face and uniform, stepped from the forest gloom and hesitated to scan the clearing. Through his gun sights, James read the name strip on the trooper's gray-green tunic: FULCHER. Fulcher was a good-looking kid. *Wouldn't it be a lot saner if only the old and ugly were killed in war?*

James tapped off a single shot. The bullet struck the boy's torso with the sound of a hammer hitting a ripe watermelon. Air expelled from his lungs in a bursting shriek as the bullet slammed him back and down, out of sight among the trees.

Return fire made the woods sparkle from muzzle flashes. The Germans were shooting at random, having no idea from where the fatal shot had originated. In the confusion, James slithered out the back of the briar patch as silently and as near invisible as a wily old whitetail buck. He had grown up hunting and fishing and prowling Oklahoma's Cookson Hills, and was as much the woodsman as any of the half-wild Cherokee boys he ran with.

He located a second hide a hundred feet back, this behind the gnarled bole and roots of an old swamp giant. Again he waited, knowing that every minute he delayed or diverted the pursuit of Regina and the professor gave them that much more time to escape.

He wiped dirt and sweat from his brow, but he still felt chilled. He craved a Lucky Strike.

The game was about to get tougher. The Germans spread out and advanced more vigilantly, sneaking and peeking through the bogs. All along his front James listened to whispered sounds, furtive rustling, shifty footfalls. He waited, eyes darting, knowing his next target would be more difficult. The best he could expect was a blur of movement, perhaps the top of a helmet or the flash of a gray-green uniform. He had to make every bullet count.

A shadow separated itself from the forest twilight in front of James's eyes. He snapped off a shot. The shadow disappeared, although James couldn't be certain if he had scored or not.

This time his muzzle flash must have given him away. A machine gun cranked up and chewed a waist-high swath through the forest. Twigs and leaves fluttered down on his head as from a blast of wind.

He beat a hasty retreat, first slithering away, then bolting to his feet and running like a spooked buck while every hunter in the woods opened up on him.

The terrain along the river had the characteristics of a tropical rain forest and offered excellent cover and concealment beneath its double canopy. At some point not far away, swamp turned into open farmland. Since Regina and her uncle must stay next to the river, James deliberately led the hounds at a tangent toward more open country. He had to give the Jahnes time and every possible opportunity to get away.

He held up a third time in a muddy sump hole. It was taking the Krauts a lot longer to work their way to him. Nearly fifteen minutes passed. He strained ears and eyes to pick up a sound, a movement. The bastards were making him nervous. What the hell were they up to? They weren't about to withdraw. Perhaps they were waiting for reinforcements.

Another few minutes of this, he thought, and maybe he would have bought Regina enough time that he could slip away to safety himself. He was just beginning to hope he might get out of this scrap in one piece when he heard the Germans coming again. It started with the shrubbery being disturbed toward his front. He got ready.

He heard other movement—*from the rear*. He listened more carefully, then decided his imagination must be playing tricks on him. He was still considering it when a Kraut made the mistake of exposing himself. James popped him. The guy dropped and set up such a howling that someone shouted in German for him to shut his fornicating tater hole.

A hail of rifle and machine-gun fire lent impetus to James's retreat. He was ducking and dodging through the swamp, running hard, when he leaped over a deadfall and the woods directly ahead exploded with the deafening crash of small-arms fire at point-blank range. Sparks pecked at him from the gloom. Bees were farting all around.

Too late, he realized he really *had* heard sounds from his rear. Blockers must have circled and gotten ahead to cut him off. The only things that saved his hummingbird ass were the trees and thick undergrowth, which absorbed much of the fury of the unleashed storm of steel, lead and fire.

He bolted hard left, away from the ambush, noting as he did so that runners began paralleling him, out of sight in the underbrush but clearly audible as they crashed along with him. Desperation set in. He was being forced away from the river, out of the swamp, and toward open farmland where he had about the same chance of surviving as the proverbial snowflake in hell.

21

They formed a half-moon wrapped around his flanks and were driving him like beaters in the jungle drove game to the hunter's gun. Ahead, James saw open sky and sunlight through the trees. He was nearing the end of the river swamp. He contemplated turning back to take his chances at busting through the ring of steel to reach the river again. He was willing to give the Vistula another shot. A desperate man recognized no closed options. Christians thrown into the Roman coliseum took on lions and tigers with their bare hands.

Lions and tigers weren't armed with machine guns.

He erupted from the swamp onto the edge of a wheat or milo field. Green grew shin-high and stretched rolling and gently undulating for nearly two hundred yards before it ended against a low stone fence, the only attainable cover within sight. Beyond the fence sat one of the little Hansel-and-Gretel farmhouses, around which grazed a few cows. An old gasogene truck parked in front of the house did him no good; it wouldn't move an inch without the engine being stoked with charcoal and fired to boil up a head of steam.

Germans surging through the woods behind him and to either side began calling out to each other and yelping in triumph. They knew they had him where they wanted him. He could either run for his life across the open field—or he could dig in for Custer's Last Stand. Like Gramps always said, a treed 'coon retained the option of whipping the collars off all them mean hounds and *walking* right out of there. James recalled no occasion when a 'coon actually did it, however. His pelt almost always ended up stretched on the back of the smokehouse wall.

Barely hesitating, James blasted out of deep shade into blazing sunlight. In spite of his limp, he was still nearly as fast and quick as he had been as a jock at Oklahoma A&M. Sprinting in a zigzagging field run to make himself a more difficult target, head thrown back, arms pumping, baggy green coveralls flapping, he had eyes only for the stone fence and the cover it offered. He had a chance if he could reach it alive: Put up a brief defense to drive the enemy back into the swamp, then sneak down the back side of the fence and out the other end. Like a smart 'coon dashed in one end of a hollow log and out the other while the hounds stopped to yodel and cheer and brag.

A Polish farmer and his wife stood out back of the Hansel-and-Gretel house squinting in the direction of the wool mill and the column of smoke etched against the skyline. They turned in surprise toward the man running across the field toward them as first one weapon, then others, opened up from the swamp's border. They fled for the house as bullets began singing around their ears.

A Kraut MG-42 machine gun joined in the cacophony of discordant fury. It ripped a string of geysers past James's pounding feet, plowing up a furrow all the way to the stone fence. Bullets ricocheted off the stones, screaming into the sun.

James threw himself into overdrive. He could almost

hear Gramps saying, "Boy, never zig in life when you oughter have zagged."

The promise of the fence loomed large directly in front of him. A few more steps, a final leap over the top . . . By God, he was going to make it.

Suddenly, his head seemed to explode. He crumpled and rolled like a cottontail rabbit clubbed by a shotgun. Dirt clogged his mouth. Just before unconsciousness overcame him, he heard Germans running out of the swamp and across the field to finish him off.

22

James drifted in and out of a nightmare that paralyzed his muscles while evil incarnate crept toward his throat. Snatches of cognizance flashed through the fire burning in his head. He felt himself picked up roughly by his feet and shoulders, tossed into the back of a tarp-covered lorry, and then driven fast over rough, dusty roads. He couldn't figure the Germans. For some mysterious reason, they had opted not to execute him on the spot.

He was starting to regain full consciousness when the lorry drove into the courtyard of an old castle on the outskirts of Grudwald and stopped. The back flap of the tarp flew up. Two black-uniformed SS with death's-heads on their collars grabbed him by the feet and jerked him out onto cobblestones. The landing knocked the air out of his lungs, igniting fresh explosions of pain in his skull.

His hand came away bloody when he touched the area of pain on the side of his head, from which he determined that a grazing bullet had knocked off hide and hair and left him with at least a concussion. He wanted to lie right there on the courtyard for the rest of the century nursing his injuries and struggling to dispel the fog from his brain. Instead, one of the SS, a glowering NCO of about 40, kicked him brutally in the ribs.

"Aufstehe, Jude!" Get up, Jew.

A logical mistake. His borrowed green coveralls displayed the yellow Star of David. He didn't understand why being mistaken for a Jew had saved his life, at least temporarily, but he was in no position to question it. He would already have been dispatched if his captors knew he was a Yankee spy.

Maybe I should have sorted through the stacks of coveralls for a pair with a swastika on it.

The NCO kicked him again. Dizzy, James struggled to his feet and was immediately prodded down a flight of stone steps.

"Why didn't you kill me?" he asked his captor.

"An easy death is too good for a *Jüdisch ratte,*" the SS snarled. "You will suffer for what you have done to our comrades. Then you will die with the other vermin."

"I see you have my future planned."

The guard booted him hard in the ass and sent him reeling down the rest of the steps. He sprawled on the cellar floor, striking his face hard enough to make his ears ring, on top of everything else. The guard slammed the door and locked it, casting him into pitch darkness, but not before he glimpsed colors in the sky that told him sunset was near.

Damn! How long had he been out?

Had Regina and her uncle escaped? If so, that was his only consolation for an otherwise bad day.

No light entered the cellar. He felt around on his hands and knees, exploring. It was a smallish underground chamber with rock and concrete walls and only a single entrance, that via the steps to the heavy timber door. A thin layer of rancid straw covered the floor. A bucket in one corner apparently served as a toilet. It sloshed when he blundered into it and reeked to high heaven. The floor all around it was slimy and slick. He backed away to avoid retching. Obviously, other prisoners had been kept here.

Finding no possibility of escape for the time being, he settled in a corner opposite the slop bucket and supported his head on his drawn-up knees. It felt the size of a Black Diamond watermelon and throbbed as if a spike had been driven through his skull.

It occurred to him that he always had one final way out if everything else failed—the L-pills, still safe with the little clasp knife in the soles of his boots. He dismissed that option. *Too damned final.* He would wait to see what happened otherwise.

He found Regina's barrette, still in his pocket. It was plastic and looked harmless enough that his captors had not bothered taking it. The scent of her hair was still on it. He lapsed in and out of consciousness while clutching it in his hand.

Footsteps tromping down the cellar steps jarred his eyes wide. The door had been opened to frame a sky studded with stars. German soldiers were cursing and threatening as they hurled into the darkness of the prison a large number of shapes and forms, the identities of which James could not discern.

His first fear was that it might be after midnight and Regina and Professor Jahne had missed their flight.

Whispering to each other in Polish or Yiddish, neither of which James understood, men and boys shuffled and fumbled about in the darkness to find positions for themselves on the rotted straw. It was so crowded that anyone who might choose to sleep would have to do so standing or sitting up. People shifted about, moaning and complaining of the stench from the slop bucket as it was soon overflowing again. Someone unseen but felt slumped down next to James and said something in Polish.

"Ich verstehe nicht," James replied in German. I don't understand. *"Sprechen Sie Deutsch?"*

"Somewhat," James's new companion said in German. "You were not with us today. You were in the cellar when we arrived. Where are you from?"

"Warsaw," James lied.

"You are a Polish Jew and you do not speak Polish?"

"I was raised in Berlin."

"That is too bad. Why are you in Grudwald?"

"Vacation?"

"You choose a bad time of year, friend."

Around them the furtive and frightened whispering continued in the grim darkness. Everyone appeared to be waiting.

Soon James understood why. The Krauts arrived at the top of the steps and called two prisoners up to carry cold black coffee and a pot of *kohlrabi* soup into the cellar. Everyone except James had been issued a tin cup. The man next to James, who introduced himself as Michael Grojanowski, shared his. James found it unpleasant to eat because of the overpowering foulness of body odor and human wastes; he forced himself. He needed to maintain strength for any escape opportunity that presented itself.

"It is better not to see what is in the soup," Michael said.

While they ate, the men tried to comfort themselves by speaking of home and loved ones and the good days before the Germans and the Russians came. Even through forced cheer, however, emerged a dark undertone. Michael Grojanowski interpreted for James. He would say the speaker's name and then translate. In this manner, the dread and terror common in the darkness transferred itself to James.

"My mother wanted to lead me to a white wedding canopy," said Mier Pitrowski. "She won't have the experience of leading me to a black one."

Levi Shapiro, a thirteen-year-old boy, said, "Ah, even if I die a victim, my mother and sister perhaps will stay alive."

"I have left my dear wife and five children at home,"

declared Gershon Wiltschinski, and burst into sobs. "Who knows if I shall ever see them again, and what is going to happen to them?"

From the timbre of Michael's voice, James guessed him to be an older man. Michael did not know who had occupied the cellar previously; he supposed they were other Jews who had already been taken into the forest. He and the men and boys with him, Michael said, had this afternoon been trucked from the railroad transportation pens, told only that they were a work detail being assigned to dig pits. He shuddered.

"We are to dig graves," he surmised. "Why else would the Germans want pits?"

"For their defenses against the Russians?"

Michael doubted that. The German commander in Grudwald, edgy about the threat of a Soviet advance, was preparing for withdrawal, not for defense. Last night, his troops had had to fight Polish partisans behind their lines. This morning, Russian commandos had raided Grudwald. Michael had heard that traitorous Jews blew up a weapons laboratory at the old wool mill and that infiltrators were everywhere. All this was accelerating the German withdrawal—but first the "Jewish problem" in Grudwald had to be resolved, posthaste.

An order had been issued this morning for all remaining Jews in Grudwald to assemble. Alarmed, the leaders of the Jewish council had warned the Jews to escape if they could. Several managed to flee, even though German troops had ringed in the town. Furious Germans took members of the Jewish council to a nearby forest and shot them. That was the beginning of the roundup. For most of the rest of the day, Jews were either being herded to the compounds near the railroad tracks for deportation or they were taken elsewhere. How it was determined who went where and why was anyone's guess. Michael thought it might be a matter of expediency: Only so many Jews could be liquidated and the crime concealed before the Russians came. The rest would be deported.

"Since we have not been shot, and since we are being fed," Michael concluded, "I must believe that our special detail is to bury those who will be killed tomorrow."

He fell silent after that and, trembling, seemed to curl up inside himself like a caterpillar inside its cocoon. He aroused presently to translate a prayer segment by Gershon Wiltschinski.

"We have a great God in heaven and must pray to him," Wiltschinski said. "He will not desert us. We must all now together say the prayer of confession and penitence before death."

There were sobs and sighs as they recited the prayer in Yiddish. *What a cheerful bunch of campers,* James thought.

A guard pounded on the door, shouting, "Quiet, you Jews, or I shoot."

The Jews continued to pray quietly, in choked voices.

"Who knows who among us will be missing tomorrow?" intoned Michael. "We gravediggers shall dig our own graves."

23

Shortly after daybreak, the prisoners were served a breakfast of black coffee and chunks of stale bread. Some were
close to tears. All were depressed.

Afterward, gestapo and SS on duty ordered them up
the stairs into the courtyard, where two lorries and several other vehicles waited with drivers. James lost contact
with Michael Grojanowski without seeing what he looked
like. Surrounded by at least thirty SS and *Wehrmacht*
with machine guns at the ready, the Jews were ordered to
line up and be counted. Two men were then singled out
and sent into a second cellar to bring out the corpse of a
Jew who had hanged himself during the night.

They came back up out of the cellar, one at the head of
the body, the other at the feet, and threw it into the nearest lorry. James and about twenty other men had to climb
over the stiffened corpse to stand at the front of the open
truck. Six SS men with machine pistols climbed into the
back of the lorry.

Other gravediggers filled the second truck, and the

convoy departed the palace. It consisted of two lorries crammed with Jews, an escort of gestapo in a black limousine, and a truckload of SS men. It proceeded for about three kilometers through a summer morning disturbed only by the cawing of crows and the shrill cries of long-tailed magpies, a morning so lovely and peaceful that it seemed nothing bad could happen. Only the gloom that enclosed the convoy, like that which accompanied a funeral procession, betrayed its nature and darkened the morning.

The artillery duel near Warsaw was enjoying a lull, but it would likely start up again. Smoke from the burning wool mill had dissipated. German soldiers at a checkpoint watched the convoy as it passed, covering their faces with their arms against the dust. James glanced up at the cobalt sky. By now, the Carpetbaggers should be landing in Italy with Regina and Professor Jahne. At least the old scientist was out of reach of both the Germans and Russians. James's mission had been accomplished, even without him.

He looked around at the strained and haunted faces of the men and boys in the truck with him. How ironic somehow that his fate should be linked to that of the Jews because of a yellow star on a pair of filched coveralls.

The convoy turned off the road onto a path and soon stopped at a clearing in the woods. Jews were ordered to get down and line up in a double file where they were issued shovels and pickaxes from a pile. Crews of SS set up MG-42 machine guns around the clearing; all muzzles pointed inward toward the arriving work party. Two men threw down the suicide corpse. It was left crumpled in the grass like a bag of old dirty clothes while the crews went to work digging a long, wide trench, the dimensions of which—thirty feet by ten—had already been marked off with lime.

The overseer was a stocky SS colonel with thin-slashed lips that matched the cruel scar down the side of his face. He goose-stepped up and down the line of workers while he snapped his whip against the high tops of his shiny leather boots. Those who failed to work fast enough for him soon felt its liberal sting on their bent backs. James suffered it once. He controlled his temper, but silently vowed, God give him the strength and opportunity, he would exact revenge before he drew his last breath.

Soon the gravediggers were laboring in a ditch deeper than their heads. They worked in silence except for a terrified sob now and then. One fat individual with a pasty face and soft hands was unable to keep up with the speed of the work. The SS colonel with the scar and the whip shouted for him to get out of the ditch, undress, and get down on his knees. He then flogged the fat man until his bruised body looked as black as a spleen.

James flinched every time the whip bit into its victim's flesh. The OSS had been briefed about German atrocities committed against the Jews, about Hitler's so-called "final solution," but until now it had all seemed too horrific to be true. James was almost ashamed that Gramps hailed originally from Germany, a country that produced sadists such as the scar-faced colonel, and that Teutonic blood flowed through his own veins.

The fat man was ordered back into the ditch. Unable to rise and walk, he dragged himself to the edge and tumbled to the bottom, where he landed on his back next to where James was digging with a pickaxe. The sound of a pistol being cocked was as loud as the crack of a gunshot might have been. From the corner of his eye, James saw the colonel pointing his gun at the fat man. The fat man glared up at his tormentor in final defiance.

"I am perishing," he said in perfect German, "but Hitler will die, the Germans will lose the war, and you, Herr Colonel, will be tormented eternally by the devil's red-hot whip."

The SS colonel shot him through the head. Blood and skull fragments spattered James's legs. Helpless fury welled in his throat like sour bile, but he and the other conscripts doubled their efforts and did not so much as look up, for fear of suffering similar consequences. They moved the stiffening body from place to place as necessary in order to deepen the ditch.

At precisely twelve o'clock, the SS colonel ordered in German and in Polish, "Put your tools down. Get out and line up in double file to be counted."

They climbed out of the ditch. Guards surrounded them. James feared they were about to be executed and their bodies shoved on top of the fat man's in the mass grave they had dug. Accepting the inevitable, he coolly calculated how many steps it would take him to reach the SS Scarface's throat. He had been trained to kill quickly and efficiently. His only regret was that he would be unable to prolong the Nazi's agony before he died.

His muscles bunched for the final effort—but before he could act, the gravediggers were pushed away from the ditch and given cold bitter coffee for lunch. They sat on the ground for a half hour, lined up in two files, ordered not to move. They even had to excrete on the spot. The man sitting next to James was as bony as a starving hound and looked to be about fifty or so. He wore faded farmer overalls and a ragged flannel shirt that hung from his frame as from a clothesline.

"You are the stranger?" he said to James in German, whispering from the side of his mouth. "From last night, I mean."

James recognized the old-sounding voice as that of Michael Grojanowski.

"Good to see you," James likewise whispered. "I would have preferred under better circumstances."

"Whatever happens is God's will."

James chanced a sharp look at his companion. "It's not *my* will," he said. "Michael, we outnumber them."

"What can we do with our bare hands against their guns?"

"They can't get us all. Some of us will make it to freedom."

"I am praying," Michael said.

"Prayer is not enough. We need to pass the word. You speak Polish. I don't."

A guard came along and jabbed the butt of his Mauser against the back of Michael's head. "The next time I catch you talking," he warned, "the both of you will join your tub-of-lard friend in the ditch."

After that, Michael glanced away in fear every time James tried to catch his eye.

A lorry that looked like a large gray box with hermetically sealed rear doors arrived. It pulled up near the open ditch and stopped. The driver was a man of about forty who wore SS death's-heads. He got out of the van and smoked a cigarette while he gravely surveyed the big open ditch.

James and seven other men were directed to open the double doors. The rotted-eggs odor of gas almost overpowered them as they approached it. Mixed with the gas was the even more overpowering stench of human excrement.

The box was full of dead, naked bodies. Men, women, children, babies, old, young. All stacked on top of each other, arms and legs intertwined in a final orgasm of terror and pain. Strewn among the corpses were clothing, bedding, books, violins, toys, watches and other belongings. They must have thought they were getting on a bus with their valuables—up until the time they were ordered to strip off their clothing.

"You Jews!" Colonel Scarface shouted. "Get in there and turn everything out."

When the sickened workers hesitated, the colonel fetched his whip and screamed, "The devil with you, I'll give you a hand straight away."

He struck out in every direction with his whip, slashing at heads and ears and faces. Another SS joined him with the butt of his Mauser. When one man suffered a stunning blow and couldn't get up, the colonel drew his pistol and shot him through the forehead. A replacement was ushered over.

Although horrified at the scene, which seemed straight out of Dante's *Inferno*, the men dived in to perform their task.

There were no seats in the box. Straw mats on the floor were spread on top of a wooden grating like that in a public bath. From the cab into the back extended two tubes through which poison gas could be pumped from a generator. The inner walls were steel with two glass-covered peepholes between the cab and the rear to allow the driver and his assistant to observe with a flashlight when the victims were dead.

Damned Germans! They were so businesslike in everything they did, including murder.

Corpses were thrown out of the van on top of one another like rubbish on a heap. Other workers tossed the bodies into the ditch, while still others in the bottom of the pit packed them in like matches in a box, per instructions from the SS colonel. Children and babies were used to fill in the gaps. Every order was accompanied by screams, blows, curses or the popping and snapping of whips.

The resumption of the artillery duel near Warsaw seemed to make Colonel Scarface more anxious. James bided his time, waiting for an opportunity to make his move against the sadist. He would die, if need be, with a bang and not a whimper, taking at least one Nazi bastard with him to hell.

There were fifty corpses in the van. A second van arrived full of bodies. It was emptied the same as the first. Reason and hope told James that Gabrielle was not among the Grudwald victims, but he still searched the faces of the young women.

Lime was thrown into the pit between layers of corpses. After the second van was empty, the eight gravediggers inside the trench stacking bodies were forced to lie on top of them facing downward. Their clothing became smeared and stained with blood, shit, and other body fluids, apparently deeming the wearers too filthy to live any longer. Breathless muttering and whispering rose from the trench like a breeze through dead leaves as the Jews said their last prayers. An SS man produced a machine pistol and shot them in their heads one by one. Blood and bits of human beings sprayed from the pit. The breeze died.

The SS colonel shook the hand of another officer and congratulated him on a job well done. He looked self-satisfied as he stood spread-legged, snapping his whip in the palm of his other gloved hand, while guards and SS surrounded the remaining workers and forced them back toward the edge of the trench. The gravediggers looked horrified, demoralized, resigned.

"We are leaving this world," said Michael Grojanowski, shoulder to shoulder with James. "We are all getting out of this hell."

"We are going to send *them* to hell with us," James hissed back. "At least some of them, we will. We're going to fight. Pass the word to the others. Quickly."

Michael's eyes widened. "They have guns," he protested, as though James hadn't understood him before. "We don't."

"We're going to die anyhow. Which is better—to die like men on our feet or like pigs on our knees?"

Some of the SS were setting up machine guns about fifty feet away, all aimed at the gang of gravediggers.

"*Tell them!*" James barked underneath his breath.

That shook Michael out of his fear-induced lethargy. He nudged the man next to him, whispered something in Polish. That man's eyes narrowed. He stiffened with newfound courage and passed the word to the next man, who then passed it on down the line. In that manner, the mood began changing right before the surprised Germans' eyes.

Scarface looked suddenly alarmed. After all, Jews weren't supposed to behave like this.

The gravediggers had closed into a half circle, with the trench full of carnage to their rear and the Germans to their front, facing outward like a herd of buffalo on defense. Half crouching, they looked terrible and menacing in their desperation. The nearest guards began moving back to give the machine guns an open field of fire.

"On my command," James said, glaring at the colonel whose whip had gone still. "That one is mine."

24

While all this was going on, a German open-topped staff car entered the clearing unnoticed by the gravediggers, guards, and SS Colonel Scarface. An SS officer in black got out of the car. He was tall, with blond hair and a raptor's beak of a nose. His piercing blue eyes settled on the wiry, redheaded Jew who appeared to be leading some kind of standoff with his captors.

"*Halten!*"

The command defused the moment and froze everyone in place. The SS officer marched briskly into James's view, his spine as stiff as the riding crop he carried. Although Colonel Scarface outranked the newcomer, who wore a major's insignia, he sprang to attention and thrust out a palm. "*Heil Hitler!*" Major Fischer, whose life James had spared at the wool mill, ignored the salute and walked directly to James. Clearly, from the deferential way Scarface behaved, Fischer carried some kind of referred power.

A little sniff of distaste pinched the major's nostrils as he looked James up and down. Blood, mud and human excrement soiling James's coveralls, boots and skin made him feel further defiled under the scrutiny. Major Fischer fanned a hand delicately in front of his face to stir the foul air. James remained half crouched, muscles tensed like a cocked pistol ready to go off.

"It would appear *this time*," Major Fischer said, "that you have cooked your own goose."

James noticed that the gravediggers appeared ready to disengage with the introduction of this new factor in the equation, as though willing to grasp at any straw of hope. James decided that his own best course of action was to reach for that straw and let the thing play itself out for a few minutes. Still wary, he forced himself to loosen up. He didn't want the Germans to see how the adrenaline rush had left him with a case of jitters.

Major Fischer scratched the side of his jaw in a thoughtful way. "What did you mean when you said I owed my life to a Focke-Wulf pilot?" he asked.

"Because of him, I promised myself to let a Kraut live," James said. "You happened to be the next Kraut in line."

Fischer's lips curled slightly in amusement. "Who *are* you?" he asked.

"A Jew."

"You don't behave like the *Juden*."

"How do *Juden* behave?"

Major Fischer splayed his hand toward the yellow-starred gravediggers, who once again looked cowed and submissive. "Look for yourself. They would let you die for them—as Christ died for them and was rejected."

He laughed, a sound that was half snarl, half in amusement. "*Jude*, surely you understand that you and I cannot permit this course to continue. *Mein Gott!* Who knows where it will end? You allow me to live, I return the favor, and soon the chain is extended to such length that we are no longer killing each other. How can we have a war when no one kills each other?"

"Somebody calls a war and nobody comes," James agreed.

"Precisely."

"No more building things up during the recovery period between wars, then tearing them down again."

"You are a Jew who thinks. Good. Now think about this one carefully. I am looking for the old man, *Doktor* Jahne, whom you took from the laboratory. I think you are more capable of answering that question than is the colonel. Was he captured with you and brought here? Is his body among the dead?"

"Dr. Jahne is no longer in Poland," James said truthfully.

"And you would know this because . . . ?"

"Why would I lie? You've been unable to find him."

The SS major looked long and searchingly into James's eyes. "I could turn you over to the gestapo."

"You could."

"They would torture you until you soiled your own drawers before they helped you die."

"Possibly. They would still get the same answer."

Major Fischer thought about it. "I believe you," he said finally. "I also believe that the *doktor* remains in Poland, although you likely do not know where he is. Otherwise, you would not be separated from him."

He abruptly took a step and stood over the pit where he surveyed its grisly contents, his features stony and controlled. Colonel Scarface walked up and stood beside him. Fischer asked him a few questions, none of which James overheard. Colonel Scarface shook his head. Major Fischer turned from the grave. He looked pale.

"Have the men cover up that ghastly mess," he instructed.

"But, Herr Major . . ."

"Escort this Jew to my car." He pointed at James.

"But . . ."

Fischer glared, daring him to disobey. Scarface fell to as ordered. Two SS with machine pistols steered James to the staff car. Fischer climbed into the open backseat and closed the door, leaving James and his escort standing. The driver stared pointedly ahead.

"You understand why I cannot invite you to sit with me?" Major Fischer said. "You are not dressed for the occasion."

"True. I am dressed only for burying massacred Jews."

Major Fischer sighed. "We do only what must be done for the survival of civilization. We Germans are doing the work for which our entire world will one day be grateful."

James remained silent. He looked back at the pit, where the gravediggers were busy throwing dirt in on top of corpses. Colonel Scarface stormed up and down shouting and blustering, frequently betraying his nervousness by either stopping to look at Major Fischer or looking in the other direction toward the artillery duel at Warsaw. In his mind's eye, he probably saw the advance of the Soviet army.

"You are no Jew," Major Fischer said to James. "I know Jews, and you are no Jew."

James let it go.

"The Jews are the world's misfortune," the SS officer went on. "They stand against us as our deadly foe. There is no such thing as coming to an understanding with the Jew. There is one hard and fast rule: them or us."

James inclined his head toward the toiling captives. "I can see how they are a grave menace to the Reich."

Fischer ignored the jab. "Even Martin Luther, the founder of Protestantism, would agree with the Führer regarding the Jewish Question," he said. "In 1543, Martin Luther set out what he called his 'honest advice' on how to deal with the Jew. He said their synagogues should be burned, and whatever did not burn should be covered and spread over with dirt. They should be put in stables like livestock and made to toil by the sweat of their noses. If even then these 'poisonous, bitter worms' were still considered dangerous, they should be stripped of their remaining belongings and driven out of the land for all time."

James wondered why he was being told all this. Was there a guilty conscience beneath that Nazi exterior, attempting to justify the unjustifiable?

"There is only one problem," Major Fischer said, looking directly at James and letting his upper lip express his disgust. "There is no other land that wants the Jew and will take him."

He reached over the back of the seat with his riding crop and tapped his driver on the shoulder. He had grown weary of lecturing. The driver started his engine. Major Fischer looked at James again.

"It doesn't matter whether you are a Jew or not," he said. "It doesn't matter who or what you are. It is irrelevant at this point. Nonetheless, never let it be said that a German officer of the Reich is not generous or does not repay his debts. I grant you your life in repayment for mine. Plus, I throw in your comrades' lives as well, since the life of a German officer is of far more value than the lives of a bunch of Jews."

He paused. "Don't thank me," he concluded. "You will be transported with the other vermin from this town. Before it is over, you may wish you had died today. But whatever happens in not my concern. I have rendered my obligation to you and it is out of my hands."

James's bulldog mouth was unable to resist a last word: "We shall meet again in hell, Major."

"That is possible. I will tell you at that time how I managed to find *Doktor* Jahne even without your help."

He tapped his driver on the shoulder and the staff car drove off, tarrying only long enough at this place of death for the major to relay instructions to Colonel Scarface regarding James and the remaining gravediggers.

25

By the time the gravediggers finished filling in the trench, swarms of flies attracted to the gore were buzzing the clearing, gathering in clumps on spilled blood and human wastes, sucking fluids and laying eggs that would turn into squirming masses of maggots. Guards herded the reprieved gravediggers back into the lorries. The convoy lined up and set out on a return route toward Grudwald.

Michael Grojanowski was crowded into the same truck as James. He looked pale and withered, much older than he had on the trip out. He seemed unable to comprehend the miracle of his survival.

"*Ich habe nichts getan,*" he whispered. I have done nothing.

"Being a Jew is enough," James replied.

Michael retained his hope. "We are being transported to a labor camp," he said. "I overheard the SS major say so when he was speaking to the colonel with the scar. The Russian army is making gigantic strides forward. Hitler won't be able to do us any harm now, even if he wants to. Do you agree?"

How quickly and completely, it seemed to James, that Jews were willing to surrender even the faintest spark of resistance in exchange for hope that enemies sworn to exterminate them might have a change of heart at the last moment, or that a savior in some form might intervene. As the convoy sped toward town and an uncertain fate, the prisoners muttered verses from Psalms and prayed for those who had died that day and been buried in the mass grave. Among those receiving benediction were the trench workers shot in the head, including the thirteen-year-old boy, Levi Shapiro, who had worried about his mother and sister, and the man whose mother had promised him a white wedding canopy. All afternoon, wails had issued from the throats of workers who recognized someone they knew among the gassed corpses, and now prayers were said for them too.

It frustrated James that these people believed that reciting a chapter from Psalms did more to affect the course of events than killing Germans. In his estimation, there was truth in the old adage that those who beat their swords into ploughshares ended up plowing for those who didn't—or they ended up extinct. Why couldn't Michael and the others see that the Nazis were out to destroy every last Jewish man, woman and child?

"They will place us in a labor camp until the war is over," Michael whispered next to James as the speeding lorry jostled them against each other. "It won't be easy, but we will be safe there."

The convoy topped a hill and there was Grudwald spread out in its little valley. The Jew roundup was still in progress, with a sense of urgency that had not been present the morning before, when James had fled the town with Regina and the professor. Gunshots banged here and there. Bellowing German troops were hurling themselves about, kicking in doors and herding small groups of Jews. The convoy had to pull off onto the sidewalk to avoid running over the body of an old woman lying in the street. The Jews in the trucks mumbled their prayers faster than ever.

"If they were going to kill us, they would have done it out there," Michael asserted. "Don't you think?"

James took Regina's blue barrette from his pocket and clasped it as though it were his only hold on reality. He was no Jew, but, like a Jew, he was going passively into that dark night. Perhaps a man shouldn't criticize the Jews until he had walked in their shoes.

26

The convoy circled the town and stopped at the railroad sidetrack near where James had first slipped into Grudwald with Regina to rescue Professor Jahne. Railway transport cars still sat in a line, attached now to a black locomotive. The locomotive was building up a head of steam. It sat hissing, smoking, and shuddering a little as railroad men and *Wehrmacht* soldiers rushed about in a high state of urgency. The doors to the transport cars had been slid open, but so far, no cargo was being loaded.

For the first time, James saw the barbed-wire compound that Regina had told him about. The fence was more than 10 feet high and enclosed a half acre or so of packed earth next to the railroad. People were massed inside the fence. More were being crammed inside as soldiers marched Jews down from the town and pushed them toward the prison's only gate, where SS officers had a little engineer's table set up to dutifully record every prisoner's name in a log. Nazis had an obsession with counting and keeping records. One would think they wouldn't want to keep records of victims scheduled for murder.

Overseers and SS were everywhere, all armed with rifles, machine guns, or the ubiquitous "Jew stick." Machine-gun squads surrounded the enclosure, while others kept watch over the train. The Germans appeared in a hell of a hurry, almost in a frenzy. Cursing, they lashed out with their clubs to flail anyone within reach. Children, old men and women—it made no difference. It struck James as madness that at the same time the Russians were advancing and threatening to entrap the Germans, the Germans remained so obsessed with the "Jewish problem" that they couldn't leave with the job unfinished. Apparently, most of the Jewish population of Grudwald and surrounding towns, including refugees who had fled Warsaw to hide out in the countryside, was being prepared for transport. Gassing one van full at a time took too long.

James found himself ordered to line up at the gate to the compound with his fellow gravediggers and other Jews. He wasn't quick enough to avoid the vicious swing of a guard's stick. He ducked in time to save his head, but the blow across his shoulders sent him staggering. Isolated shots throughout the crowds left bodies for others to step over and warned him that all he could gain by fighting back was a bullet through the brain. He would have to wait for an opportunity. What he needed were some garlic bulbs, a flask of holy water and a howitzer.

Michael proved less fortunate and not as quick. A stick caught him on the back of his neck and felled him like a slaughtered ox. James grabbed him and dragged him into line before the guard had the chance to deliver another blow. While James's shoulder only ached in time to the pain in his head from his earlier bullet wound, Michael was out on his feet. James was afraid the Germans would execute him on the spot if he failed to respond and keep up with the line. He supported the other man with an arm around his waist and shook him to bring him back around. Slowly, Michael began to recover.

A burly junior officer walked up and down the lines counting the people. He stopped and looked searchingly at a tall young woman in a red dress who had wonderful eyes and long, braided hair. Then he smiled and beckoned.

"You," he said. "Take a step forward."

She was so paralyzed with fear that she could not move. He repeated the order and asked, "What is the matter with you? You are so pretty. Don't you want to live?"

She finally took a step forward. He told her, "What a pity that you are a Jewess. You are too pretty to die. There is the street."

She hesitated. Could he really mean it? Then she started to walk. Other women in the lines watched her with mixtures of jealousy, envy and terror. She walked slowly, step by step, as though uncertain of what she should do. She did not look back. Her arms were stiff at her sides.

Suddenly, with a high, strange laugh, the junior officer whipped out his revolver and shot her in the back. She fell, screaming, and he walked over and shot her in the head to shut her up.

"*Jüdisch ratte prinzessin,*" he scoffed.

Some of the other overseers laughed. Others turned away. The lined-up Jews looked straight ahead, all the blood draining from their faces. Bitter rage welled in James's throat, but he forced himself to look straight ahead with everyone else. Madness seemed to be infecting the entire world.

The SS officers at the engineer's table proceeded as though nothing had happened. James gave them his name: "Albert Einstein." The SS wrote it down. They eyed Michael when James provided his name, since Michael was still unable to speak.

"Something he ate," James said.

The two men entered the compound with the terrified

masses, Michael leaning heavily on James for support, and worked their way through the packed throngs as far away from the gate as they could. The people were very scared and very quiet. They stared out of pinched and frightened faces through haunted, hunted eyes.

James was searching for a space to ease Michael to the ground when someone called out his name. "James! Over here!"

Startled, he looked up. He saw short black hair, eyes like points of anthracite coal, and a small, striking woman waving at him.

Regina!

They had missed their airplane.

Regina had selected a spot inside the crowd away from the fences and out of sight of the guards, a measure calculated to hide her injured uncle, considering the Nazi predatory penchant for weeding out the weak. Professor Jahne lay on a pillow made from his overcoat, his ankle bound in a strip of black cloth torn from the hem of Regina's skirt. Regina stood guard above him like a hen over her last surviving brood, shoving and pushing to keep fellow prisoners from trampling him.

James maneuvered Michael through the mob and eased him to the ground next to the professor. Michael groaned and tried to sit up, but was still not quite right. He sagged, then stretched out on the ground next to the old scientist. Professor Jahne sniffed his disapproval and gave James a sour look.

"Young man, you are the source of nothing but trouble," he said.

"Some people are called to it."

Tears filled Regina's eyes. She embraced James soundly. "I thought we would never see you again," she cried in English. "I was sure you were dead."

"I was sure you were in Italy."

Disheartened, his only thought was that he had failed

his mission to get Professor Jahne out of Poland after all; he would now be dying for *nothing*.

"This isn't exactly old home week," he said. "I would rather not have seen you here."

"I am sorry that we let you down, James," Regina said.

"We were unable to outdistance them due to my impairment," the professor apologized, although he sounded resentful about it. "I attempted to explain that I am *the* Professor Erwein Jahne and that the Führer personally appointed me to Strasbourg University. However . . ." His white beard quivered with indignation.

"I would not let him," Regina put in. "I was afraid they would shoot him immediately for trying to escape with his research papers."

She explained briefly how they had come upon a group of Jews in the forest attempting to flee the roundup in Grudwald. Before they could go their own way again, a German patrol fell upon them and seized the entire bunch. Regina thought it safer for the both of them if they kept her uncle's identity a secret. Hauled to the compound, she gave their names as Gerhard Goldberg and his daughter Ursula.

That explained why Major Fischer had been unable to find the Jahnes, so far.

"Good for you," James approved.

He was looking around while she talked, his mind working again after an initial despondency. What mattered now was not *how* Regina and Professor Jahne were caught, but instead how he might succeed in his mission in spite of the setback. The difficult we do immediately, as Winston Churchill liked to say, whereas the impossible takes a bit longer.

He had to admit that things for the moment looked impossible. They were being held inside an impenetrable wire fence guarded by machine guns and caught up in a transport to an unknown destination, which had to be one of the death camps scattered across western Poland

and eastern Germany. Of course, if all else failed and it became necessary, he always had the L-pills secreted in the soles of his jump boots.

Grudwald settled down as the Jew hunt came to an end and the sun sank low in the western sky. Lines being processed past the SS at the engineer's table thinned out. Some soldiers herded in a few final strays; there was a single gunshot from somewhere and a fire still sent thin smoke into the sky. Otherwise, Grudwald might have been an abandoned little city.

"It is like a Passover," Regina said quietly, "during which *Goyim* smear blood above their portals to prove they are not Jews so that the Angel of Death will pass them by."

A quiet settled over the compound. Even the praying ceased. There was nothing to do but wait to see what happened. The sky gradually printed sad streaks of rose and orange. Nightfall would soon spread across the town. Most Jew transports began under cover of darkness, as though they were a shame that must be concealed. James recalled Gabrielle telling him how the gentiles in France resented the midnight trains and even blamed them on the Jews.

"Those damned Jews!" went the complaints. "They won't even let us sleep at night."

Regina offered to treat the bullet graze on the side of James's head as best she could with another bandage torn from her skirt.

He grinned. "How much skirt?"

"You have a fever. If we had thick slices of a large hot onion, we could wrap them on the soles of your feet to get rid of it."

"My Grams' home remedies were often worse than the affliction."

The locomotive on its track hissed and snarled impatiently through the stillness. Nearby faces faded into the encroaching purple of nightfall. Everywhere grew an awareness that the waiting was almost over.

The professor, who had been dozing off and on, exhausted as he was from his travails of the past two days, suddenly opened his eyes wide.

Michael moaned. *"Bald schiessen sie nicht mehr,"* he said. The shooting will soon be over. He sat up and looked around. "We are being taken to a labor camp," he whispered, still clinging to his hope.

James grabbed Michael and shook him hard, out of pure frustration. "Damn you!" he said. "We are being delivered to the ovens. Why won't you Jews fight?"

Regina threw her arms around James and gently pulled him away. Michael cast his eyes toward the ground, looking much put upon and ashamed.

"Do not take it out on this poor man," Regina said. "That is not fair."

The four of them—James, Regina, Michael and Professor Jahne—sat close together for comfort, a sort of family that had bonded out of chaos and uncertainty. After a while, Regina said to James, "Have you heard of Sobidor?"

He had, but she didn't give him time to answer. "Hitler chose it as a death factory in eastern Poland near Chelm. In September 1943, a transport arrived at Sobidor, included in which was a Red Army officer captured by the Germans. Three weeks later there was a spectacular revolt and four hundred Jews escaped."

"It was planned and led by the Soviet," James said.

"That is the point," Regina concluded earnestly, her face near his, grim and convincing. "The Jews *will* fight. They only need someone like the Red Army officer to lead them and show them how."

27

The transport began. Shouting and cursing erupted from the main gate as it swung open and guards began driving Jews to the waiting train in the dusk of the evening. Young and old people, men, women, children, infants wrapped in blankets, all thronging like a flock of bleating, frightened sheep—nearly 2,000 surviving Jewish souls gleaned out of Grudwald and neighboring towns being hustled to the big boxes on steel wheels.

Some people stared straight ahead, stoically suffering abuse from their herders. Others mourned, wailed, or recited prayers, wringing their hands and begging the guards not to do this thing. Women tore their hair and clung to bewildered children, who shuffled along among the legs of their family members, gazing up with eyes big in silent fear.

Yawning doors on the transport cars received them. There were no windows in the cars, only a few air gaps covered with gratings made of chicken wire. SS men with weapons ready to shoot stood on footboards on either side of the cars. Some lay on the roofs with machine guns. The Jews were being transported as though they were dangerous criminals.

As soon as guards filled up one car, they banged the doors closed, bolted them and chalked on the door the number of people inside: *300.* Precisely. Not one soul more, not one less. German efficiency in action.

"Tempo, schnell!" the SS shouted, wielding their clubs and whips. On the double, quickly.

Terrified people looking out through the air gaps in the cars asked hopefully, "How far is it to the place where we will be working?"

No one answered them.

James and Regina, together holding on to Michael and Professor Jahne to keep from being separated, let themselves be carried along with the slow, surging tide. Michael had recovered from the blow to his neck and complained now only of a splitting headache. He looked bonier than before; he had had no spare flesh to lose in the first place.

James remembered Regina's blue barrette in his pocket. She had told him it belonged to her mother. He pinned it in her hair over one ear for her. The gesture made her eyes fill.

"We may as well dress for the occasion," he said with more spirit than he felt. He continued to scan the scene with his eyes, seeking a way out. OSS agents were trained never to give up, even when things looked the most hapless.

Ahead of James and his little "family" in the crowd moved a young mother and her child. They clung desperately to each other to avoid being torn out of each other's arms. The mother was slight of build with dark hair and dark eyes. Her simple yellow housedress hung loose on her petite frame. It was faded to the same hue as the star sewn above her breast. The little girl appeared about six or seven and wore a dress the same color and style as her mother's, selected no doubt so that all would know they were a pair. She was so scared her dark braids trembled and her liquid eyes darted about like those of a lost fawn. One of her front teeth was missing.

Just as they reached the open doors, an overseer threw the child inside on top of all the other people and slammed the doors between her and her mother. After all, *300* meant *300,* not *301.* The mother charged the car, arms outstretched, clawing at the heavy door with her fingernails and screaming in German, "My child! *Mimi! Mimi!* Let me go with my child!"

Muted sobs came from inside. *"Mutter! Mutter!"*

People watched as though hypnotized. Some appeared annoyed at the mother for disrupting the process and putting them all in jeopardy. Oblivious of everything except her daughter, she continued to pant and bawl in anguish, the sound of an animal being beaten. She clawed at the door until a German guard ran over and struck her with the butt of his rifle.

That failed to stop her. She jumped up again, head bleeding, and hurled herself against the door again and again, as mindlessly as a moth against light. The guard and the overseer began to laugh at what to them seemed a comical interlude.

Recovering her sanity, she stopped, snuffling, and took a gold ring off her finger and offered it to the guard in exchange for his permitting her inside with her child. The guard took the ring, looked at it, tested it with his teeth. Then, satisfied, he stuck it in his pocket. He grinned at her and, at the same time, kicked her in the stomach with a jackbooted foot.

He continued to kick her after she fell to the ground until she was reduced to mewling semi-consciousness. James and one or two other young men started forward, but riflemen on the roofs of the cars stopped them with a warning volley of shots fired into the air. A machine gunner with them bolted his gun and pointed it at the masses, his finger on the trigger, waiting for the order to open fire.

"Our time will come," James muttered under his breath.

People were herded down to the next car. They stepped over the babbling mother on the ground, too fearful to aid her. Defiantly, James and Regina helped the distraught woman to her feet and brought her along with the rest of the family. The Germans seemed to have lost interest anyhow, once the fun ended. Michael took Regina's place in serving as Professor Jahne's crutch.

"We'll reunite with your child at our destination," James reassured the mother in German, a language she spoke so fluently that he assumed it was her native tongue.

"Do you think it is possible?" the woman asked.

Let her have her hope.

C ouplings between the cars took up the slack, pitch-ing the human cargo first forward, then backward en masse, as the filled train got underway. All inside the cars had to stand, everyone brutally jammed together, because there was no room to sit. The locomotive began to chug, blowing out sparks like frantic fireflies from its stacks. Mounted floodlights aimed over the entire length of the train during periods of reduced speed helped prevent escape attempts.

At the train's first lunge forward, James's foot caught an uneven spot on the floor and he would have fallen except for the crush of human bodies around him. He braced his back against the nearest wall, below one of the air gaps. Regina and the rest of the family, which now included the mother separated from her child, gathered close to support each other against the teeth-jarring jouncing of the car on its steel rails. It was dark enough inside that James could not see Regina very well, even though his face was buried in the dry scent of her hair.

Conversation was virtually impossible—even group prayers were drowned out by the clatter of wheels and the rattle of cars. The grieving mother managed to convey her name—Elena—and explain that she spoke German, and *only* German, because she was from Frankfurt. She and her daughter Mimi had traveled to Warsaw prior to the uprising to visit relatives. The Germans wouldn't let them return home.

Hot weather, high temperatures, and lack of air created conditions that challenged even healthy, strong, young people in the cars. People fainted, but they could not fall or lie down, so they remained upright until they revived. Since there were no toilet facilities—simply one bucket in each car, which no one could reach except those next to it—the stench of urine and bowels released from stress quickly became overwhelming.

Professor Jahne, an old man not in the best of health, his depression exacerbated by the conditions and his injury, had spoken hardly a word since James's reunion with him. He seemed introspective, withdrawn. A renowned professor, a scientist of the Reich, was not treated in such a manner! James could almost feel the old man's bitterness growing. Still, bitterness might sustain a man when nothing else could.

The train passed on through the darkened countryside, a black monster with its locomotive's single headlamp making of it a cyclops blasting through Hades.

"How can they treat people so inhumanely?" a loud voice protested. To which someone responded with a dark joke, gallows humor being a form of accepted Jewish resistance: "A German officer came to a Jewish house to confiscate the owner's possessions. The German agreed not to seize the weeping woman's things if she would guess which of his eyes was artificial. 'The right one,' she said. 'How did you know?' he asked. 'Because that one has a human look.'"

The train stopped once at a station to take on more water and coal. People fought to reach the air gaps, through which they offered station railway men as much as two hundred *zloty*, more than a day's wages, for a loaf of bread or a cup of water. One woman threw her watch out on the platform and begged to be given in exchange a glass of water for her dying child. The station men were afraid to give it to her. They kept the watch.

The transport resumed its long journey with a series of lurches. James again stumbled over the irregularity in the floor. He explored it with the toe of his boot as the train lined out at a more even pace. Surprised, he discovered an opening where part of a plank was missing. He stuck his foot down through it and felt the speeding wash of wind across it.

Regina stirred. "What is it, James?"

He had heard how German SS at concentration camps sometimes received arriving transports with the greeting, "The only way out is up the smoke stacks." Maybe there was a way out *before* they arrived.

28

Regina seemed less than enthusiastic about his discovery of a possible means of escape, and that puzzled him. Nonetheless, she and Michael shoved themselves against the suffocating press of humanity to give him room to explore further. By playing circus contortionist, he wriggled to his knees over the aperture. The roaring clacking of steel wheels and air that smelled and tasted of cinders, oil and locomotive smoke blew in through it. His hands traced the opening. It was about two feet long and about six inches wide, not quite big enough to permit passage of anyone larger than a very small child. But if he could remove the adjacent floor plank, it might be possible for some of the prisoners to drop through onto the railroad bed and escape without the guards on top or on the sideboards becoming aware of it.

Like the Boy Scouts, an OSS operative had to *Be Prepared*. Among the scores of devices created by the R&D (research and development) department of the OSS to aid field agents were such devious items as maps on the backs of playing cards, lipstick tubes and buttons with hidden compartments, women's corsets lined with razor-sharp stilettos, candlesticks that exploded, cigarettes laced with truth drugs, a plastic explosive called "Aunt Jemima" that resembled baking powder and could be blended into muffins or biscuits, a pencil that fired a .22 caliber bullet . . . and the L-pill and the old knife-in-the-shoe-sole trick.

He extracted the flat knife from its secret compartment in his boot sole and set to work digging at the embedded bolt heads that secured the wood to the car's frame. It was tedious work. He had to be careful not to snap the blade. His eyes were of no use in the effort; he had to feel with his fingers while he avoided being trampled.

The air was foulest near the floor. Human waste was being kicked and sloshed about. With the stench came the sounds of human misery that also seemed trapped at the bottom—a wailing and weeping and praying and gnashing of teeth, directly from Dante's *Inferno*. Old Preacher Seabolt back on Drake's Prairie might have thought it the end-time.

Somewhere up front a child was bleating at the top of its lungs. Somewhere else people were quarreling over what to do with the body of an elderly person who had suffocated to death. Professor Jahne's constant wheezing and moaning made James wonder if the old man was even physically capable of escape if offered a way.

He kept at his task, not knowing how much time he had left before the long, black train reached its unknown destination. He wore blisters on his hands. His head throbbed from wounds and fever, his shoulders ached. Gradually, he became aware that his venture had not gone unnoticed, even in the dark. Word of mouth spread the news to every corner of the car.

At first, people sounded approving of what he was doing. Then a different note entered the discourse. He didn't need to comprehend Yiddish or Polish to understand the rising chorus of dissent. Regina, Uncle Erwein, Michael and Elena babbled along with the rest, every-

body shouting back and forth until James feared guards
on the roof were bound to overhear.

He wriggled to his feet, wiping his filthy hands on his
coveralls. A plumber must have the shittiest job in the
world.

"What the hell is going on?" he shouted directly into
Regina's ear in order to be heard above the noise. "Can't
you tell them to pipe down?"

"They are afraid," she said.

"We're all afraid."

"They are saying everybody cannot get out before the
guards notice."

"I don't expect everybody to try."

"James! Slow down and listen. The Germans hold everyone collectively accountable for the actions of individuals. If even one of us escapes and the rest cannot,
they will shoot all who are left behind. That is why they
are so frightened."

"Regina, I didn't come here to save Jews. I came here
for you and your uncle. Just a few more minutes. Get
ready."

*Let the damned Jews argue it out among them-
selves on whether or not they would even try to escape.
Couldn't they understand that all were going to be killed
anyhow?*

He went back to work. Fortunately, the wood was old
and dry rot had set in. He finally wrenched a board free
to enlarge the escape hole. Urine and other waste made
it slippery. He dropped it on the rushing ground between
the tracks below. Steel wheels and the rumble of the train
covered the sound. He ran his hand around the opening to
check for splinters or other hindrance to a smooth exit.

Angry, frightened people were crowding in from all
sides. James ignored them and gathered round the members of what he was subconsciously thinking of as his
family in order to issue last-minute instructions. He stood
astride the opening in the floor to protect it.

"We'll go out one at a time," he said hurriedly. "It'll

have to be done fast to avoid becoming separated. This is the order of exit: Elena, Michael, Professor Jahne, then Regina. I'll be last. Feet first, then let go immediately. Don't try to get up until the train passes over you and I tell you it's clear. Stand up too soon and the guards might see you silhouetted against the skyline, or they'll turn on their floodlights. Any questions?"

James mistook their silence for concurrence. "Good. We're going out the next time the train starts up a steep grade and slows down."

"Elena will not leave without her daughter," Regina interjected.

"Then she stays. Okay, Michael, that makes you first."

"James . . . ?" Regina started to protest, but she was cut short by a commotion that broke out around them.

From the sounds of it, a number of people were attempting to force their way to the opening while still others were trying to block them. Someone, a big man, from the feel of him, poked James in the chest with a hard finger and shouted Polish in his face. Regina translated.

"He is saying that no one leaves. There are old people, children, sick people and babies who will be unable to get out. The Germans will kill them if anyone escapes. So, since everybody can't go, nobody goes."

The train hit a grade and began to slow, straining up the hill. There might not be another opportunity. Things were about to get nasty.

James still had the knife clinched in his fist, but he didn't want to have to kill this guy unless he had to. Instead, he inscribed the man's outline with his hands to find the target, then lunged sharply and viciously upward with his knee into the groin. The man grunted in pain and surprise, folded over and then fell backward into the cushion of human flesh. That put him out of commission, and because of the darkness, no one could see exactly what had happened.

The train continued to slow. "I am prepared," Michael

said. He had found a hero and was going to stick with him. At least James had gotten through to one Jew.

"Then we're outa here, *kemo sabe*."

"James . . . ?" Regina again. "My uncle is old, he is sick, and I think his ankle is broken. We will only slow you down. You will have to go without us."

"I can't leave him," James shouted back. "Don't you understand that?"

"What difference does it make now? The Germans do not want him anymore. They are sending us to a concentration camp. Do *you* not understand that?"

James dared not take the chance of leaving the old scientist behind alive. Sooner or later, Krauts somewhere might come to their senses and realize who the professor was, no matter what other name Regina told them. After all, Major Fischer, for one, was already scouring the countryside trying to find him. If nothing else, once the old man's identity was discovered, the Germans would force either Regina or her uncle to disclose where James cached the tin box containing the scientist's research papers along the Vistula River. Those papers were almost as valuable to Hitler's A-bomb program as the old man himself.

"You have a job to do, James," Regina said, reading his dilemma. "I know. Duty first and all that. Just like the Germans."

James was gearing himself mentally to do anything necessary to make sure neither the Germans nor the Russians got their hands on Professor Jahne after he disappeared through the bottom of the train. His palm sweated on the hilt of his knife.

"You do understand, James, that you will have to kill me first in order to get to my uncle?"

He thought of the pretty girl with the braids and wonderful eyes whom the SS officer shot in the back at the compound gate. Was he any different, any better, than the SS if he *murdered* the professor—after first *murder-*

ing the old man's niece? How many years of nightmares would a deal like that be worth after the war?

The train reached the top of the crest and began picking up speed.

"We must go now!" Michael urged, pulling on James's arm.

"The next move is yours," Regina said.

Steel wheels clacked faster and faster, the sound filling the car through the opening in the floor.

James took a deep breath and exhaled slowly. He gripped the knife. In the darkness, Regina's hand rested lightly, questioningly, on his arm. He dropped his chin on his chest. Mission or not, he folded the knife, knowing full well that he might be passing up his last chance to either accomplish his mission or avoid a Jew's fate. He really *did* need to get his head examined. There was nothing that covered anything like this in any of the OSS manuals.

29

He was beginning to think like a beer bottle himself: empty from the neck up. Uncle Henry would never accept an excuse for failure. Not with the fate of the war and the world in the balance. But that was reasoning in the abstract. Reality was an old man and a young woman, *real people* in the way.

"What else can we do?" Michael approved, automatically accepting James's decision.

"I could hang myself and beat the Krauts to it," James said.

The long, black train roared on through the night. And because everyone could not go out through the hole in the floor, no one went. An OSS agent, conditioned to make the tough decisions, hadn't the guts to do what must be done. As a result, he had failed his mission. The Allies would never receive the necessary technology to build the A-bomb first; the world's leading nuclear scientist and his research papers were the same as lost. Years later, some archaeologist, hunter or hiker might discover the tin box along the Vistula River—long after the Germans had bombed the rest of the world into submission and Professor Jahne's bones were in the earth. The most James could hope for now was to try to keep the professor's identity hidden from the enemy in case some Nazi bureaucrat woke up and came looking for him.

Daylight was breaking when the transport arrived at a small deserted station with a white sign in big Gothic letters: NISKO. Below the name appeared the inscription ARBEIT MACHT FREI. Work Makes Freedom.

Nisko, the camp, was in an enormous clearing bordered on three sides by woodlands. In view from the station was a triple barbed-wire fence more than 10 feet high. The train switched to a sidetrack, where the locomotive slowly backed its cars through a gate with a sign: SONDERKOMMANDO.

The gate was shut as soon as the train passed through into the wire fortress, which was guarded by a large number of SS men, German guards, Polish auxiliary police, and minefields. Already, escape seemed humanly impossible.

Transport doors flew open, letting in the blinding morning light. Inside the cars, the Jews were hungry, thirsty and broken in spirit. Putrid fluids trickled onto the track. A group of a dozen or more German officers emerged with whips in hand from a white shack to unload the cars, count the prisoners and check manifests, while liberally employing their whips to stragglers. Crushed from all sides, a number of older people were found to have died standing up during the night. Emptying the cars allowed their bodies to slump to the floor, where they were left.

James jumped down to sandy soil that looked gray rather than brown. Before the whips reached him, he helped Regina and Elena disembark. Then, with Michael, he caught Professor Jahne to prevent his falling and attracting the attention of the guards.

Overwrought with the expectation of reuniting with

her child, petite Elena braved the wrath of guards and overseers by darting into the confusion and making her way forward to the car where she had last seen Mimi the evening before. Her pale yellow dress flashed in and out of the crowd as she ran, shouting her daughter's name: *"Mimi? Mimi?"*

Soon there were two yellow dresses, one much smaller than the other. They held each other and wept for joy. Rather than stay forward with the other transport, Elena guided her daughter back to James and his little group. Regina hugged the both of them. There were tears in her dark eyes.

Elena introduced the six-year-old to James with, "Darling, if anything should happen to Mommy, I want you to stay with him and do what he says. He is a good man, and you can trust him."

Mimi's fawnlike eyes took in James from head to toe, as though deciding his character for herself. Then she held up her arms and insisted on James's stooping down so she could hug his neck.

Great! Quite the core of a New Resistance: Two men, a crippled old man, two women, and a little girl.

"Here come the Deutsch boys," James warned.

Quickly, they lined up with the other new arrivals in several ranks on the square in front of the white shack. The entire transport was ordered to undress. James shucked his green coveralls and boots and stood in line barefooted and naked except for his boxer shorts. He hoped no one examined his boot too closely and found the knife and L-pills; they were a dead giveaway to his identity. He hated giving them up.

The morning sun shone over the fence upon the pathetic and embarrassed Jews, upon rows and rows of wooden barracks-like buildings beyond, and upon a water tower painted bright red with a white swastika on it. Next to James, Regina stood at rigid attention in her panties, looking defiant, chin and bare young nipples up. Some of the *Einsatzgruppen* men were looking her over with obvious designs upon her and the other young women. James's jaw clinched.

Elena, on Regina's other side, sobbed softly while she clutched her daughter close. James could count every one of their ribs. Their hip bones jutted through baggy pink panties. Mimi had soiled hers during the night. Blood stained Elena's from the beating she sustained at Grudwald when overseers wrenched her from her daughter's side.

Michael, as pale and bony as a skeleton, seemed to be getting older and older day by day. His face looked as sharp and pointed as a starved greyhound. An emerging black beard obscured his jaw, while the graying hair on his head was starting to fall out.

Professor Jahne appeared a little ridiculous and pompous standing in his underwear with his ample white belly and white beard quivering in indignation. An SS slashed him across the face with his whip and moved on when the old man started to protest such treatment being rendered a representative of the Führer's scientific community.

"Shut up!" Regina sharply admonished. "You must not remind them who you are."

Guard officers ordered everyone to deposit his or her clothing, footwear and all valuables and money in separate piles. Those attempting to withhold anything would be shot. Talking was *verboten*. Then the ranks were given a "right face" and paraded past a group of women with shaved heads who issued uniforms from a long table. A uniform consisted of a black-and-white-striped shirt, striped trousers, and a pair of straw sandals like those worn by criminal internees. James's stripes hung off his wiry frame, but they were an improvement over the blood-crusted and filthy green coveralls. It was only after the lice started biting and sucking that he would yearn for his old clothing.

Even little Mimi was issued stripes. Her mother had to roll up the cuffs to keep the legs from wiping out her tracks. Regina, James thought, could make even baggy black-and-white stripes look fashionable. He wasn't sure that was a good thing, judging from the way the *Einsatzgruppen* ogled her.

A gang of *Sonderkommando* foremen—Jewish prisoners selected for special work details—entered the square and waited for new laborers to be assigned. A German officer stepped up and shouted, "Carpenters, cabinetmakers and bricklayers—forward!"

"Workers' brigades," Michael explained. "See the big man in front?"

James nodded, a tip of his chin.

"I know him," Michael said hurriedly. "Leopold Socha is from my hometown. He signaled me to volunteer."

"Go!" James said. He himself had to stay near Professor Jahne.

"Not without you."

"Don't be a fool. Do it!"

Reluctantly, Michael stepped forward with about 40 men. Other people with special skills were called out of the ranks. James saw Leopold Socha speaking with head bowed in submission to an officer of the Elite Guard. The soldier turned and approached James.

"You are a bricklayer," he snapped. "Over there."

James had no choice. Disobedience or defiance in any degree led to immediate execution. He looked back as *Einsatzgruppen* marched the rest of the transport off toward the barracks, leaving behind in piles their clothing, shoes and valuables. Regina's eyes sought his. Her lips formed words: *God bless and keep you, James.*

He thought he would never see her again. Or Professor Jahne. The way things were going, maybe he should consider giving up his secret-agent license.

The Germans assigned him to a group that included Michael and the gang boss Socha and was charged with carrying bundles of clothing from the square to the storehouses. They had to run a gauntlet of lined-up overseers who beat anyone they could lay their whips to, especially the newcomers. By noon, James's face was a bluish mass out of which peered his bloodshot eyes. Even Grams would have had difficulty recognizing him.

During a brief pause for lunch—a greasy gruel of some sort and a chunk of black bread, Leopold Socha squatted on the ground with Michael and James. He had bristly black hair, a prominent beak for a nose, and a face only a mother could love. His broad nose crooked from side to side down his face, the cheek bones looked crushed, and a jagged scar extended the width of his mouth on one side. Like everyone else, he was scraggly and unshaved. Once a big man, he now looked big only in comparison to the others because of his large frame. Otherwise, he was as emaciated as everyone else. He was about 30, but a hard-lived 30. He spoke German in addition to Polish and Russian.

"Be sure to eat the bugs and worms," he advised, tongue in cheek. "They're protein. You'll need it."

"It's a good thing I'm not much of a gourmet," James replied, gulping down the soup, worms, larvae, bugs and all. He was famished, having eaten nothing since coffee and bread the morning before, at the castle cellar.

A guard was watching them. Socha clearly had something on his mind. He lowered his head over his bowl. Lips barely moving, he said, "Grojanowski explained about yesterday at Grudwald. He thinks you are military. You were going to fight them. A desperate action, but it took guts."

"Maybe it's because I'm not Jewish."

That stung Socha. "Don't judge until you know what you're talking about," he growled. "You are being selected."

"Selected for what?"

"You will be told in due time. You are not selected to be kept alive—but you can sell your life at a higher price if need be."

30

Thin drifts of gray smoke sifted upward into the darkening evening from somewhere on the far side of the camp, emitting a sharp odor James associated with hog butchering time on the farm. Pig fat rendering too long in a kettle over a hot fire smelled like that. Michael Grojanowski turned his head away, not wanting to know what it was. He had suffered terribly from the masters' whips during the day and had now collapsed with the rest of his labor party in a holding pen near the storage buildings while they waited to be let into the compound with the general population. A mean-looking *kapo* named Groner, who had a bad left eye, kept watch over them with a stout club. A *kapo* was a prisoner with the status of a policeman inside the camp.

"If we keep our noses clean and bow to hard work and stay out of trouble," Michael said, clinging to his stubborn Jewish hope, "we should survive here until the war ends."

Leopold Socha seemed to know better. He caught the

expression on James's face as James contemplated the smoke.

"Don't look in that direction," he admonished. "You won't find your friends in the smoke, yet. You'll see them again. Every week or so another transport arrives. Unlike most camps where we are segregated from the females, here at Nisko all are housed together for expediency. And here all work for the German war effort until we become *them.*"

He indicated the frightful, otherworldly creatures moving about inside the greater compound with inanimate slowness, many of them staggering along one step at a time with no apparent destination. They were virtual skeletons with skin stretched over them, more emaciated than human beings could be and still live. Wrists, knuckles and elbow joints bulged, arms looked like broom handles, eyes were sunken into their skulls so that they appeared as empty caves. Unmistakable evidence of the degradation humans would endure in order to survive.

"These Jews are almost ready for the open ditch and a bonfire," Socha said, gesturing toward the smoke. "By the time we are ready for the smoke, the Germans will have improved the procedure."

James had witnessed the death vans. Now he looked in the direction Socha had and observed what appeared to be the foundation and lower levels of a huge brick building rising out of the ground. A coldness formed in the pit of his stomach. Michael's face turned pale and he shuddered.

"What is it?" He could hardly get the words out, so great was his dread of actually knowing.

Socha explained simply, as though in conversation about ordinary matters: "The camp commander must get the ovens built as quickly as possible in order that his superiors will be impressed with his efficiency in burning bodies. Corpses don't burn well piled into ditches."

Michael's ears had picked up a single word: *Ovens.* James had read secret OSS reports of the existence of

Nazi crematoriums for humans, but he had never expected to see one. Certainly not from this vantage point. Socha nodded matter-of-factly, without visible emotion.

"Once the ovens are completed," he said, "the assembly line of death will go into full production to fulfill Hitler's promise of a 'thorough solution' to the Jewish problem. The mockery of it is that we are constructing that loathsome edifice with our own hands, through whose chimneys we will all soon pass."

The implication of *bricklayer* dawned on James with a horrific jolt. Socha was the labor boss in charge of building the furnace; James was a member of his crew.

Jews, Socha went on, were being evacuated, ahead of Russians advancing from the east and Americans and British from the west, and rushed to camps like this one, in Germany and western Poland. The war might be going badly for Hitler, but he still had time to take care of the despised Jews.

"I have seen how the ovens work," Socha said. He took a deep breath as he dredged up memories better left buried. Clearly, he had been through the process before, somewhere—and somehow had survived. "Women and children go first, wearing only their underclothes. Men follow behind them. All are heavily guarded, and are told they are going to the baths to be disinfected for lice. There are two separate parts of the building. Sometimes there are two buildings. One is for women and children, the other for men. Obviously, I personally have not seen what it is like inside at the time, but I have been in them before and afterwards.

"Everything looks as a bath should look. There are faucets for hot and cold water, even sinks to wash in. The doors are clamped shut as soon as the people are inside. Gas comes hissing out from vents in the ceiling. Horrible shrieks are heard, but they never last long. They say mothers cover their little ones with their own bodies to try to save them."

Socha shifted his brooding, angry gaze in the direction of the construction site.

"The bath attendant observes through a small pane in the ceiling. It is all over in minutes. The floor opens and the dead tumble down into small carts and are trundled to the ovens by the *Sonderkommando*. Everything is organized in accordance with German technology."

The world *had* gone mad.

An eerie silence hung over the camp, disturbed only by the occasional slamming of a door, a shout from a guard, the sound of a vehicle in the German administrative and guard section outside the main gate. The camp was settling down for the night. From somewhere near the smoke rose the babbling and honking of . . . *geese?*

Socha confirmed it. "Krauts use them for their feathers and for covering up the cries of the damned," he said.

He lowered his head wearily between his knees. Groner the *kapo* was watching them closely, as though suspecting a conspiracy. James felt exhausted. His battered body ached all over. By now, Uncle Henry must have given him up for lost after he and Professor Jahne failed to catch the Carpetbaggers' redeye flight out of Poland.

He *was* lost. Lost in hell.

Socha met James's eyes. The experience was like a blow to the midsection, it contained such rage.

"What is your name?" he asked.

James thought it better to stick to the name he had facetiously provided the SS: "Albert Einstein."

"It is a Jewish name. Yet you do not speak Yiddish . . ."

"I wasn't raised in a Jewish home."

He thought Socha was about to explain why he had been "selected." Before the labor boss had a chance to say anything else, however, Elite Guard officers rushed toward the holding pen. Groner snapped to attention and began running among the prisoners, swinging his club like the bully he undoubtedly was.

"*Achtung!*" the guards shouted. "*Juden*, on your feet!"

"How much time before the oven is finished?" James asked Socha.

"Two weeks. Perhaps less," Socha said, before Groner and guards with whips rushed to drive them through a gate into the main prison.

31

The unpainted wooden barracks at Nisko were each about 100 feet long. Doors and windows were nothing but empty eyes. A hut outside for every two buildings served as a latrine, overflowing with human waste and reeking enough, as Gramps might have put it, to gag a maggot. Men and women used the same one.

The red water tower that presided over the camp provided the only splash of color. It stood on its tall spindly legs like one of the sinister Martian machines from H. G. Wells's *War of the Worlds*. Groner escorted James and the other workers past the tower to their barracks. He said nothing, but he kept his club ready and an eye on James and the Jews with distrust and hostility.

Incontestably, cruelty was the law of the universe. Veteran internees they passed on the way wore impossibly vacant looks and mere scraps of their original stripes as they shuffled along, desperate to beat the sundown curfew to their rabbit warrens. Socha dropped off at his Barracks 3. Groner continued with James, Michael and the other "bricklayers" from the day's transport to Barracks 8. The stench from the burning human pits cloyed stronger among the barracks than elsewhere, as though to remind inhabitants of their own fate.

So far, James was little impressed with Leopold Socha and his hushed whisperings and implication of some secret conspiracy for which James had been "selected." From his experiences with Jews so far, he doubted that any of them were going to fight in sufficient numbers to actually accomplish anything. If there was going to be an escape from Nisko, it was up to him to machinate it—and he must take Professor Jahne with him, if possible.

Groner stopped in front of a building with bare-trodden ground in front and a large number *8* painted above the door. The *kapo* motioned with his club for the Jews to go inside. He followed them in. Socha had earlier warned James about him.

"*Kapos* patrol the grounds at night," he had said. "Most of them are not Jews but are thugs and criminals sent from German penitentiaries. They have unlimited power inside the camp. They make wagers on who can beat to death the most Jews. Groner is the worst among the worst."

James hesitated inside the door of the barracks, aghast at what he saw. Sufficient light entered through windows to permit a limited first view. Michael's long face turned white; James thought the scarecrow was going to throw up.

Barns for cattle were more suitable as living quarters for human beings than this long, dark stable of misery. Piles of feces stood here and there on the straw-covered floor. Wooden bunks stacked like shelving accommodated the sick and starving. People sneezed, coughed and scratched lice, but otherwise seemed dead to this world and merely waiting for the next. Zombie eyes stared out of the gloom at the newcomers.

James felt relieved when he heard Regina calling to him from out of the dimness at the rear of the barracks. He had been afraid he might lose contact with the professor. Groner poked him with the end of his stick and followed them to where Regina had selected and staked out a sleeping shelf that would accommodate the family near a rear window. Late afternoon light suffusing through the window revealed something different about her appearance, but he couldn't tell what it was until he came near.

He stopped in astonishment. Her hair had been shaved down to her scalp. He blinked. Regina, looking self-conscious, splayed her hands across her head as though to hide beneath them. Before either could say anything, Elena and her daughter popped down out of the bunk. Elena's head had also been shaved, but little Mimi's braids were spared. Not due to any generosity on the part of the Germans, James was sure, but merely because she didn't have enough hair on her small head to make the effort of taking it worthwhile.

"I went to the hairdresser's while you were away. Can you tell?" Regina said in English, to exclude Groner. Her lips trembled. "Do you think Jurawski would like it?"

"You could grow a mustache and you'd still be beautiful."

"You always say the right thing. I suppose they stuff pillows or flight suits or something with our hair. Nothing is too good for the German troops."

Groner's presence made the reunion awkward. Mimi looked as though she yearned to run to James and hug him, but she held on to her mother's striped pants instead and sucked her thumb, watching the *kapo* fearfully from her big fawn's eyes. Professor Jahne swung his legs over the side of the communal bunk and sat there glaring at Groner. Groner laughed, more a sneer, and raked Regina up and down with his hard eyes.

"Hair or no hair," he said in German, "I won't kick you out of my bed."

James slowly turned to confront him. The *kapo* was fully a head taller than the American and possessed the neck and shoulders of a boar hog. Clearly, *kapos* enjoyed a better diet than other inmates.

"Watch it, little man," Groner snarled, dismissing him with a flick of his stick.

James held his ground. Groner frowned and looked over James's head. "You do me favors, I do you favors," he promised Regina. "I can keep you alive. Think about it."

He glared at James from his good eye, but something about the way the smaller man's dark brown eyes returned his gaze, something dangerous, made him swallow and look uncertain. He tapped James on the chest with his stick.

"Nothing will keep you alive, runt," he threatened. He shifted his weight from foot to foot underneath James's unwavering eyes, then turned and stalked out of the building.

James was certain they hadn't seen the last of this creature.

With Groner gone, Mimi threw herself into James's arms and cried, "Alber'! Alber'!" She couldn't pronounce *Albert* because of her missing front tooth. Everyone gathered around to tell one another what had happened to them during the day. The girls and Professor Jahne displayed fresh serial numbers tattooed on their inner forearms. James and Michael would receive theirs tomorrow, since they had been busy on the work detail today.

"Hurt," Mimi complained. "I cried."

They were all going to be burned in the new furnace when it was completed, but in the meantime the Germans were permanently marking their intended victims. What kind of disturbed minds did such things?

"I'll probably be numbered 666," James commented.

A *kapo* came by and pounded on the door frame with his stick to silence the building's occupants. James boosted Mimi onto the top shelf. Professor Jahne received her. A thin matting of loose, dirty straw covered the bunk. The rest of the family climbed in around the little girl as though to protect her from threat as best they could. James lay on his side, looking out the window. Regina curled up to his back. Mimi insisted on sleeping next to James, where she felt most secure; she wriggled in between Regina and James and squeezed his neck with both arms.

"I love you very, very much," she whispered.

Great! Exactly what I need! He had been dispatched to Poland to wrest one old man from the Krauts—and here he was, playing guardian angel to an assortment of Cowardly Lions, imps, maidens and cripples.

James stared out the window at the night, watching, guarding, feeling the weight of his responsibility and his mission, feeling lice crawl. The others soon fell asleep. The bunk was so crowded that if one turned over, all had to turn. Their collective future looked bleaker than the darkest night of winter.

He could not sleep. The ghouls of war took over every time he closed his eyes. Each time he drifted off, some panicked sensory recollection sprung open his eyes. There were flames everywhere. Flames changed to tanks and armored cars and they were chasing little Mimi. Mimi turned into Regina, Regina into Gabrielle. The big *kapo* Groner with the stick was among the Germans. His hair flowed in flames, and his lips were drawn back to expose a dragon's breath, and he was about to catch Gabrielle . . .

Seized with terror and dread, James sat bolt upright.

"James, what's the matter? Wake up!" Regina said.

"I was having a bad dream."

"We are all having bad dreams tonight," she said, and put her arms around him and Mimi.

"My hair will grow back," she whispered. "Am I so ugly?"

James turned over carefully as not to wake the others. He reached and drew Regina and Mimi closer.

"When I was a little girl like Mimi," Regina murmured, "I was afraid of the dark."

32

The new transport quickly fell in with the camp's routine. A typical workday at Nisko began with a cup of boiled dingy water for breakfast. At noon there was the murky liquid called soup. The day ended with a piece of bread. No wonder inmates were nothing but skeletons by the time overseers deemed them unfit for labor and sent them to the slaughter pit.

As expected, James and Michael were assigned to Leopold Socha's crew as bricklayers after receiving their tattooed numbers. There were only two 6's in James's. Regina was assigned to work at the commissary tailor's, while Elena and her daughter replaced the previous keepers of the geese—the keepers' bodies—rumor had it—having been among those burning in the pit on the day the Grudwald train arrived. As for Professor Jahne, who could barely walk on his fractured ankle, he hobbled along with his niece to the tailor's, where a sympathetic crew boss, another prisoner like Socha, gave him a sit-down job at a sewing machine, making army uniforms.

Those who could not work were sent to the pits without mercy. As far as the camp administration was concerned, Gerhard Goldberg was just another worthless old Jew.

The old man found it agonizingly humiliating to adjust to the fact that his country had turned on him, one of Germany's most respected scientists. It was demeaning, he complained, to have to hide his true identity. If he simply gave the Germans his true name, he argued, that alone would save them all. James feared every day that the old man would walk up to some guard in that lofty manner of his and declare he was *Professor* Erwein Jahne, whom the Führer himself had appointed to Strasbourg, and demand that he be released. Perhaps the old man had a point, if Major Fischer was indeed still looking for him, but while the name *might* save him and his niece, it meant immediate execution for James and the end of any chance of the Allies obtaining a German nuclear scientist to help them beat Hitler in building the A-bomb.

Regina kept a close eye on her uncle and warned him to keep his mouth shut. Privately, she confided to James that she was afraid the old man wouldn't last long, what with abuse, starvation, and poor living conditions compounded on top of his age, injury, and failing health. All the more reason that James must work quickly to find a way out, hopeless though it seemed at the moment.

What he should have done when he had the chance was shove the stubborn old goat through the hole in the bottom of the railroad car—or leave him behind with the knife in his heart to render him useless to the Krauts.

Whenever the work whistle sounded in the morning, internees were expected to run, not walk, to their assignments. Mimi always insisted on giving James a goodbye kiss on the cheek before she and her mother bustled off toward the geese pens. The adults of the family attempted to put on a cheerful front for the little girl's benefit.

"Whistle while you work," James urged Regina as she and her uncle hurriedly departed for the tailor's.

"Any particular requests?"

"*So Rare,* by Jimmy Farrell?"

"Never heard of it."

"That's okay. I work best anyhow under constant supervision and when cornered like a rat in a trap."

"Pick up some lamb chops for supper on your way home from work tonight, dear," Regina joked with forced cheer, covering up the depression and constant fear they all felt. She looked back, her shaved head covered by a scarf she had made from a discarded scrap of gray-green soldier's uniform. To the scarf above one ear she had clipped her mother's blue barrette.

Precocious Mimi, with her braids and impish smile, became the family's bright spot of the day and a reason for everyone to hurry "home" after work. Both she and her mother adopted James as their strong male figure and continued to stay as near him as possible. Droll little Mimi learned that she could make James laugh by spouting off one of what seemed like a countless number of fractured aphorisms she picked up somehow: "The First Commandment was when Eve told Adam to eat the apple."

Of them all, only bony, sad-faced Michael actually seemed to seek the bright side. He assumed that since all of them had a "job," they were valuable to the Germans and therefore safe.

One morning, guards and overseers lined up Leopold Socha's men and marched them off to the interior railway spur line. There, six large platforms stood laden with bricks for the crematorium. Each man was expected to take a load of the bricks and run with it a distance of over two hundred yards, put it down in a designated spot, then run back for another load. German overseers and *kapos* stood near the platforms as well as all along the way, employing their whips and clubs to correct the slightest mistake. Anyone who failed to catch a brick tossed to him was lashed, as well as anyone who tarried even a moment. The air resounded constantly with the popping of whips as prisoners ran back and forth, stumbling, panting for breath, eyes glazed, soaked with perspiration. Groner seemed to enjoy the game more than the others, especially whenever he got a crack at James with his club.

Except for that one morning with the bricks, the crew laboring at the crematorium site was left in relative peace as long as the crew boss, Socha, kept his men working at a brisk pace. Socha shouted and threatened, but everyone knew that was just for show as long as no one malingered. James was given the job of mixing mortar and keeping it supplied to the bricklayers. It provided him the opportunity to examine his surroundings.

The foundation and outline of the new facility was well established, including the eight interior ovens. It was going to be a huge building, with heat ventilators leading from each oven to a massive smoke stack that, when finished, would rise nearly as tall as the red water tower. The back of the construction site adjoined one side of the compound, only five paces separating it from the barbed wire. Another five paces separated the inner fence from the electrified outer one. A spindly-legged guard tower stood beyond that. It overlooked the compound on one side and a cleared field on the other that presumably was mined.

The pit area, where those either murdered or dead of "natural" causes were burned and buried, occupied an isolated corner of the compound beyond the geese pens. On most days, the tendrils of smoke spread a ghastly odor throughout the camp. James sometimes caught glimpses of Elena and little Mimi running about in the pens with other women and girls. Geese kept up a constant racket that helped mask the gunshots and screaming of victims.

Although he wasn't sure how all this information was going to serve him, James stored it safely away in the back of his mind for future reference. Similarly, he made mental notes on the comings and goings of guards, overseers, and *kapos*, and on the times when sentries changed shifts.

Even in their quarrels, which were almost nonexistent among the long-termers, barracks residents knew enough to keep everything muted to avoid attracting attention. That was why James and Michael found alarming the commotion that erupted from the back of Barracks 8 as they entered the door one night during their third week of confinement. Feet scuffled in the straw, followed by the sound of a slap, and then Regina's scream of suppressed fury.

James sprang forward between the shelved human zombies and charged to the back of the long room. Light through the paneless window framed a gorilla of a man in a free-for-all with a much smaller form. The gorilla had hold of Regina's wrist, but she was kicking out fiercely in an attempt to rearrange his balls.

Professor Jahne lay sprawled on the floor, where he had either fallen or been pushed, helplessly watching the struggle. Elena and Mimi crouched together in terror underneath the window, holding each other tightly. Neighbors on their bed shelving turned their backs on the disturbance. It was always safer not to know what was going on.

"Jew bitch! I will soon break you to the saddle!" Regina's attacker snarled in German.

James recognized the voice: *Groner.*

Michael hung back, as was his pacifist nature. James charged right in, as was *his* nature. Grams was always saying her grandson would rush in where angels feared to tread.

Groner heard James coming. He whirled, still holding on to Regina's wrist with one ham of a hand. This guy looked huge and well fed—and in his free hand quivered his *kapo*'s stick.

"Back off, little Jew boy," he growled.

More often than not, James's opponents underestimated him, generally to their regret. They saw the red hair and freckles of a schoolboy and the wiry frame of a lightweight. What they did not see was how he had won a state boxing title at Oklahoma A&M, later brawled it out as an Oklahoma City cop with some formidable bad guys, and then excelled in "gutter fighting" techniques during OSS training at the "Country Club."

He feinted to the gorilla's right and ducked underneath the vicious swing of the *kapo's* stick. Instantly he straightened, and with a snap of his foot, rearranged the balls Regina had attempted to target. The cyclops bent double with a *whoosh* of breath. A sharp left jab to the nose and a right hook to the point of the jaw put him down for the short count.

James ended up with Groner's club in his own fist, standing spread-legged and ready between the gorilla and his intended victim.

"Want to try another round?" he taunted as the *kapo* clambered painfully to his feet.

Groner's nose spurted blood. It was obviously not the only part of his anatomy that had been rearranged. Hunched over what was left of his manhood, dry-retching from the center of his being, he stumbled away, dragging his feet. He hit the front door in a lumbering gait and disappeared outside.

Regina grabbed James in a bear hug, overjoyed to see him. "You keep showing up just in the nick of time," she said. "A girl could get to expect it."

"Like a new penny."

He hurled the *kapo's* stick out the window. Better to be unarmed than give the German guards an excuse to shoot him. He was counting on Groner being too embarrassed over having had his ass kicked by a lowly Jew to report the incident.

Elena assisted Professor Jahne up off the floor. He had nothing to say, but the hand he rested briefly on James's shoulder expressed his gratitude more than words. Mimi stood looking up at James, arms akimbo, braided head tilted back as she regarded him with wonder. She made everyone laugh by reciting a fractured platitude in her innocent little voice: "Jews are a proud people and we have often been troubled by unsympathetic genitals."

Groner's genitals should be unsympathetic for quite some time.

A murmured voice in Yiddish from a neighboring shelf cast ice water on the victory celebration. Regina translated: "It would have been better to let him have his way with her. This is something you will all regret. He will have his revenge. Groner is a dangerous man."

James flared. "Translate this," he instructed Regina. "You are a man and you would watch without coming to a maiden's aid?"

"It is not my affair," said the man, going through Regina.

"What does it take to make you people stand up?"

"You are new here. Soon, you will beg him to take her. She will beg to be taken in exchange for a crust of bread. You will even give the little girl to him."

33

News of James's encounter with Groner spread rapidly throughout the camp the next day, as bad news will. Some silently applauded a Jew's getting back at their keepers. Others were fearful of reprisals directed against all, which was the Nazi way. Often as he worked, James felt Leopold Socha watching him curiously and with new regard. Socha soon found an excuse to tarry where James was mixing mortar.

Scowling and shaking his fist for the visual benefit of the overseers, he said quickly in a low voice, "You did a job on that son-of-a-swine Groner. The bastard has had it coming for a long time. I need to tell you this: Watch your back. Groner is treacherous. Do not put anything past him. He will get even, one way or another."

James played along with the charade of having his ass chewed by the boss. He worked faster, nodding without looking up. "I've already been warned. They say you can tell a man's friends by the enemies he makes."

"Albert Einstein, you have friends in Nisko."

One of the overseers walked toward them. Socha glanced up, saw him, and roared at James, "You worthless piece of shit! Keep the mortar coming or there'll be lashes, do you hear?"

"Yassuh, boss man, yassuh."

That satisfied the overseer, who returned to his post.

During the noon break, Socha approached James and Michael and sat down with his bowl of "soup." Michael's sunken eyes and drawn face were beginning to resemble those of inmates who had been there much longer.

"How is the work going?" Socha asked carefully as an overseer walked by.

"I'd like to speak to the union rep about hours and working conditions."

"I'll pass it along."

They ate together in silence; any extended conversations were forbidden.

Ten minutes elapsed and some of the men had not received their rations. A guard named Franz ordered the cook to sit on the ground with his hands straight down and his feet tucked under. As punishment, Franz beat the cook over the head and shoulders with his whip in time to some march he was whistling. The unfortunate victim's body quivered from time to time, but he dared not cry out. He moaned almost inaudibly. Soon his face was smeared with blood.

Michael choked on his soup. Socha turned away from the scene and, stone-faced, continued to eat. To James, the soup tasted as though it was mixed with blood. He drank it anyhow. He had to keep up his strength the best he could.

Some workers still did not receive their meals. The cook was too beaten up to get off the ground. He was dragged away, never to be seen again.

"There goes the first whistle," Socha said, standing up. "Time to get ready."

The second whistle blew and everyone hurried to his work place. Socha got in a last quick word.

"There's a meeting tonight, Albert Einstein," he said. "Someone will come for you."

34

The Countdown Begins A Game 198

For a brief instant they and everyone turned to the open place, bathed in the last rays of the day.

There, a mocking smile. "About time!" he said. "Almost welcome the news."

34

A wave of dark excitement flooded the camp near quitting time. A rumor spread that hangmen's nooses were dangling from the water tower's scaffolding, a development that meant the camp was about to be collectively disciplined for some infraction of the rules. Just before sunset, *Einsatzgruppen* officers, guards, overseers and *kapos* scurried all over the grounds rounding up work crews with bursts of shouts and curses and wielding of whips and clubs. They drove frightened flocks to the big courtyard where a raised stage had been erected between the rows of barracks and the blood-red water tower. There was no supper for anyone; those who survived tonight's punishment would go to bed even hungrier than usual.

The hangman's nooses proved to be no rumor. Six of them dangled from the water tower in a makeshift gallows, in full view of the frightened gathering. Some people stared at them in horror and dread. Others ducked their heads and refused to acknowledge their presence. Michael seemed on the verge of panic.

"We've done nothing other than what we've been told," he exclaimed.

"Do you think they give a rat's ass?" James snapped back, annoyed by Michael's constant whining and endeavors to please his keepers.

There was a set order for musters like this. Each barracks had its own rank in formation. Tonight, it seemed, only the first ten barracks were involved. James and Michael soon located the rest of the family in the milling of ragged, terrified humanity.

Mimi spotted them first and broke away from her mother to throw herself into James's arms. The tot's round cheek felt wet against his. Regina seized James's hand, while Elena clung to Michael. Professor Jahne complained bitterly about the indignity of it all. All around them gushed a flood of hasty whispered conversation, most of it in Polish or Yiddish.

"They are saying someone's attempted to escape," Regina rasped as the prisoners were ordered into their respective barracks ranks. "The Germans are going to do a selection."

In the Barracks 8 lineup, the cowardly neighbor who had declined to come to Regina's aid against Groner glared accusingly at James and shouted in Yiddish, "I warned you this would happen. This is all your doing. Yours and Groner's. Groner is seeking his revenge on the lot of us. Let our blood be on your hands."

Regina translated. "He says everyone thinks Groner staged a phony escape plot in order to get back for what happened to him last night."

James didn't want to believe that what he had had to do was about to lead to the executions of innocents. He was forced to accept it, however, when Groner strutted by in his black-and-white stripes. From his carriage and the way he wielded his big club, he might have been wearing a splendid uniform studded with brass. He sought James out and glared at him. James returned his gaze.

The big *kapo* sported a bruise on the point of his jaw

where James had slugged him. His nose was black and blue and crooked in the middle of his face. His balls were probably the same color. He carried his bad left eye slightly closed, a mannerism that made him appear even more sinister. He aimed his big stick at James, cocked his thumb as though it were the hammer of a pistol, and let the hammer down. The depraved grin of triumph and revenge he left with James was the same as a confession. The sly *kapo* must have arranged all this to get back at James and at inmates who had laughed at his misfortune during the day.

"The dreadful brute!" Regina hissed. "You should have killed him, James."

He should have.

"Now he will kill us," she said.

Clutching James's hand tightly, Mimi shuddered and moved closer. An ill wind heralding the coming darkness blew across their sweaty faces. James's several injuries were healing, his fever had broken, and the breeze sniffing between the rows of internees made him shiver. He smiled reassurance down at Mimi. She took his hand in both her tiny ones.

While *kapos* like Groner patrolled the flanks of the muster, guards with ready machine guns kept on the alert further back. How could a hundred or so Germans possibly control a mass of two or three thousand prisoners? It *couldn't* be done, James pondered, if he could find a way to organize inmates into an army, and then convince them to act en masse, like an army.

He realized, however, that organizing large numbers under conditions that prevailed in the camp was a virtual impossibility, human nature being what it was. Jews with their innate optimism and trust in God made the task an even greater impossibility. They had rather wait and pray, even while ovens were being made ready to receive them.

A group of minor SS officers in black marched onto the raised stage and stood at attention while they awaited the arrival of the camp commandant. Soon, a stout SS lieutenant colonel with a riding crop and a Hitler mustache fashionable among officers goose-stepped across the courtyard and climbed to center stage. He reverted to a modified parade rest, hands behind his back, but his minions remained at the position of attention until after a second officer briskly mounted the stage and joined the first.

James did a double-take, hardly daring to believe his own eyes. With mixed feelings of dread and uncertainty, he recognized the stiff-spined posture, wide shoulders, and piercing blue eyes of none other than Major Fischer. Regina's swift intake of breath affirmed her own recognition.

There could be only one reason for Fischer's being in Nisko. He was still looking for Professor Jahne and must have somehow traced him here.

L ieutenant Colonel Muller, the camp commandant, possessed the kind of deep voice that carried as if through a bullhorn. While he posed on the stage, bellowing at his silent captive audience, Major Fischer stood aloof, behind and to one side, chin tilted upward, haughty eyes searching the ranks of prisoners with all the compassion of a hawk selecting a field mouse for dinner.

"We house you," Lieutenant Colonel Muller thundered. "We feed you, even when to do so takes food and comfort from our brave Aryan soldiers fighting on the fronts for the survival of our civilization. And how do you demonstrate your gratitude for our benevolence? Is there any shady undertaking, any form of foulness in which at least one Jew does not participate? Put the probing knife carefully to the abscess that is International Jewry and one immediately discovers, like a maggot in a putrescent body, a little Jew or two blinded by the sudden light."

The man had a way with words.

"Today, my observant staff has exposed a plot engineered by the little deceitful minds of Jews. Did you think to escape from these accommodations freely provided you, which, at any rate, are too good for the likes of vermin from the ghettos? Even with such provocation, I have nonetheless assembled the camp to demonstrate how we have your greater welfare at heart. You are all guilty of plotting . . ." —he repeated the phrase for added emphasis— "You are *all* guilty. However, in the interest of fairness, we have decided to punish only those who had knowledge of the detestable plot against our generous Führer."

Eyes were riveted on the water tower and its waiting nooses. Here and there, inmates who had been through similar previous ordeals began sobbing.

"The guilty parties have ten seconds to identify themselves and redeem the guilt rightly shared by you all," the commandant bellowed, cocking his elbow underneath his chin so his watch was visible to everyone, even in the failing light of sunset. "The ten seconds begin . . . *now.* Ten . . . nine . . . eight . . ."

People recited psalms amid an explosion of crying and wailing. Recriminations and pleas for the culpable to give themselves up in order to protect the innocent flew in all directions. Discussions about God broke out. Some said there was no God, else He would not curse His chosen people in this manner. Others argued that their lives were in the hands of God, and the chosen people must accept His will with love and understanding, all the more so since the days of the Messiah were surely approaching.

"Seven . . . six . . . five . . ."

Regina held her breath. Elena looked about to faint. She held on to Michael. James saw Leopold Socha standing as rigid as a fence post in his own barracks' ranks. Groner the *kapo* strode back and stood at the end of Barracks 8's formation, his eye expectantly on James and Regina. Machine-gun bolts ratcheted in anticipation of the end of the count. A squad of *Wehrmacht* in formation trotted onto the stage and fanned out across the front, pointing their MP-40s and Mausers.

"Four . . . three . . . two . . ."

A great wailing and gnashing of teeth rose from the multitudes. Still, no guilty party stepped forward. Perhaps it was because there were no guilty parties, no plot to begin with, simply a fabrication by a prideful man bent on reprisal.

"*One!*"

A hush fell over the assembly.

"By your intransigence, you compel me to take drastic measures," Lieutenant Colonel Muller shouted. "You can blame no one but yourselves."

Major Fischer lit a cigarette. Muller gave a signal. An officer in charge of a troop of black-clad death's-headsmen waiting in front of the stage rushed forward with his detail and immediately began moving into the ranks of inmates, seemingly selecting at random those to be marched away to the gallows. People waited with bated breath to see if they would be chosen.

A man screamed mightily when his 14-year-old son was dragged away. He begged the Germans to hang him instead of the boy. A soldier butt-stroked him in the solar plexus with his rifle and left him writhing on the ground.

An old woman of around 70 stepped out when she was tapped. She stared straight ahead at the nooses. Her hair was loose and her eyes had a glazed look, wide open, filled with terror. She walked slowly, quietly, while the sergeant of SS yelled, "*Vorwärts! Vorwärts! Los! Los!*"

A tall, thin man with a furrowed face and long, flowing beard stoically accepted his fate. He looked like an old-time Jewish patriarch. The entire burden of past centuries seemed to rest on his narrow shoulders.

"Stand up straight!" the SS officer ordered. "What is your occupation?"

"Chief rabbi," said the thin man proudly.

"Chief rabbi! You won't be chief rabbi here anymore. Do you hear me?"

No response came from the Jew's lips.

The SS officer struck the chief rabbi full in the face with his fist. Professor Jahne involuntarily cried out, as if he were the recipient of the blow.

"Did you hear me, Judas?" the officer roared. *"Vorwärts! Vorwärts! Los! Los!"*

One woman was noticeably pregnant, and in the last weeks of her pregnancy at that. She reacted to her selection only with uttered groans, as if in labor. Groner and some other *kapos* dragged her away while they laughed and took turns punching her in the belly.

Next came a young deranged girl of about 16. She walked toward the water tower giggling and gesturing inarticulately with her hands.

"Vorwärts! Vorwärts!"

James overheard a whispered argument behind him between two men debating the necessity of surviving the suffering today in order that God might avenge the Jews against the Germans later. He resisted the urge to shout at them: *What's wrong with* now? *If we act* now, *all together, we can take them!*

Shame burned in his face as though the fever had returned. He wasn't even Jewish, yet here he stood as unresisting and submissive as the others, doing *nothing* while monsters dragged away innocent people to hang them. He himself had relied on the same old argument against action: *What could one man do against machine guns? One man acting alone was simply another corpse with a bullet in its brain.*

"Vorwärts! Vorwärts!"

How many would it take to satisfy the Nazi bloodlust? There had to be a method to this madness of selection. Germans always had a system; they seldom did anything randomly.

The officer and his SS were at Barracks 7 and starting down the ranks when James caught on. They were seizing two people from each barracks, always the tenth person out of the first and third ranks.

James did a quick count. He and the family were in the unfortunate third rank and . . . He re-counted to make sure. Little Mimi was number ten.

Without hesitation, he pulled the little girl across his front and exchanged places with her. Elena failed to understand at first, but when she did she burst into tears of gratitude. Regina's eyes filled with tears. There were lots they might talk about, but there was no time left.

With one simple dodge, he was sacrificing his own life for that of the little Jewish girl who clung desperately to his hand.

35

"What is your name, *Jude*?" the SS officer demanded, stopping in front of James.

"Albert Einstein."

"You, Albert Einstein. Step forward. Go with the others."

James had to wrench his hand free of Mimi's grip. Stuttering and mumbling through her tears, the child repeatedly and desperately recited one of her fractious proverbs because she knew it amused him and because she thought it might somehow delay the inevitable. "Th–the g–greatest miracle in the Bible is when Joshua told his son to s–stand still and he obeyed."

James passed his hand swiftly over her braided dark hair, then met her mother's eyes. "Take her, Elena," he said.

Elena pulled Mimi away from James. Mimi sobbed as though her heart was breaking. Although only six years old, she understood enough, had witnessed enough, to know that when the armed men in black took someone away like this, he never came back.

Professor Jahne looked stunned and stared like a mindless robot. Regina held James's gaze as fiercely as Mimi had clung to his hand. The gray-green headscarf had slipped low over her ear on the side of the blue barrette. She didn't notice. Her lips mutely voiced the single word over and over: *"No . . . no . . ."*

He shook his head slightly to warn her not to make a fuss, lest the Germans take her too, out of pure cussedness.

"Vorwärts! Vorwärts!"

James turned away quickly and joined the steady, slow procession toward the gallows. The last thing he wanted was for Regina or anyone else to see weakness in him. He didn't know how much longer he could control his emotions.

Ultimately, he realized, the sacrifice he was making was an empty gesture, buying the little girl a few more days or weeks at most. But at least he could give her that. He thought he should feel noble, brave—something other than humiliated or degraded. At the moment of tribulation he was finding out things about himself. For one thing, he was discovering that it was easy enough to carp from the sidelines. But when it came down to the nut cutting, he was going along to the hangman as placidly as the Jews.

The chief rabbi, the pregnant woman, the deranged girl, the 14-year-old son, the old woman, James, a 4-year-old girl whom a *kapo* put on a leash and led like a dog, and all the others, numbering 20 in all, marched the long forever across the courtyard between the bristling guns of their tormentors. The sunset seemed especially gorgeous. It had rained earlier, a light shower that cleared the air and made sky colors unimaginably bright. Or was it so lovely only because it was the last sunset the condemned would see?

James averted his face as they filed past the stage, not wanting Major Fischer to recognize him. It sustained his mission for Professor Jahne to remain caught up in the concentration camp system as Gerhard Goldberg, lost inside it until both he and his brain full of research on the atom bomb went up the new crematorium's smokestack. Gerhard Goldberg, old, wasting away, shouldn't last many more days. Maybe he would be sent to the pits before Major Fischer ferreted him out of the camp's population.

James thought he could feel Major Fischer's penetrating gaze on his telltale orange hair and his slight limp. There was nothing he could do to hide either characteristic. He kept his face to one side, not daring to look to determine whether he had been recognized.

Twenty victims, but there were only six nooses hanging from the blood-red water tower. That meant they were to be hanged in three shifts with a remainder of two. There must have been a breakdown in the Germans' celebrated efficiency.

Groner and the other *kapos* drew the dirty job of the actual killing. They were even more despicable than guards and overseers in that they were prisoners themselves abusing other prisoners. A smirk appeared on Groner's face when he saw James brought forward with the other condemned.

That made James's mind up for him. He would not be hanged. He would die like a warrior and not like a . . . *not like a Jew.* As he had been selected to die for the collective guilt of the Jews, he selected Groner as the man he would take with him for the collective guilt of the *kapos*. As soon as the opportunity presented itself, he would kill swiftly with his bare hands as he had been taught. Groner would die an instant before the guards either opened fire or the *kapos* descended with their deadly clubs. Regina would be safe, at least from Groner.

Groner's bad eye twitched and he looked away.

All the Jews were forced to watch. Faces were ashamed and hearts ached, but there was nothing anyone could do as the first six victims were culled from the group. They consisted of three ragged, skeletal men, the 14-year-old boy, the Chief Rabbi, and the pregnant woman, her shaved head glowing red in the sunset. The rabbi walked up, climbed the little ladder stool beneath one rope, and defiantly placed the noose around his own neck and drew it snug. The fourteen-year-old boy passed out from fear and the *kapos* had to carry him to his ladder stool and lift him up in order to engage the rope. He fell off the ladder and dangled, kicking spastically until he strangled to death. From the ranks of Jewry issued a father's great howl of grief and agony.

The *kapos* kicked the stools out from under the feet of the other five. They jerked and gurgled. Many women fainted at seeing the horrible sight of their fellow prisoners writhing on the gallows in the sunset beneath the red water tank and its giant white swastika.

Now for the next batch of six. James directed his full attention on Groner, whose eye was drooping and whose thin lips formed a cruel smile as he made his way toward James. Three more steps and he became buzzard bait.

Suddenly, Lieutenant Colonel Muller's voice hammered a command across the camp. *"Genug!"* Enough.

Sport was over for the night. The order caught everyone by surprise, Groner no less than the Jews. The big *kapo* looked both shocked and disappointed, while James was as much confused as relieved. He shot a glance toward the stage in time to see Major Fischer whispering something in the camp commandant's ear. Before the SS officer turned and walked away, he looked directly at James with such intensity that James knew he had been recognized.

It took the OSS agent another moment before he comprehended the cunning behind tonight's event. It was diabolically brilliant. They had never intended to hang all 20 of those selected. They had made their point with the first six, retribution exacted from the collective. By sparing others already condemned and seeding them back into the population, the commandant assured himself even further control over his charges. Saved at the last moment from the rope, the reprieved would not only *not* participate in anything that violated camp rules, they would in turn persuade others that living even a few more days, a few more hours, was preferable to immediate death.

"*Juden ratten!*" snarled the hard-core sergeant of SS. "Return to your places. *Vorwärts! Vorwärts!*"

James turned away with the others.

"Red on the head. You stay, little man."

Before James realized what was going on, three *Wehrmacht* surrounded him and escorted him from the prison courtyard to the small white hut near the main gate, where the transport had been processed in on the first day. One of the soldiers knocked on the door and announced himself. A voice inside bade them enter.

Major Fischer sat on the far side of the small room, illuminated by an oil-burning lamp, his shined boots crossed at the ankles and propped up in the middle of a desk. He smiled genially and was smoking a cigarette. A Beretta pistol lay within his reach.

"It's just to make sure there are no misunderstandings between you and me," he said of the pistol.

James eyed him warily. "I said we would meet again in hell, Major. It looks like we have."

36

Major Fischer swung his boots off the desk and sat up straight with the Beretta between his elbows and his death's-head officer's cap to one side. This was the first time James had seen him bareheaded. He wore his hair cropped short. It was so Aryan blond it looked white.

He casually toyed with the Beretta on the desk. He picked it up, slid his finger into the trigger guard, and pointed it at James. Cigarette smoke curled out of his nostrils like twin poisonous serpents.

"Do you know how easy it would be for me to put a bullet through your brain?" he said. "The only thing I would feel would be the pistol's recoil."

James refused to give the Nazi the satisfaction of a reaction. The pistol was nothing compared to the hangman's noose. He waited.

Finally, Major Fischer returned the pistol to the desktop and leaned back in his chair. He ordered the *Wehrmacht* Elite Guard unit that had brought James to wait outside.

As soon as they were gone and the door was closed, he gestured toward a wooden straight-backed chair in front of the desk. "Sit down, *Albert Einstein*."

He must have looked up the name James had given himself. It seemed to amuse him. "Couldn't you have chosen a more original name?"

James shrugged. "No one's noticed."

"Who are you, Albert Einstein? Really?"

James showed him the fresh tattoo on his forearm. "It's the same answer as before. A Jew."

"A *Jude*? Please sit down. Would you like a cigarette?" He shook loose a cigarette and extended the pack toward James.

James was having a hard time figuring out what this was all about. He took the proffered cigarette and bent over the desk for the major to light it for him. His eyes fell on the pistol lying there within his reach. Major Fischer's pale eyes flicked from James to the Beretta, then back to James. One brow lifted in amusement.

"You wouldn't make it out the door," he said.

James nodded and sat down in the wooden chair, crossing his legs to show how relaxed he was. *This bastard wanted something from him. What?* Life really was one damned thing after another. He inhaled smoke gratefully, then looked at the cigarette. "It's no Lucky Strike. Now what do we do? Sit around and chat like long lost buddies?"

"You are no *Jude*, Albert Einstein," Major Fischer said. "We share some things in common."

James took another slow drag from the bitter German cigarette. "And what would those things be, Major?"

"You speak excellent German." He stubbed out his cigarette in an ashtray and replanted his boots on his desk. His intense blue eyes drilled through the clouds of cigarette smoke. "You really didn't think I would be deterred by so simple a ploy as changing Professor Jahne's name to Gerhard Goldberg now, did you, Albert Einstein? It appears to me that you have gone to a great effort to keep Professor Jahne well and alive."

Fischer apparently had what he wanted. So why were they having this conversation?

The cat-and-mouse game proceeded.

"I think you are working for the Allies and that you were dispatched to Grudwald for the same reason that I went there—to rescue Erwein Jahne. We have ways of making you talk, Albert Einstein."

"I saw the movie."

"That's something else we have in common—a sense of humor."

So far, James had seen no signs of levity in the grim-faced SS officer.

"The events in Grudwald were not merely flukes of cosmic proportions," the German went on. "I can't accept coincidence as an explanation. Russians attack Professor Jahne's German escort. Russians and Germans kill each other. Lo, you end up with the prize—"

"After I spared your life, Major."

"The score is even on that matter, if you recall."

From Fischer's expression, James's bulldog mouth was coming dangerously close to overloading his humming-bird ass. Circumspection being the better part of valor, James held his tongue to let the Nazi play his cards. Clearly, he thought he was holding kings, if not aces.

It unexpectedly occurred to James that Major Fischer's intervention may have been the reason he was spared from the first six persons in his most recent encounter with the Grim Reaper. To give himself an ace in the hole, so to speak. *Why?*

Fischer partly answered the question with his next breath. "Albert Einstein, if you cooperate, you may be more valuable to me alive than dead."

"Life is cheap in the Third Reich."

The Nazi's face hardened. "It shouldn't be, for a scientist who holds the secrets to winning the war. The ideological fools! They would send him to the ovens. But you and I together, Albert Einstein, we can save him."

"I thought the purity of the race was everything to you hard-core Nazi types." Why couldn't he stop goading the man?

"Winning the war is everything," Major Fischer said, trying not to appear insulted. "I believe with the Führer that as long as a people remains racially pure and is conscious of the treasure of its blood, it can never be overcome by the Jew. Never in the world can the Jew become master of any people except a bastardized people."

"I've read *Mein Kampf.*"

"I am no ideologue," Major Fischer protested. "Like you, I use my brain. Damn the incompetent bureaucrats in Berlin."

"With their low personal standards, which they consistently fail to achieve."

Major Fischer smiled tightly. "Professor Jahne is not merely any old Jew, although Eichmann in Berlin treated him like one. They transported him with other Jews to get him out of Germany, which they assumed the Führer desired. Fortunately for them, they retained sufficient good sense to set him up in a lab in Poland rather than send him to a camp. I heard he was in Warsaw, but after that bloody business there, the gestapo, on their own authority and in secrecy, took him to Grudwald. Do you know how long it took me to find him? Months! I only found him there by accident when I was ordered to make sure a laboratory was destroyed ahead of the Russian advance. The fools! Germany has a scientist who can win the war for us, and they are treating him like—"

"A common Jew? It sounds to me like your Third Reich is in chaos. I'll buy you a beer one day in Berlin."

"*Dagegen!* I'll buy you an ale in London, Albert Einstein. All I have to do is return Professor Jahne to Strasbourg in time."

James waited. Let him finish laying down his cards.

"I have known men like you, Albert Einstein, and sometimes I have admired them," Major Fischer continued. "A mercenary, if I'm not mistaken, who will sell his services to the highest bidder. I am making a bid you cannot afford to refuse. I am bidding you your life."

"That's high bid so far," James acknowledged. "Who do I have to kill?"

"Who do you have to keep alive?" the German corrected. "Lieutenant Colonel Muller, the camp commandant, is one hardheaded bastard and jealous of his authority. We are butting heads, as you may guess. His orders are to accept transport of Jews and release none without proper authorization. It may take days, perhaps as long as two weeks, for me to receive authorization from the chancellery to remove Professor Jahne from the camp. In the meantime, Muller extends privileges to no Jew. He is working on the Final Solution as fast as he can. If he finishes his crematorium before I get authorization, the old, the weak, the injured—all those unable to work—will be driven to the baths. That includes Professor Jahne.

"Albert Einstein, I am being honest with you because I think you have no choice except to do what I ask. Your job is to keep the old man alive and be prepared to carry out my orders immediately if he is threatened. The only way I may be able to save him is to break him out of the camp, an action for which Muller will hang me if I am caught. It is a risk I must take for the Führer and for the fatherland. In order to accomplish it, I am forced to trust you to help arrange his escape. That makes you more valuable to me alive than dead."

"And if I do help you, I will be provided passage to London?"

"Herr Einstein, turn down my offer, or betray me, and you are going to die during the next selection like an ordinary Jew, messing his pants on the end of a rope. If

Professor Jahne lives to return to Strasbourg, you and his niece live. If he dies, you die. Simple enough?"

An appeaser, the great Churchill said, is one who feeds a crocodile in hopes it will eat him last. But appeasement could be used to buy time—and time was rapidly running out on OSS Agent James Cantrell and his lost mission to obtain the atom bomb for the Allies.

37

The others greeted James's return effusively with laughter and tears, especially Mimi. Miracle of miracles. Someone actually came back from the dead. That night, after all the others had gone to sleep and James and Regina were battling their nightmares, he told her about the meeting with Major Fischer, speaking in whispered English. Since Fischer appeared to wield little power at Nisko, had few allies and even fewer resources—else why depend on a prisoner to help him?—James thought he might be able to use the SS officer to get himself, Regina, and her uncle out of the camp. Of course, there was no way James was going to let Fischer actually take Professor Jahne, but escape seemed far more possible through Fischer than attempting it on their own.

"If he keeps his word, the three of us will at least have a chance," James explained, whispering. "If there was some way we could contact . . ." —he started to say *Jurawski,* but caught himself — "partisans and arrange for them to meet us outside the fence, I think we can double-cross Fischer and pull this thing off."

There was an old saying in the OSS that if you had 'em by the balls, their hearts and minds would follow. Major Fischer only *thought* he had James by the balls.

"I have heard a rumor that there is a secret shortwave radio in camp," Regina whispered. "Socha would know. He is the one conducting all the hush-hush. If . . . if Jurawski still lives, I know how to contact him by radio."

"It's a thought. I'll work on Socha."

"What about the others? Michael, Elena and Mimi?"

"We can't take them. Do you understand?"

"You realize what will happen to them if we escape and they are left behind? They will be in the next selection."

What did she expect of him?

"James?"

"Yes. Damn it."

"They will hang them. Mimi too."

His mission was to make sure Professor Jahne ended up in Allied hands—or ended up dead.

"James, listen. They eliminate everyone or anything that gets in their way. You are not like them. I *know* you are not like them."

"We have to do something," he protested, choked with frustration. She was using the same argument employed on the train to deny escape: Either everyone went or no one went, in order to prevent those left behind from suffering retaliation. "Why do you think the Germans assign collective responsibility? It's to make sure no one does anything, that no one even tries as we are all driven to the ovens."

She agreed. "But we cannot do something if our actions cause innocent deaths."

"So we recite psalms and march all together up the smokestacks?"

"Rather than leave Mimi behind, James, it would be

more humane if you turned over now and choked her to death in her sleep."

The thought horrified him.

"Can you do it, James? Go ahead, kill her now."

Normally, Regina and he slept in each other's arms, with Mimi sometimes between them. Such contact was essential in maintaining one's humanity under squalid and inhuman conditions. James now turned away from her.

She refused to understand. Mission came first. Mission always came first.

Corpses remained rotting on the makeshift gallows beneath the red water tower, grisly reminders of the fate that awaited anyone who disobeyed rules or condoned such disobedience. To James, they were also a memento of his own guilt, since it was likely that his altercation with the *kapo* Groner had led to the hangings. The sight of them brought up ghastly images of little Mimi and her mother being hung there as well, if he concluded his plans with Major Fischer.

James and Regina spoke no more about the subject, although he sometimes caught her watching him speculatively, as though wondering what he had decided. Each morning when everyone departed the barracks for their job sites, Regina straightened her head scarf and blue barrette, brushed wrinkles and filth from her stripes and then put on a smile to help keep up morale. It became routine for her to cheerfully suggest that James stop at the store on his way home to pick up something for supper. The others soon got into the spirit. Ordering supper was the highlight of the day. Everyone contributed. Steak or lamb chops or hamburger, perhaps whitefish on Fridays, green beans and peas, hot loaf bread, apples for a pie—even as hunger stripped the pounds off their ribs and began to reveal the skeletons beneath their skin.

Mimi's big brown eyes grew larger and larger in her pinched face, and her arms and legs resembled toothpicks scabbed with runny sores from biting lice. Regina's face looked less and less childish and more ruthlessly cold woman turned gaunt. Michael's optimism slowly evaporated; he and Elena prayed a lot and held each other for comfort. Wiry to begin with, James had little fat to lose, and he could tell his muscle tone would soon go.

Of them all, Professor Jahne was the most affected. Already virtually crippled from an ankle that would not heal, he weakened day by day. His melancholy thoughts kept shifting back over his life when they were all crammed together in the dark on their bunk shelf to sleep.

"I am living for my dreams at night when I have wonderful glimpses of how it was back then," he murmured, more to himself than anyone else. "All the years have passed, and I sometimes wonder where they went, although I am sure I must have lived them. The winter of my life catches me by surprise. I remember my wife, but I remember her at the end and not when she was young, not when she was the alive and vibrant woman I married. All of us enter into the winter seasons of our lives, and we are surprised and therefore unprepared for the aches and pains, the loss of strength, the slowness of our muscles and mind to respond. We gradually lose the ability to do things, and soon, as the winter progresses into the coldest months, what we have left are our memories and our dreams. Hope has gone. The winter of one's life is shorter than the other seasons . . ."

Regina tenderly put her arms around him. "It is still a long way to December, Uncle," she said gently.

"I do not think I shall see December."

Clearly, James had to do something soon. Lieutenant Colonel Muller continued to cull the weak and debilitated from the work force. Soon, no matter how Regina tried to cover for her uncle, he would be noticed and it would be his turn for either the death pits or the new crematorium. James waited for a word from Major Fischer, but none came. Often in the evening when he went to the latrine, he saw a light burning in the window of the little white shack by the main gate and assumed Fischer must be working late as he waited for authorization to come from the chancellery to remove one Gerhard Goldberg from the prison population.

James hardly expected Major Fischer to keep his pact if authorization came before the necessity to break Professor Jahne free.

It wouldn't be long now until the new building was up and ready to put Lieutenant Colonel Muller big time into Hitler's assembly line of death. The brick walls rose quickly, until it was time to install the roof. Steel ovens the length of human beings were shipped in by rail for installation, as were large butcher blocks, which one of the *Sonderkommando* said were used to crush gold fillings from the teeth of the dead.

As he slaved every day toward his own eventual destruction, James observed, made mental notes and tried to formulate an alternative plan of escape to that offered by Major Fischer. Guards left little room for inmates to think for themselves, and even less opportunity to resist. Elena said overseers counted the geese every morning, and woe to the keepers if even a single gosling turned up missing. The life of a goose was more valuable than the life of a Jew.

After only weeks of internment, few inmates were mentally willing or physically capable of either escape or resistance. Resistance at most was minor and inconsequential, as when Regina and the workers at the commissary tailor's sent off a cargo of German military uniforms with trousers sewn together, pockets missing and buttons on backward. It wasn't much, but Regina was proud of the effort, even if it did come back eventually to bite her in the butt.

James attempted to approach Leopold Socha a number of times, but the work boss declined to renew his invitation for James to be "selected" and, in fact, remained aloof and suspicious after the night of the lynching, when James was escorted to Major Fischer's office. He was proving slow to come back around. Hate, said a man named Horowitz who had been transported to Nisko with Socha from the Majdanek camp in Poland, was what kept Socha going while his fellow internees withered away and died.

"Leopold has much hate, like acid burning inside his heart," said Horowitz, speaking in Polish through Michael. "I was there and saw the genesis of his hatred. His baby daughter was only seven years old when she was selected out after we first arrived at Majdanek by train. Everyone knew that those too young or too small to work were sent to the baths. His wife and his daughter were very afraid. Leopold was dragged away to labor, but his wife refused to go. She insisted that she be taken with her daughter. 'Do not be afraid, Daughter,' she said, 'for I will be with you.' And so she was, and so both were killed. Since then, Leopold has lived for one thing—to escape and, once free, to kill all the Germans in the world."

James needed Socha's trust and help to even consider an escape option other than Fischer's. James finally cornered him.

"Do not speak of such things," Socha hissed. "People who are desperate with hunger and fear make excellent spies for the enemy. There are spies where you least expect them."

He looked at James, the scarred length of his mouth compressed, and asked pointedly, "Why were you taken to the SS major's office, Albert Einstein? And returned alive?"

He walked off without giving James a chance to explain.

38

Another transport arrived at Nisko from the east. To make room for fresh labor, old used-up labor had to be taken to the pits in the isolated corner of the camp behind the geese pens. Professor Jahne was to be selected for this action, but a *kapo* named Brzecki somehow learned of it in time to inform Regina, whom he had been trying to impress. Considering the acrimony between the camp commandant and the SS major, James doubted Lieutenant Colonel Muller would have informed Fischer of his intention to kill the old man. Since Brzecki had already compromised himself by speaking to Regina, James had little difficulty in coercing him to further commit himself by delivering a message to Major Fischer. Fischer somehow managed to save the professor, this time.

Gunfire rattled from the corner of the compound for what seemed like hours; upset geese continued their racket for even more hours after that. Following the guns came the smoke and the stench like burning hog fat that burned eyes throughout the camp. Inmates were quieter than usual, and paler. They averted their eyes from the smoke.

Carrying his big stick, his bad eye drooping, Groner made a point of swaggering past James at morning muster and headcount. "Next time I will see you go up in smoke," he taunted.

"How are the old gonads hanging, Cyclops? Or are they still up in your mouth?"

Groner threatened with his club, but James stared him down.

"Think about this, Red on the Head Like the Dick on a Dog," the *kapo* snarled, then turned his attention to Regina, whom he undressed with his leering eyes. "When you are smoke, I will screw her until her eyes bulge out. Perhaps I'll even screw the *little* bitch and her mother as well."

"Don't count on it," James said softly but with iron-like underlying menace. "It gets very dark in the camp at night. Be afraid."

L ater in the morning, Major Fischer had James brought to the little white shack near the main gate. Socha watched with a frown on his face as a prison-guard unit ushered him away.

Major Fischer was kicked back as before with his boots on the desk and his hands clasped behind his head. This time the Beretta remained holstered. He ordered the guards to wait outside, offered James a cigarette, and invited him to sit.

"We managed to spare Professor Jahne," he said approvingly. "That was quick thinking on your part, Albert Einstein. I will have the *kapo* Brzecki rewarded."

"I think he considers it reward enough that he wasn't hung."

Fischer swung his feet off the desk and leaned forward, getting right to the point.

"After this," he said, "I dare not wait any longer for the

chancellery to act. That buffoon Muller will not cooperate, he's so afraid of making the wrong move and stalling his career. How much more stalled can it be, for the love of God? He's the keeper of a bunch of dirty Jews wearing filthy stripes and stinking up the universe! Cleaning latrines would be a promotion."

"Maybe you should water him twice a week."

"That old man is going to the pits the next time, and there's nothing I can do about it," Major Fischer went on, ignoring the wisecrack. "All Muller wants is to get rid of me—and he gets rid of me by disposing of the Jew scientist."

"Enemies make strange bedfellows."

"Indeed." He leaned forward conspiratorially. "Five mornings from now," he said, his voice low and tense, "you and the old man and his niece will volunteer for a wood-cutting detail that goes outside the gate. I've arranged it with the overseers. You will do nothing to make the guards suspicious. There will be a distraction when it is almost dark and time to return to the camp. Never mind what it is. You'll recognize it when it happens. As soon as it occurs, bring Professor Jahne and the girl and run as fast as you can to the logging road. Turn away from the camp. A vehicle and a guard of loyal SS will meet you there."

"What happens to the girl and me?"

Major Fischer exhaled sharply in flat streams of cigarette smoke. "You will be freed, both of you. You name the place."

"London?"

The major chuckled. James knew he was lying. Once he had what he wanted, he had no further need for James.

"I'm curious," James said. "What's in this for you personally that you would take such a chance? Muller will hang you if we're caught."

"Correction, Albert Einstein. He will hang all of us."

"We Jews are already dead."

The major's cold blue eyes gleamed like ice as he contemplated the question. Finally, overcome with the prospect of success and needing at least someone to appreciate his cleverness, he opened up.

"The Führer will award me the Knight's Cross once it comes to his attention that I rescued the world's foremost atomic scientist from these bumbling idiots. Dr. Fleischmann at Strasbourg is near a breakthrough in building the most powerful weapon known to man. He requires Professor Jahne's expertise in order to complete it. With this weapon in possession of the Third Reich, the Allies will have no choice but to sue for peace. Germany will dominate civilization for the next thousand years—and I will be the reason for it. I will be well rewarded with a high position in the Führer's government."

That explained it. The guy was a megalomaniac.

A brittle smile twisted Major Fischer's thin lips. "Don't disappoint me, Albert Einstein. Remember. Five mornings from now."

39

James struggled to arrive at a decision while he labored at the crematorium. Major Fischer was about to provide him a one-in-a-million chance. He felt confident he could bend circumstances to his own advantage once he had the professor outside the compound. Even without the radio Socha supposedly possessed, certainly Regina and her intimate knowledge of partisans operating in Poland could link them with a band. All they had to do first, once they were outside the wire, was elude both the wood-cutter guards and Major Fischer's men.

He had no qualms about betraying the SS major, as he was sure Fischer would betray him. Enemies indeed made strange bedfellows—who shouldn't trust each other.

On the other hand, there was Mimi, her mother and Michael. They depended on James, trusted him, even loved him as a sort of savior and hero. Talk about nightmares, if he had to leave them behind for the noose and the furnace. The decomposing bodies hanging from the water tower would be cut down and replaced by fresh sacrifices—Michael, Elena and Mimi. For the rest of his life, he would see the little girl's large, dark, trusting eyes and hear the way she created Biblical aphorisms to amuse him: "Samson was a strong man who let himself be led astray by a Jezebel like Delilah."

Could he live with that?

During their lunch break, he squatted next to Leopold Socha with his cup of soup.

"Do I still have friends in Nisko?" he asked before Socha could move away.

"Your friends are wary of your association with the SS major."

"Unless you trust me, Leopold," James added hurriedly, "there is going to be an escape in five days that will bring another German selection."

Socha hesitated, his broad, battered face gone cold. "I'm listening."

Briefly, James outlined how his relationship with Fischer began at the wool mill in Grudwald and what Fischer was demanding of him now. When he finished, Socha looked thoughtful.

"You amaze me, Albert Einstein. Why are you not going along with him? Most anyone else would."

"Personal reasons."

Socha's brooding eyes searched James's face. "The little girl?"

He was more observant than James supposed. The silence that followed was answer enough. Socha's mouth thinned and extended into his scar. He looked down at his soup.

James said, "I can't go if it means leaving others behind to take reprisal for me." He knew that made him a sentimental fool; he had a job to do, no matter the collateral damage.

Socha studied James for a long minute, as though debating whether to speak. The overseer was watching them.

"There was a French girl in Majdanek when I was there," Socha said, watching James for a reaction.

James looked up sharply, his heart beginning to thud. That encouraged Socha.

"She was captured during the invasion at Normandy—"

"Gabrielle!" James blurted out, unable to contain himself, his voice charged with rising emotion.

"Gabrielle? Yes. There was an American named James. She thought he might be dead, but she talked of how he would come for her eventually if he was still alive."

The first whistle blew. They scrambled to their feet to avoid the whips.

"Where is she now?" James demanded. "Is she alive?"

Socha shrugged and watched the overseer and guards start to crack their whips. James's link with Gabrielle seemed to make up his mind for him, which spoke highly of Gabrielle. "The meeting is tonight," he said. "Someone will come for you."

40

The meeting site for the self-named "Camp Executive Committee" could not have been less glamorous. It was a latrine, since latrines were the only places inmates were allowed to go after curfew. Brzecki, the *kapo* enamored of Regina and now made loyal to the inmates, led James and Regina to it after nightfall. It was the only completely enclosed facility within the compound. It even had a door. Brzecki pointed to the darkened little structure and warned them that they should be extra cautious; Groner might be on to them. Brzecki remained patrolling in the area to act as lookout.

A candle burned inside the latrine, its flame flickering deep hollows around the eyes of the five skeletal Jews crammed inside waiting for Socha's visitor. Three of them, including Socha, sat on the long board that, with round holes cut in it, served as commodes over the waste pit. One leaned against the wall. The fifth squatted on his haunches on the floor. There was barely enough room left for James and Regina to push themselves inside.

"Close the door. Quickly," Socha said.

They found themselves trapped in the stench. "This is getting to be a shitty job," James commented.

Leopold Socha's battered face in the poor light turned him into Frankenstein's monster. Horowitz, the wizened little Jew who had been at Majdanek with Socha, perched on the commode board to Socha's right. To Socha's left sat Dupre, a French-Jewish bricklayer with long eyelashes and a goatee. The other two men, strangers to James, could by appearance have been any inmates. Both were starved-looking, hollow cheeked and missing teeth. Their names were Eisenberg and Grossbert. The only way James could distinguish between them was that Grossbert was almost completely bald, while Eisenberg had tufts of black hair clinging to his scalp.

"Why did you bring a woman?" Dupre challenged James in Yiddish.

Regina translated the resulting exchange, James speaking in German. "As you can see, I don't speak Yiddish or Polish. She's my interpreter."

"You are a foreigner."

"So are the Krauts."

"You speak German."

"*Je aussi parle le français et l'anglais,*" James said, looking at Dupre. I also speak French and English. Dupre smiled.

Socha interceded to end the interrogation. "This man is not a Jew, but we can trust him," he said. "I have reason to believe that God may have answered our prayers in sending him. I have heard of this man from a reliable source. And a brave source at that."

He could only mean Gabrielle. James ached to question Socha further about her, but Socha had, for some reason, seemed reluctant to talk about her. It would have to wait until another opportune time.

Obviously, the Committee had met enough to establish some procedure. James's purpose for appearing tonight, however much curiosity it aroused, would have to await its proper point. First, Socha disseminated news about the war with the authority of one who had received it from a primary source. Good. That meant he had a clandestine radio and was tuning to either the BBC or the U.S. Armed Forces Network. Maybe not all Jews, James mused, were sitting around on their butts waiting for God to save them after all.

The Russian offensive, Socha relayed, was still stalled east of Warsaw. Supply difficulties and the arrival in the east of German reinforcements, specifically the Hermann Goering panzer division from Italy, were preventing the Russians from breaking through. But even the panzers couldn't hold out much longer.

In the west, Generals Montgomery and Patton had busted free of the hedgerows and were preparing a *blitzkrieg* of their own across France toward Belgium and Germany. Patton was promising to take a leak in the Rhine before Christmas.

Other business included a discussion on what had led to the hanging of the six innocent Jews at the water tower. Since no escape plans were being considered at the time, and no individuals had attempted to escape, the Committee concluded that the *kapo* Groner must have somehow engineered the action in revenge for his run-in with the new arrival Albert Einstein.

That led attention back to James. Socha stood up next to the guttering candle.

"Albert Einstein," he began, "has been offered an opportunity and a means of escape . . ."

That was as far as he got. The recent hangings were too fresh in their minds, the corpses left on the gallows a powerful deterrent to even thinking of sedition. A whispered outburst of disapproval and heated objections made it almost impossible for Regina to keep up her translations for the American.

"No one attempts escape without authorization of the Committee," declared Horowitz. "In light of recent events, the Committee is not authorizing further escapes."

Finally, Socha held up his palm to restore order. "Let Albert Einstein speak," he said. He nodded at James.

James searched the consumptive faces of his audience. Socha trusted these men; James would have to trust them as well and be as open and honest as he could.

"I was sent here to bring back an important Jewish scientist who is now in this camp," he began, pausing between sentences to allow Regina to work her linguistic magic. "Who I am and why this scientist is important is of no concern. What is of concern to you is that, five days from this morning, I will escape with him from Nisko, which will result in the Germans hanging some of you in reprisal—unless . . ."

He waited for the protests to cease. " . . . *Unless*," he finally interrupted, "this Committee will help me devise a plan to leave *no one* behind."

Regina's translation caught in her throat. She had not known the reason for tonight's meeting, nor had she suspected what James's decision might be regarding Major Fischer's ultimatum. When she finally got it out, it elicited another round of disbelief and skepticism.

"That is impossible! It's suicidal to even contemplate a revolt!"

"There was a successful revolt at Sobidor last year," James said. "Four hundred prisoners succeeded in breaking out."

"Almost all were killed by land mines and thousands of pursuing Germans," Horowitz countered.

"Yes. But some managed to escape to freedom. How many have escaped from Nisko?"

Muttering and averted eyes.

"Tell me!" James insisted. "How many has this Committee freed?"

"None yet," the bald Grossbert conceded. "But if we revolt, we will be executed in masses."

Angry, James thrust a trembling finger in the direction of the water tower. Regina enthusiastically echoed the tone of his words.

"Each day you pass those corpses hanging on the gallows and you will not look at them. You deceive yourselves by saying it will not happen to you. In one week—hear me, *one week*—the crematorium will be completed. It's a big oven—and it's not going to be used to bake manna from heaven. It's going to be used for baking Jews. Do you understand that? One way or the other, sooner rather than later, those Nazi devils are going to kill all of us. The question is, Do we fight back? And if so, when?

"Or do we stick our heads in the sand, chant psalms, pretend it's not going to happen and blindingly follow one behind the other to the bath houses? I'm telling you this now because I already have enough nightmares. I don't want on my conscience Jews hanging from the gallows because of me. But I'm also telling you, whether you go or not, I'm leaving this cesspool in five days. I'm asking you to give yourselves a chance, perhaps the only chance you'll have."

Tears surged into Regina's eyes. "I am proud of you, James."

"I'm a fool. Don't translate that. Tell them this: I say we fight. Some of us will survive. Maybe even most of us if everything goes right." He concluded in a ringing voice deliberately held low: "I know not what course others may choose, but, as for me, give me liberty or give me death."

What the hell. It had worked once before.

The Committee discussed, argued, and discussed some more. James grew impatient. Brzecki came by, stuck his head in and warned that Groner and some of the other *kapos* were walking about the area. Socha finally spoke up for the group.

"We can listen. What do you want us to do?"

James described his observations from various points in the camp, especially from the crematorium construction site, and explained the plan forming in his mind.

"It might work," Socha said speculatively after the Committee members put their heads together again. "We have nothing to lose. What do you need?"

That was what James wanted to hear. Regina squeezed his hand as he began listing his requirements: geese manure, at least 200 kilos; 10 gallons of truck fuel oil; rifle or pistol cartridges; trousers from the tailor's with the cuffs sewn closed; some paper . . . Could these items be obtained and concealed until they were needed?

Puzzled at such unusual requests, the Committee decided nonetheless that it could be done. Jews who were mechanics working at the German motor pool could obtain fuel oil. Female Jews used as bunkmates by some of the guards should be able to steal a few cartridges. Goose shit, trousers, and scrap paper were relatively simple commodities to obtain. Brzecki could be persuaded to hide larger materials in one of the *kapo* shacks.

"The Germans trust the *kapos*," Eisenberg said, "and they move about freely. But who knows whether Brzecki is trying to work his way in in order to betray us?"

"Blackmail," Socha said. "He's in too deep to back out."

The next few minutes were utilized in deciding logistics, tactics, command and control.

"Each barracks will need to be organized," James instructed. "One trusted man will be placed in charge of each. His job when he receives the signal is to clear out his barracks and direct his people to the escape route. There will be one commander in overall charge of the barracks leaders."

Socha designated Horowitz. Horowitz nodded.

"Regina will organize the women and children," James said. She nodded her acquiescence. "We'll also need other department heads. Who will take materials and concealment of materials?"

"Eisenberg gets along well with Brzecki."

"Eisenberg it is. Weapons?"

"Grossbert."

"Transportation?"

"Dupre."

"Socha and I will coordinate the department heads and act as co-commanders. We will work out the details with each of you in private. Understand, there must be total secrecy. If one word leaks out, we'll all be hanging by our necks from the water tower."

Horowitz massaged the skin of his throat and made a face.

"Leopold, do you have contact with the outside via radio?" James asked.

Socha hesitated. "We are talking to Polish partisans," he admitted.

"Are the partisans capable of radio communications with the Allies? I have a code that can be relayed in order to designate a target and request a bombing run. That will make it a lot easier to get a large number of people out of this hellhole during the confusion."

The Jews looked impressed, more confident. With that kind of support, they might pull this off after all. That was one of the reasons James disclosed it now.

"It can be done," Socha said.

"Good." James was clearly in charge of the operation. "Another request: Can the partisans send vehicles to pick up people, as many as possible?"

"Jurawski has always refused to assist Jewish escape attempts—"

Regina looked as though someone had slapped her in the face. "Jurawski! He is still alive?"

"There was fighting near Grudwald. Some were killed, but most of the bands escaped."

Regina lowered her eyes. She wiped them with the palms of her hands. Her voice sounded choked. "If you tell Jurawski that 'Regina' is here," she said, "he will come."

James squeezed her hand. They were two people thrown together whose hearts were elsewhere.

"One final thing," James said. "Everything and every-one must be ready to go in three nights. That's our open window."

The Jews exchanged worrisome looks. He hoped they *would* fight.

41

Over the past several days, Professor Jahne, taciturn and
unsociable to begin with, had become more and more
withdrawn and uncommunicative. He brooded constantly.
He was losing weight and his stripes now hung from a
body that not so long ago could have been described as
portly. His beard was unkempt and stained from lack of
grooming. His eyes took on a haunted quality. The few
comments he uttered were bitter and angry. The others
in the family sometimes caught him glaring at the *kapos*
patrolling with their sticks and clubs or at the German
guards with their machine guns between the separate
fences and in the watch towers. No longer was he quick
to rationalize or defend against remarks denouncing Germany and the Führer.

Regina thought he was getting ill. She worried that
he might not have the strength to escape when the time
came. She wanted to tell him about the Committee's plan
for the revolt in order to provide him hope and the will
to persevere. James vetoed the notion. It would be safer
for everyone if the first the old man knew about it was

when he was shoved through the break in the wire minutes ahead of Allied bombers dropping their loads on the
camp. It was James's opinion that the stubborn old bird
was finally coming around to seeing the Third Reich for
the rotten abomination it was, instead of what he had per-
ceived it to be a decade or so ago, when his prestige at the
University kept him isolated and protected.

For some reason, despite the professor's gruff and off-
putting idiosyncrasies, little Mimi began to warm up to
the grandfatherly-looking scientist. He returned her affection to some degree and would sometimes run his hand
across her braids or let her hug him briefly around the
neck. It was this growing relationship with the little girl
that started to scrape the scales of denial from his eyes.

"That they would treat little children so shamefully is
beyond the pale," he muttered through his growing out-
rage.

Self-deception and delusion do not fade readily once
they have become ingrained upon a person's value
system. Professor Jahne at last broke completely free one
morning, prior to headcount, while inmates were still
milling around the prison courtyard with their cups of
hot stained liquid and bread crusts. He had awakened in a
particular grumpy mood and refused to speak to anyone.
Even Mimi kept her distance. He nibbled at his crust of
bread and glowered like a boar hog with a toothache. It
was almost as if he'd gotten up that morning and seen a
world gone bleaker and nastier than he could ever have
imagined.

Suddenly, he dashed the contents of his cup to the
ground and attempted to clamber to his feet. Regina
caught him before his bad ankle dumped him back on the
ground. From somewhere deep inside his body erupted
a pained roar of long-suppressed agony and despair and
disillusionment. The rest of the family rushed to surround
him and calm him before the *kapos* or guards took matters into their own hands. A prisoner must never express
himself in such a manner; it was bad for morale.

"Uncle Erwein. It's 'Gina. Look at me. You must not let them hear you."

"Fornicate the bunch of them!" he roared. "They're monsters! We're being caged by monsters."

That seemed to deflate him and make him feel better. Just in time. Groner was climbing on top of an upturned kettle, looking over heads to find the delinquent who had so little respect for his fellow inmates and his benevolent keepers.

Mimi clutched James's hand and cringed against him. As with most of the camp's children, the slightest disturbance or break of routine sent her darting for cover as fast as a kitchen mouse when the cat was about. Michael and Elena watched Groner from the corners of their eyes. Regina stroked her uncle's neck and cheeks to restore calm to his tortured soul. Lice worked among his unkempt white hair and beard. He let out a long breath, still finding it painful to accept the events in his life that had led inexorably to his being treated like any other Jew.

"I was blind," he said. "I had eyes, but I refused to see."

"Many of us were blind in the beginning," Regina consoled him.

"I *chose* to be blind."

His gaze was fixated on the withering corpses still hanging from the water tower, but he was looking right through them to a distant time and place.

"In 1921," he went on presently, expressing the need to talk through his epiphany, to confess, to atone, "I was assistant to the great Albert Einstein, who had arrived in Germany only a few years previously and was neither particularly conscious of his Jewishness nor sensitive to anti-Semitism. However, as early as that, Dr. Einstein saw prophetically what was coming. He told me that he would be forced to leave Germany within ten years.

"I scoffed at him. What a fool I was. I became an important scientist crucial to harnessing atomic energy, indispensable to the Reich. When I heard Jews were being driven from their professions and homes and imprisoned in ghettos, hubris automatically steered me around the thought that such a fate could also overtake me. After all, I was as German as . . . as Hitler himself."

"Uncle Erwein . . ."

"Silence, child. Let an old fool say what should have been said long ago. I was deliberately blind for so long. So many wasted years. I refused to believe the Nuremberg Laws applied to Jews like me. I remember with horror November of 1938. *Kristallnacht*, it is now called. Even in Strasbourg, I was jarred awake in the middle of the night by the sounds of shattering glass, the smell of burning synagogues, and the cries of agony from Jews being dragged from their homes and beaten to a pulp. For the space of a second, I became keenly aware that something terrible was happening, something terrifyingly brutal.

"Yet, almost at once I accepted what happened as over and done with, an aberration, thus avoiding critical reflection. I was too busy with my work. Besides, I assured myself, such things happened only to the old beards and backward orthodoxes. They did not happen to Jews like me, who had assimilated and taken on the manners, dress and idiom of modern Germany."

The old man's face was cheek sunken and as gray as his beard. His eyes burned with the fever of accepting how he had been betrayed. He had started, and now he must get it all out before the work whistle blew.

"In one university after the next," he said, "academic associations were captured by nationalists, *volkisch*, and anti-Semitic forces who adopted 'Aryan clauses' calling for the exclusion of Jews. Both students and staff at our universities were severely restricted. I thought I was exempt due to my status and my work.

"Ghastly rumors floated about of mass shootings and death of Jews by starvation, torture and gassing. It was said Jews were being taken to uninhabited, devastated regions in Russia where they were left to starve and freeze to death. Rumors circulated of 'death camps,' where Jews were in the process of being exterminated. I ignored them. I should have listened to the American Jewish literary critic Ludwig Lewisohn. He called Nazism the 'revolt against civilization.' He wrote how the whole thing would be a ghastly farce if it did not constitute such a grave danger for the planet. It was corrupting the souls and hopelessly curdling the brains of an entire generation of Germans. He was right."

In one respect, it was difficult to see in the stricken, beaten-down old man in filthy stripes the renowned Professor Erwein Jahne, the most brilliant atomic scientist in the world. Long suppressed, perhaps, the human side of the scientist seemed to be emerging, reborn into the light.

"I was too busy to notice," he said. "My country valued my work. I failed to see the threat in people who felt the need to extract from Jews the greatest possible contribution to winning the war, then discarding them when they were used up. They came for my neighbors. They came for my colleagues. God help me, they came for my brother and his family. I assured myself that the Führer was unaware, that he would correct it and right the wrongs when he learned what the Nazis were doing in his name. I was blind. I never thought they would come for me. But one day they did . . ."

His eyes focused on a *Sonderkommando* that had appeared at the red tower to remove the corpses that had been hanging by their necks since the evening of the selection. Michael gasped. The blood left his face. "They are going to replace the old crop with a fresh crop," he whispered.

"There will always be a fresh crop," Professor Jahne said. "I am no longer blind."

"Welcome to the real world, Professor," James said.

The Professor looked at him. "Yes. Young man, if you can get me out of this purgatory, I will build your atom bomb for you."

James had schemed and plotted to bring out the old scientist and turn him over to the Allies for what he could do. That had all changed within the last few minutes. Now, he wanted to save the old man for what he *was*, for the human being he was about to become.

42

Work whistles blew. Jews trotted and shambled off to their labors as rapidly as their physical condition permitted. They avoided glancing at the empty nooses even more studiously than they had shunned the corpses. An empty noose was more menacing than a full one; it suggested the need for someone's head to fill it.

"We obeyed the Ten Commandments of Moses," Michael commented. "The reason we are having trouble now is because we have neglected the eleventh: Thou shalt choose for thyself proper grandparents."

"I know the Seventh Commandment," Mimi piped up. "Thou shalt not admit adultery."

Her mother corrected her. "The word is 'commit.' You don't even know what adultery is."

"I do too. It's grown-ups. You're an adultery. Adulteries are mean to each other. I want to stay a little girl from now on."

* * *

Four weeks were hardly sufficient preparation time for an operation of this nature, much less four days. Nonetheless, four days were all they had before Major Fischer took over on the fifth morning. The plot rapidly began to take substance. The first three days and nights were utilized in preparing to obtain, in obtaining and in concealing the materials on James's list. The fourth night would be the true test of whether it all came together and worked out, with Fischer left holding the bag.

Regina and other women at the tailor's smuggled out men's undergarments and uniform trousers sewn together at the cuffs. Late at night while everyone else slept, Regina, Elena and other selected women from the geese pens fashioned long-legged pantaloons from the men's underwear that could be used to carry out manure underneath their baggy stripes without being noticed. Regina, Eisenberg and Michael packed the take in the specially prepared uniform trousers and hid them in the crawlspace beneath Barracks 8, accessed through a loose floorboard. By the following night the women should have collected the required 200 kilos, stuffed rock hard into four pairs of German combat pants.

"The dryer it is, the better," James said.

"I am praying for salvation," Michael confided. "So far, He hasn't answered."

"He sent us goose shit. What else do you want?"

Michael merely stared. Why would anyone *want* goose shit?

James also had to explain it to Socha. "Poultry droppings are rich in ammonia nitrate. Ammonia nitrate with an accelerant and a priming charge is a powerful explosive."

"How powerful?"

"Sufficient to blow the back wall of the crematorium through the fences and part the Red Sea."

Socha remained skeptical.

Dupre's mechanics from the motor pool stole 10 gallons of fuel, which Eisenberg persuaded Brzecki to hide in a closet in one of the *kapo* shacks, where it was unlikely to be discovered until it was missed. Horowitz and Regina appointed leaders in the barracks, both male and female, whose job it was to evacuate the Jews when the order came.

"What about the people too weak to walk on their own?" Horowitz asked.

"Leave them," James said.

Horowitz's mouth gaped. "We can't just—"

James felt like one hard-hearted sonofabitch. "Our job is to give those with the best chance of making it the opportunity to escape. If we try to take everybody, especially those too sick or weak to walk, then nobody gets out. That's the way it has to be."

Through Jewish women certain German officers took as bunkmates, Grossbert managed to come up with a handful of 9mm cartridges. "Will these be enough? My girls don't know if they can get more without creating suspicion."

"They'll have to do."

In the meantime, Socha was busy on the clandestine radio he kept buried beneath his barracks. He and Horowitz and several others Jews, whom the Germans had since assisted in meeting their Maker, had smuggled it in pieces from Majdanek and then reassembled it. It was relatively safe to use late at night and as long as outgoing messages were kept brief. As far as Socha knew, the Germans did not have RDF capability in the area.

He managed to contact Jurawski's partisans on the first night. Jurawski wanted nothing to do with the escape until he learned that Regina would be among those fleeing the camp. Overjoyed, he then promised to bring what vehicles and men he might successfully smuggle through German lines and checkpoints. Since Jurawski couldn't possibly provide enough transportation for everyone, James ordered Dupre, the Frenchman, to work up a loading plan naming those with first access to it. At the top of the list were Professor Jahne, James, Regina, the Executive Committee and their department heads.

Although Elena and Mimi were not essentials and therefore not on the loading plan, James privately vowed not to leave them behind. Not even if he had to turn Professor Jahne over to Socha, Jurawski and Regina for exfiltration and *walk* with the little girl and her mother all the way across Poland.

Socha also persuaded Jurawski to pass along a message in code from James to Allied Command in London via France. James feared he had been missing so long that Uncle Henry might not be able to provide on such short notice the bombers he had promised as part of the initial operations order. The wait was long and tense before the reply came that the B-17s were still available. They would strike the designated grid coordinates at precisely 2300 hours the day after the next.

That meant the Jews had to be out through the fence and safely away from the camp before the first bombs dropped and gave the Germans more to think about than chasing escaped prisoners.

"Until now, it has been impossible to obtain outside aid for the Jews' underground and resistance movements," Socha marveled.

James saw no need to tell him this operation had nothing to do with assisting or freeing Jews; one old scientist with knowledge of how to build a superweapon was far more valuable to the war effort than any number of prisoners held in Nazi concentration or extermination camps. All this was for *him*.

As the Committee department head in charge of processing weapons, Grossbert, a former soldier in the Polish army, faced daunting obstacles. The German armory lay inaccessible outside the gate, and it wasn't as if Mausers were left lying carelessly about for Jewish females to steal while they filched ammunition. The success or failure of the breakout attempt depended on the leaders obtaining at least one or two rifles at the start of the action.

"All I can suggest are clubs and stones," Grossbert said.

"Not good enough," James countered. "We'll have to take rifles from guards near H hour. Come up with a plan."

Too many people were involved in the plot for James's comfort, but an operation of this scope required the involvement of numbers. Therefore, it was fraught with the possibility of compromise. An air of expectancy, of excitement, of *hope* crept over the camp. The trick was to make sure the guards and traitorous *kapos* did not sense the change in the air before things kicked off. Brzecki came by the latrine late at night to cast a warning as the Committee reviewed and hammered out final details.

"Groner is sniffing about," he cautioned. "I think he suspects something. He's trying to bully people into talking about you, Albert Einstein."

Socha's knife-slashed mouth tightened. "He will be dead before we leave this place, or there is no God."

James slapped him on the shoulder. "Don't do anything to screw up the escape, my friend."

The two leaders were left alone in the latrine together for a few minutes after the others departed. James yearned for more news about Gabrielle. Although he was prepared to accept the worst—that she might be dead—he dreaded having his fears confirmed. At this point, it was better that he not know her fate, that he nurse his hope, however slim it might be, until this was all over. He had to keep his head clear and his wits sharp for the next night.

Socha sensed what was on James's mind. "Regina and you, you are together," he said. "Yet, there is also Gabrielle and the warlord Jurawski . . . ?"

"It's a long story."

"We in the camps all have our long stories."

James could not force himself to ask about Gabrielle, not now. As Socha volunteered nothing on his own, James was left with his anxieties. He felt nightmares coming on.

He lay awake most of the rest of the night on the bunk shelf with people who had come to mean something to him, to the degree that he was even willing to risk his mission for them. Regina, who slept in his arms to conserve space, awoke and found him sleepless.

"Another nightmare?" she whispered in English.

"No. You?"

"We are all nervous about it. Do not worry. We have prayed."

Mimi whimpered in her sleep. Michael snored. James ran his hand across the returning stubble on Regina's shaved head.

"It will grow back, James."

He would probably never see it. They lay together, awake, each in thought.

"Tell me about Gabrielle," she said finally.

He didn't want to talk about Gabrielle with her.

"Are you in love with Gabrielle?" she asked.

He hesitated. "Are you in love with Jurawski?"

She hedged. "I knew if he was still alive he would come for me."

"You didn't answer my question."

"You did not answer mine. Perhaps there are no answers for people like us, who must live with the assurance of a future only five minutes away. James, on this night, at this moment, I love you more deeply and completely than I have ever loved anyone. Do you understand?"

"Yes." He felt the same way about her.

She kissed him tenderly on the mouth, snuggled deeper into his arms, and both of them fell asleep at last. Neither suffered nightmares.

43

More guards than usual were about, they and the *kapos* sniffing around like jackals on a scent, spreading anxiety and foreboding, reaching for the slightest excuse to employ whips and clubs.

"Someone has talked," Socha whispered as James trundled a wheelbarrow full of wet mortar to the bricklayers. "Spies are everywhere and will betray for a scrap of bread."

"If they knew anything for certain, the hanging would already have started," James pointed out.

"They know *something*, Albert Einstein. I will not be hanged. I will take some of them with me."

"Easy, Leopold. You'll get your chance. We must survive until tomorrow night."

Unadulterated hatred blazed in Socha's eyes. "I have much to pay them back for," he promised.

If one of the guards or *kapos* foiled a conspiracy, either intentionally or by accident, he received rewards of more food, better living conditions, praise and wider choices among the young Jewesses in the camp. Certainly a bounty worth the effort, and one which the *kapo* gorilla Groner seemed determined to collect. He was like a hound who knew the 'coon was hiding somewhere. He just didn't know where. Eye droopy, bullet head squared obstinately on his thick shoulders, he cast about relentlessly all day trying to pick up a track.

Apparently foiled at every turn, he finally resorted to the proven standby of those without subtlety or imagination: threats and violence. He cornered Michael Grojanowski against a wall of the crematorium. His back against the bricks, the emaciated Jew turned the color of soiled athletic socks. He began to age right before the other workers' eyes.

It was noon break before James had an opportunity to talk to Michael. "What did he want?"

"I told him nothing, Albert Einstein."

"What does he know, Michael?"

"I don't know what. Something. He kept asking me what you were up to. I told him I didn't know what he was talking about. He said for me to think it over, for he would be seeing me later. I am really scared, Albert Einstein."

Weather forming in the Alps was ushering in a murky, dismal sky. A single plump raindrop landed on Michael's bony cheek like a tear.

"I swear I won't tell him anything," Michael whispered.

Socha tarried near James's mortar-mixing pit the next time he had a chance. "Michael will break if he's pressured," he predicted. "I have known Michael since before the Germans came. He is weak willed."

James nodded. "Your suggestion?"

The work boss had eyes as hard as agate. Nothing ever seemed to soften them. "He should be eliminated before he can talk. Tonight."

James briefly considered it. The hard, calculating OSS part of his brain warned him that disposing of Michael might be the most prudent course, that he would regret it later if it was not done, but he still couldn't make himself take the step. Michael had become "family," sharing and surviving with the rest.

"Wait," James said.

"We can wait too long and all end up hanged."

"Wait."

The rest of the day, rain continued to threaten. There was fearful talk of another action to fill the empty nooses hanging from the red water tower.

The prospect of rain made James uneasy. He winced as though stabbed by a knife every time an isolated raindrop struck him. As a kid on the farm, he had always liked rain. He used to rig a shelter on the creek bank out of an old square of canvas and huddle underneath it, listening to rain throb on the canvas and watching it pattern the surface of the creek. Rain now, however, came with a double edge if it lasted through the next night. While it would mask movement when the breakout began, it also made setting off his improvised explosives chancy and would undoubtedly force Allied bombers to scrub their mission. Either eventuality doomed the escape attempt and placed James in the position of having to confront Major Fischer again.

Quitting time was called earlier than usual. Workers muttered in nervous hope that it was because of the weather and not because of another action. That hope was dashed when the inmates were ordered to remain in ranks in the prison courtyard after headcount. Stocky Lieutenant Colonel Muller, with his fashionable Hitler mustache, established himself onstage in front of the water tower and the empty hangman's nooses. Lights were burning in Major Fischer's little white shack, but he did not appear.

Muller tapped his riding crop against one hand and glowered at those whose lives were subject to his every whim. He stood there, lightning flickering behind him with a dragon's worth of teeth, while squads of *Wehrmacht* and *kapos* spread out among the barracks and tore them apart in an unexplained search for contraband.

Prisoners heard bunks being ripped apart and their pitifully few possessions thrown out in the dirt. No one dared turn his head to look lest he betray guilt and be hanged for it. There was no talking. The entire inmate population held its cumulative breath as searchers ransacked barracks after barracks.

James hoped it was merely another "rat hunt," one of the random searches the Germans conducted frequently and without advance notice. One bullet found, one piece of commandeered clothing, truck fuel, the trousers full of geese shit—and the revolt died aborning. Another selection would fill the nooses. More ropes would be required. James couldn't avoid the water tower this time.

Thunder cracked and rumbled hard while fleets of clouds the color of iron washed out the day's remaining light. Jagged streaks of lightning united heaven and earth. James looked up in time to catch the first raindrops on his face. The sky convulsed and poured down a fierce deluge that immediately soaked the miserable masses, set them to shivering and turned the courtyard to running water and sticky mud. James had always liked the rain, never more than at the moment.

"Thank you, God," Michael murmured, lifting his bony face.

Commandant Muller hurried off the stage, mustering what dignity he could manage while being drenched by what Gramps would call a "toad strangler." SS toadies, themselves about to strangle, rushed up with open umbrellas and escorted the Nazi officer out of camp.

That ended the rat hunt. Apparently, there were no incriminating results, for a minor officer released the inmates from formation with the insulting shout, "Are you Jews too stupid to get in out of the rain?"

Relief proved premature. As the family dashed through the rain toward Barracks 8, Groner suddenly materialized out of nowhere. He snatched Michael and evaporated into the storm before anyone had time to resist.

44

Something like a little rain would not have deterred the Germans from taking action against the Jews had they really possessed anything incriminating against them. Commandant Muller's overreaction must have been based on an unsubstantiated tip, or even on something no more concrete than the subtle change of mood that appeared to have overtaken many of the inmates. Although Michael had not been in on the escape meetings and knew little about the plan other than the part he played in helping hide goose shit, what he *did* know was enough for Lieutenant Colonel Muller to take action if he broke under torture. And he *would* break. The man was always on the point of breaking.

Of the entire camp's cadre, Groner seemed most determined to suck up to the prison commander, get to the bottom of things and earn big rewards. He had to be stopped.

James saw the rest of the family to Barracks 8 for their own safety. The barracks was a shambles, but nothing that couldn't be repaired. Shivering people with teeth chattering from the soaking were trying to get dry by stripping and wringing out their clothing.

"Keep everyone here," James ordered.

Regina hesitated. "James . . . ?"

"I'll be all right."

Little Mimi refused to let him go. "Alber', don't leave us."

James knelt on his knees in the filthy aisle between bunks and enveloped the thin child in his arms. He took her by the shoulders and pushed her away a little so he could see her pale oval face in the dingy light. It seemed lately she was always afraid. She had a right to be. She had seen how people "disappeared." In her six years she had experienced things no adult should have been compelled to endure.

"I won't ever leave you, honey," James promised. An OSS agent wasn't supposed to get emotionally involved.

"They are bad, bad people," Mimi wailed.

Elena and Regina gathered with James to comfort the child. Tonight's threat of more horror at the water tower had almost been too much for her.

"Mimi, do you hear rain falling on the roof?" James asked.

She sniffled. "Yes."

"I'll be back before you stop hearing it."

"Promise, Alber'?"

"Promise."

Elena held Mimi. Regina walked James to the door. Rain fell in a driving sheet outside the doorway and lightning tore across the black skies. She touched James's cheek with her fingertips. "You are not nearly the hard-boiled egg you make yourself out to be," she said. "Even from the beginning, I never believed you capable of shooting either my uncle or me."

"Yeah? Well . . ." He was hard-boiled enough to do what had to be done. Sometimes.

* * *

Sheets of rain like barely transparent veils blowing in the wind combined with the blackened sky and nightfall to cut visibility to mere feet. James could barely make out the outlines of barracks on either side as he hurried in the direction of the water tower and the first *kapo* shack.

Since most of the *kapos* were common criminals and not Jews, and therefore treated better than Jews, they had their own accommodations scattered about the compound. Six of them. James had fixed their locations in his mind. Late at night or whenever it rained, *kapos* gathered in one or another of the shacks to play grabass and cards between patrol rounds. Brzecki had assured the Committee that the purloined fuel would be safe, hidden in the shack he shared with one other *kapo*, because his fellows considered him soft on the Jews and never came to play cards with him.

James wondered how many of the *kapos* knew about Michael's having been snatched. It complicated things considerably if all were in on it. However, if Groner planned to keep all the glory and reward to himself, as James suspected, then there *might* be a chance for damage control before things got out of hand.

That was the only thing he could count on.

Socha was waiting at the latrine. His big shadow separated itself from the wall. James immediately switched to fight mode.

"It's me, Albert Einstein."

"Damn. Call out first the next time."

"I knew you'd be going out. I saw what happened with Michael. We had better find him fast."

A crash of thunder and a streak of illuminating lightning forced them to cringe against the latrine wall. Rainwater pouring off the eaves with the sound of a waterfall covered their voices.

"*Kapos* won't be out in this," Socha said.

"I think Groner will drag him to one of the shacks to torture him."

Socha agreed.

"You take the three on the west end," James advised. "I'll take those over by the water tower. It shouldn't take long. If either of us spots him, we'll meet back here."

"If we don't find him?"

That probably meant he had been rushed directly to the camp commandant. "Then our asses are a hay meadow and here comes the mower."

"That's graphic enough."

They immediately split up. It was not a night, as Gramps used to say, for man, beast or Christian. James's stripes hung on his wiry frame like wet rags. But at least they were being laundered.

The first shack he came to sat in total darkness. Even though it belonged to Brzecki, he listened outside the walls, hearing nothing other than wind hammering the rain against the tin roof, the steady drum of water splashing from the eaves and loud snoring from inside.

He made his way to the second *kapo* quarters, this where Groner slept. Watery light framed out the window. He crouched underneath it and peeked inside while water ran off the roof onto his head and shoulders. Inside, four *kapos* sat around a crude table playing cards in the glow of an oil lamp. All were big-framed, tough-looking men. Their clubs were leaning against the wall by the door and their rain slickers were hanging, dripping, from a coat tree. Michael was not there. Neither was Groner.

Halfway to the third shack, James was slopping past the disciplinary barracks, where troublemakers were housed until their turns at the pits, when a flash of lightning revealed a hunched-over figure plowing through the storm directly at him. A poncho bulked out the figure and snap-crackled in the wind. Only German guards wore ponchos. James flattened himself against the wall. The figure kept coming.

Had the guard spotted him? Lightning flashes worked both ways.

The fellow paused at the corner of the disciplinary barracks. James made out his form, backlit by a glimmer of lightning. If he kept coming along the wall, using it for shelter, he would run right over James—at which point James was left with two options: kill the man, or be killed by him. Either way, Lieutenant Colonel Muller was bound to call for another reprisal selection, even if the guard only turned up "missing." It was classic damned if you did, damned if you don't.

James tried to meld into the very structure of the building. It would be a bad time for another revealing bolt of lightning. His muscles coiled. He would kill if he had to, and then try to work past the consequences.

After a moment, as though reconsidering, the guard altered his original course slightly and struck out past the disciplinary barracks in the direction of Major Fischer's little white shack and the main gate. He passed within 10 feet of James in the darkness, his head down and shoulders hunched against the weather. Lightning flickered surrounding buildings into eerie relief and reflected off the guard's back. The guard kept going, picking up his pace in order to reach somewhere dry.

Don't let the door hit you in the ass.

James approached his third and last *kapo* shack with more caution. What if he was wrong about where Groner might take Michael? He didn't want to think about it. Socha might be having better luck.

A light burned through the window. James heard loud ranting coming from inside, a single voice. He ducked below the window and peeked through from one corner.

The first thing he saw was Groner standing spread-legged in the middle of the closet-sized room, club in hand, bent forward shouting into Michael's face. Michael slumped, semi-conscious, on a wooden chair to which he was bound with rope. His face was a battered, bloody mess. Blood stained the floor and Groner's striped uniform. The oil lantern on the table behind them made the spittle spraying from Groner's thick lips sparkle.

"You thick-headed piece-of-crap Jew!" Groner roared in German. "I'm giving you a chance to live your pathetic little life for another day, another week. That's more than any of you deserve. I know the Jews are up to something. All you have to do is tell me what it is and you can go back to your little rat-hole barracks."

He jabbed the point of his stick viciously into Michael's solar plexus. Michael's skeletal frame snapped forward. James could almost hear his bones rattle. Green bile mixed with blood spewed onto the Jew's knees; there was nothing else in his stomach. Groner snatched a fistful of the Jew's thin hair and wrenched his head back. Blood ran from Michael's crushed nose. His eyes were swollen to slits, and a tooth hung from the corner of his mouth on a long slimy string of gum tissue. The poor man looked older than any man had a right to look and still live.

"Tell me!" Groner demanded, his bad eye drooping and his shoulders bunched in preparation to resume the beating.

Michael mumbled something unintelligible. He was still holding out. He had more moxie than James had given him credit for. Moxie or not, he was about done for. By the time James retrieved Socha for backup, the poor fellow would either be dead or spilling his guts. James had to act now.

It wasn't going to be easy, taking on the big sonofabitch again, but it had to be done. Determined, James slid around to the door. A little porch sheltered it. He took a long breath to pump oxygen into his lungs, then reared back and kicked the door open. He rode a gust of wind and rain into the cabin.

"*Überraschang!*" he shouted. "Guess who, asshole!"

Groner wheeled around, stick already swinging, hurling curses from his gritted teeth.

James ducked underneath the first murderous swing of the stick. The second swing caught him in the shoulder with a numbing blow that sent him reeling across the room and crashing into the wall. The cabin shook. The table holding the oil lamp slid across the floor, but the lamp, flickering, remained upright.

Groner lunged, swinging and poking at the intruder with the stick in one hand, scratching and punching with the other hand. There was no such thing as fair play in this kind of fight, no rules except to disable or kill the opponent as efficiently and quickly as possible. Old Man Fairbairn back during OSS training called it "gutter fighting." In his head, James heard Old Fairbairn shouting now: "Kill the bastard! Kill the bastard!"

A ham-sized fist caught him on the side of the head, directly on his scabbed and barely healing gunshot wound. It dazed him. He staggered back. The triumphant look in Groner's piggish eyes said he thought it was all over. If James went down, it *was* all over.

Groner's stick whistled through the air with a swing that would have decapitated. It missed, but the force of the swing drove the end of the stick through the thin wall. It stuck there. Groner jerked it to wrench it free. James saw his opening.

He feinted with a "tiger claw" directed at Groner's eyes. Caught off guard, the *kapo* staggered back a step, leaving his stick stuck in the wall. James danced to one side, shifted his weight, and went for the throat.

With a hoarse shriek of surprise, pain and shock, Groner grabbed his stricken throat with both hands. James brought the man's hands back down with a front kick to the groin. Many more of those and guy was going to end up a soprano. If he lived.

Two quick jabs to the belly chopped him down more to James's size. He finished off the flurry with a second chop to the throat, which crushed the larynx. It was easy if you knew how.

Groner crashed to the floor. Writhing, unable to catch his breath, emitting a pitiful noise somewhat like that of a kitten with laryngitis, he looked up at James standing over him. Abject terror filled his good eye.

James stepped on his felled enemy's throat and pressed until Groner's eye bulged and glazed over. He stopped breathing.

"*Auf Wiedersehen,*" James said without emotion.

Michael was in bad shape. He watched in horror through swollen eyes. He tried to speak, but all that came out were wet, spluttering sounds due to blood in his throat and loss of teeth. "I didn't tell him . . . I didn't . . ." he finally managed.

"I know." He released Michael's bonds. "Wait here. I'll be right back."

He scouted the water tower to make sure none of the guards had it under direct observation. Satisfied that he wouldn't be readily seen, he shimmied up to the crossbeam and pulled himself hand over hand to where the hangman's ropes were knotted. A few minutes later, he returned to the *kapo* shack with one of the ropes.

He noosed the rope around Groner's neck and tossed the other end over an exposed rafter joist. Using the rafter as leverage, he pulled the body off the floor. It took all his remaining strength, but soon he had the fresh corpse dangling with its feet off the floor. He tied off the rope to an open stud in the wall, helped Michael to his feet, and kicked the chair over to make it look like Groner had hung himself. Could the inmates be blamed if a mentally disturbed *kapo* committed suicide?

Michael recovered sufficiently to help James sanitize the scene. Using old rags they found underneath the bed, they wiped blood off the floor and from the shaft of Groner's stick. There was nothing they could do about the hole in the wall. They threw the rags outside to let the rain wash them. Satisfied that nothing would be made of the scene other than what it was—a suicide—James put his arm around Michael's waist to help him back to the barracks.

He looked back once before he closed the door. Groner's bad eye drooped, forever closed while the other bulged as though in terror at its first glimpse into hell. Wind through the doorway made the lamp flicker and the body sway gently at the end of its rope.

45

James turned an anxious eye to the weather after another night of fretful sleep. So many things could go wrong. So many things *had* gone wrong. What happened today, what happened *tonight* with the breakout, depended upon which other *kapos* knew about Groner's scheme to make Michael Grojanowski talk, what they knew about it, whom they had told and whether or not Lieutenant Colonel Muller accepted Groner's death as a suicide. So far, beginning with breakfast, such as it was, everything seemed normal.

Last night's downpour had turned to today's chill drizzle. Weather like this, if it persisted, meant no bombers. No bombers seriously threatened the escape plans.

Regina frowned at the lukewarm liquid in her tin cup, diluted even more than usual by the rain. She tilted her head to the lowering clouds. Light rain sprinkled her face. She closed her eyes and smiled. "I once loved summer rains," she said.

James ran the back of his hand along her wet cheek and adjusted the barrette that held her head rag closed. Fortunate indeed was the man who knew such a woman

in his lifetime. James had known two of them, both of
them from the war.

"You'll enjoy summer rains again," he said.

This morning, Michael's face was swollen something
awful, his eyes blackened, gaps where teeth should be. He
groaned as he got around, like an old man with arthritis, but
his strength was returning. None of the family had asked
about the night before, seeing that James seemed reticent
to talk about it. It was enough that Michael was back home
alive. In the darkness of the barracks, Regina and Elena
had tended his injuries as best they could. Mimi had awakened, sniffling, hungry and dreaming, conditions that had
become chronic in camp, and moved as near James as she
could get. "Alber'! You came back. I love you, Alber'."

Professor Jahne regarded Michael, then James, while
they waited for the morning work whistle. He shook
James's hand. "You are an unusual young man," he said,
and actually smiled. "Not so very different from the
Albert Einstein I knew so long ago."

The work whistle shrilled in the wake of a low rumble
of thunder.

"Stop on the way home to pick up a chicken for supper,"
Regina said.

James grinned tightly.

The crematorium was almost complete. The man-
sized ovens were installed and the big butchers
blocks set up. Construction continued on the dry interior underneath the roof. Two more days—three at the
most—and the ovens could be cranked up to *bake*. But
if things went right today and tonight, there would be no
one left at Nisko by that time.

As James worked, he kept one eye on the weather and
the other on the guards, *kapos* and overseers in order
to judge their reactions to Groner's "suicide" and pre-
dict any subsequent consequences. Rumors spread that
one of the *kapos* had been driven to hang himself due to

misery and deprivation in the camp. So far, the camp's command seemed to accept it. Everyone went about his business as though last night's rat hunt and suicide had never occurred. The Nazis had a remarkable capacity for self-deception as long as their core beliefs as outlined by the Führer were not threatened.

The rain ceased before noon. Lieutenant Muller toured the construction site during the meal break. He was all spiffed up, in tall, spit-shined boots, black death's-head uniform, and his little, truncated, Hitler mustache. James thought of him as a sadistic Puss-in-Boots.

Prisoners kept their heads bowed and refrained from looking in his direction, lest so much as a glance be taken for insolence or disrespect punishable by whipping. Socha appeared on edge. He had kept Michael busy and out of sight all morning for fear the man's telltale battered face would generate questions. James's heart pounded throughout Muller's inspection, fearful as he was that the Jews were going to be punished by another selection.

Lieutenant Colonel Muller seemed in an unusually good mood, precipitated perhaps, as inmates suggested, by a particularly comely new Jewess from Barracks 10 who had been escorted to his bed last evening. He strolled around, asked a few questions of the overseers, slapped his palm with his riding crop and then withdrew. James breathed a little easier. It appeared sleeping dogs—or sleeping Groners in this case—were going to be left sleeping.

By noon the sky was clearing, even toward the Alps in the south and west, and the camp was beginning to dry out. Socha brought his cup of soup and stood with his back to James. They were being especially cautious today to arouse no suspicions. A shaft of bright yellow sunshine broke through scattering clouds and spotlighted the two men. James blinked up into it. It felt warm and comforting on his face. He took it as a sign.

He took a sip of soup and with his back to Socha, eyes uplifted to the sun, whispered, "It's tonight. We go tonight."

46

From what Socha said, Brzecki was a recidivist thief
from Hamburg who had been in prisons and work camps
since before the war began. He had the quick hands of
a pickpocket and the sharp face of a burglar. Not being
a Jew protected him from the Final Solution. As a *kapo*
with a larcenous nature, he had proved himself suscep-
tible to bribery and blackmail. The Committee slipped
him a diamond ring here, a watch there to use as barter
with the German guards, and he belonged to the Jews. A
big hunk of that night's action would depend upon a thief
and a scoundrel.

"He's in too deep to turn on us now," Socha reassured
James. "If we go down, he goes down—and he knows it."

"When you got 'em by the balls . . ." James said.

Attempting to bust out of Nisko, James would have had
to admit in saner times, was the same ultimate desperation that prompted a 'coon caught in a steel trap to chew
through its own leg in order to free itself. All the ingredi-
ents of desperation and looniness were present: a bunch

of cowed-down, half-starved Jews; Allied bombers that may or may not arrive on time; dependence upon a Polack's love for a Jew girl to inspire him to risk partisan lives and send transportation; a few hundred pounds of goose shit; some pistol cartridges; two cans of fuel. . .

James couldn't even be sure his makeshift bomb would explode as intended. In theory, dried poultry droppings were rich in ammonia nitrate. Ammonia nitrate was a powerful explosive when combined with fuel oil and a propellant like gunpowder to set it off. But what if it didn't work, in practice?

He mustn't think about that. As Gramps always said, you couldn't get all your squirrels up one tree. You had to get what you could and forget about the rest.

James estimated they had maybe two hours to play with from the time the plan began to unfold until the bombers arrived. The time element was a guess-as-guess-can situation, since no one had a watch or a clock. The trick was in the timing. If he breached the wire too soon, giving the Germans time to respond, the break for freedom became a massacre. Too late, and everyone risked fiery death inside the camp when the bombs fell.

What the hell! Nobody ever got out of life alive. None of them had anything to lose. They were all living on borrowed time, James most of all. By all odds, he should have been dead by now, considering how many times, since parachuting into Poland, he had escaped fate by the hair of his chinny-chin-chin. But if he succeeded tonight, the secrets of atomic power would be transferred into Allied hands and President Roosevelt would receive irrefutable proof of Hitler's "Final Solution."

No matter what happened, however, James had to either get Professor Jahne out or . . . There was that big *or* again.

Then there was Mimi. He had promised the little girl he wouldn't leave her.

* * *

It was a clear night after a rainy morning. Stars were shining, but the moon would not come out until later. James, Socha, Eisenberg, Dupre, Grossbert and the *kapo* Brzecki made their stealthy way among the barracks, whose occupants should be sound asleep but weren't. Having been alerted that tonight was *the* night, internees lay awake in the darkness, waiting breathlessly for barracks commanders to give the word to make a break for the fence. Regina, Elena, Michael, and a few others comforted the women and children and kept them quiet.

The *kapos* on duty would have to be incapacitated early on, in order to allow the conspirators to move more or less freely about the interior of the camp. Brzecki had scouted the camp and located his fellow *kapos* playing cards in the very shack where Groner had been found hanged that morning. Having witnessed so much death—and in many cases inflicted it themselves—the *kapos* felt no particular loss from the demise of one of their own.

The little group led by James slipped free of the night shadows from Barracks 2 and skulked to the shack, whose light glowed through the window. Five *kapos* were gathered around the table. The off-duty shifts were sleeping in their respective cabins about the camp and could probably be counted on to remain asleep.

The card players were disarmed, their sticks and clubs leaning against the wall next to the door—just as James had observed about them the night before—all within easy reach of any attackers who burst through the door. The assault must be swift and violent to ensure none of the *kapos* had a chance to alert German guards patrolling the wire perimeter and manning the watch towers.

Brzecki indicated they should wait. One of the *kapos* was missing, having gone out to make his rounds.

"I'll go get him," Brzecki whispered into James's ear. "Be ready."

He melted into the night, returning shortly with the stray. James watched them moving from shadow into starlight and back into shadow. Brzecki should have been a Hollywood actor. He was laughing and talking, telling some story or other, with the assistance of animated hand gestures. He stopped in the open near the corner of the shack and maneuvered the other *kapo's* back toward James and the Jews hiding in the shadows. He laughed to cover any sounds of their movement, his hands on his comrade's shoulders. The victim was not as alert as he might be; *kapos* had little but contempt for a people whom they considered too submissive to resist.

Out from behind sprang a silent, deadly figure. The *kapo* was dead and into the next world before he had time to react. Brzecki turned his head away. James pocketed the short length of cotton rope he had used for a garrote. He and Socha quickly dragged the body to a corner of the nearest barracks and shoved it into the crawl space underneath. The barracks commanders were doing a good job of keeping their charges quiet; the only sound coming from inside was that of a starving child crying. Perfectly normal for any night.

"The Lord giveth, *we* taketh away . . ." Socha commented of the dead man.

The rest of the *kapo* caper might have gone just as smoothly, except for the recalcitrance of one individual. James, the five Jews and Brzecki exploded into the middle of the card players. Before the surprised gamblers had time to recover, the intruders had armed themselves with the occupants' own weapons and formed a threatening semicircle.

"Don't resist!" Brzecki said. "You won't be hurt—"

"Up yours!"

This one, bigger and uglier than the rest, had delusions of adequacy. He bowed his head like a bull and charged.

Socha sidestepped him and, with both hands on the bat he'd picked up, slammed the *kapo's* head out of the ballpark. His skull cracked like a melon and he dropped to the floor. Socha showed no mercy. He pounded him again, spattering blood.

An apparition of Jewish fury and revenge, Socha

glared at the remaining *kapos* frozen in fear around the table, his legs spread wide.

The others wanted none of him. Their hands flew up in surrender. Socha wanted to kill them all, but James restrained him. In short order, the surviving four were trussed hand and foot with bindings ripped from their own clothing.

Everything seemed to be going too smoothly for James's taste. He had always felt more comfortable with "one damned thing after another."

47

Brzecki and the wizened little Jew named Horowitz fetched the cans of fuel oil from Brzecki's *kapo* shack. Grossbert, Eisenberg and Dupre met Michael at Barracks 8, crawled underneath the building and returned with three pairs of German combat trousers packed tightly with goose manure.

Working swiftly under kerosene lamplight—and the puzzled scrutiny of conspirators and bound *kapos* alike—James used a tin bucket to soak dried goose shit in fuel oil, then repacked the mixture in the trousers and tied off the waists of two pairs. The third pair he left temporarily open to receive the fuse and igniter.

He constructed several long fuses by tightly twisting strips of cloth and paper and saturating them in fuel. He lit and tested them until he had the timing right. Last, he pried the projectiles from a half dozen pistol cartridges and emptied the gunpowder into a packet made of paper to keep it dry and separate from the rest of the bomb. He inserted one end of a fuse into the gunpowder, secured the igniter, and stuffed it deep into the third pair of trousers, leaving the fuse trailing to accept a flame. He tied off the waist. Socha looked at it skeptically.

"If it doesn't light . . . ?"

"Oh ye of little faith."

"All that a man requires is the faith of a mustard seed, Albert Einstein. If this works and tomorrow I'm free, I'll look upon geese with brotherly affection from now on."

"Kiss a goose for me. This works best if it's compressed and tightly packed. Understand? I showed you today where I wanted it."

"In the hollow behind the oven next to the back wall," Socha recited.

"We need to blow the back wall through the fences and make a hole."

"You'll be there to light it?"

"You know what to do if something happens and I don't make it. When you first hear the bombers . . ."

"I understand, Albert Einstein. That's when I set it off."

"You'll have about two minutes to get away before it detonates."

"I have matches. Don't worry so. About anything. The old man with the beard is under my personal protection."

"Also his niece and the little girl. Mimi's mother will be with them."

"They too, Albert Einstein. God speed."

They gripped hands. James preferred Socha stay with him. Driven by his personal hatred for all things German, he had proved he would fight and kill, a decided asset when it came to the next step in wresting weapons away from the guards. In James's opinion, the other Jews were still an unknown quantity who might start spouting psalms when the famous fat hit the fire. But either James or Socha had to be ready to light the bomb. James trusted no one else with the task.

Socha and Dupre set off for the crematorium, carrying stuffed trousers on their shoulders like the bottom halves of very fat men. Socha carried two, Dupre one.

Horowitz was to remain at the shack to watch the

kapos. "When you hear the explosions," James told him, "run to the crematorium. Someone will be there to show you the way out."

"I hope it's the last and only time we run to the ovens," Grossbert remarked with a shudder.

James and the others—Brzecki the thief; the balding Grossbert; gaunt, hollow-eyed Eisenberg—took up the captured *kapos'* weapons and made their way toward the main gate. Securing firearms was critical to the operation. Without them, escapees pouring through the breach in the fence would be mowed down like, well, geese on a pond, without a means of fighting back. It was Grossbert's idea to lure the guards inside the prison fence just before the escape began and take their weapons from them. It might not be the best idea, but it was the only one they had come up with.

The little contingent hid in the darkness against the barracks nearest the main gate, opposite the warehouses and the little white gatehouse that Major Fischer had been using. The major appeared to be working late as usual; a light burned in the window. At the gate, two sentries walked patrol. A machine gun and crew occupied a tower on stilts above the double gates. The floodlights on the perimeter revealed a train on the spur track beyond, but the train appeared empty. Otherwise, the camp lay deceptively silent and heavy in the darkness while captive mice played.

James looked up at the sky with its wonderful display of galaxies and constellations. It was the same sky everywhere—except in the rest of the world it was free, while here it was held hostage by a dictator's madness.

He wondered if Gabrielle was alive under this sky somewhere.

The two sentries at the gate marched back and forth in a precise rhythm and prescribed distance, one to the left, one to the right, meeting each other in the middle of the gate after each cycle. Estimating the width of the gate and how long it took the sentries to make a round permitted James to guess with some accuracy the passage of time.

If he made his move too soon, Major Fischer would get suspicious and sound the alarm. Too late, and the bombers would catch him before he could pull his men back into position to defend and cover the escape.

"If you screw this up," James warned Brzecki, "your buddies tied up back there are going to squeal like pigs. You'll hang with the rest of us. You have to persuade Major Fischer to send guards to escort me to his office. *Verstehen Sie?*"

"*Ich verstehe.*"

When the time came, Brzecki drew a deep, quivering breath and stepped from shadow into starlight and the reflected glow from the perimeter floods. Hesitating momentarily to gather his courage, he then struck out purposefully toward the main gate and Major Fischer's little house. He carried a club, the *kapo's* badge of office. He was still very much the actor.

A command rang out from the guard tower as soon as he broke the demarcation of the floodlights. "*Halten Sie an!*"

The sound of a machine-gun bolt slamming home stopped the rodentlike little *kapo* in his tracks. Even from a distance, James could almost hear the man's bones rattling.

"*Was wünschen Sie?*" the guard called out.

"*Ich mochte . . .*" Brzecki's voice broke. He tried again. "*Ich muss mit Major Fischer sprechen. Es ist . . . Es ist dringend.*" I must speak with Major Fischer. It is urgent.

"Nothing is urgent to scum like you except your own worthless hide."

"Summon the officer of the guard," Brzecki insisted, sounding more confident. "Do you want to put your own head in the noose by taking responsibility for knowing what is and what is not urgent?"

That set the guard back on his haunches. After a long moment of consulting with his partner, he shouted, "*Bleiben hier.*"

Brzecki remained in place as ordered. Shortly, a small gate next to the main gate swung open. An SS officer and two enlisted *Wehrmacht* rushed into the compound and strode past Major Fischer's cabin toward the *kapo* waiting in front of it. By this time, the flap had brought Major Fischer to his door to see what was going on. A lamp backlighted the tall figure. He called out a question.

The officer of the guard explained and motioned toward Brzecki. Fischer looked at the *kapo*. After a moment's consideration, he gestured for Brzecki to come forward. James glanced uneasily at the sky. *Hurry, hurry.*

The cabin was too far away for James to hear the exchange between Brzecki and Major Fischer. But from the body language, Brzecki was doubtlessly passing along the message about how the Jew Albert Einstein must see the major on an urgent matter. Major Fischer would understand.

Major Fischer seemed suspicious. He stepped outside and looked in the direction of the Jew barracks. He looked over at the gate behind him. It was a strange way and time for Albert Einstein to try to contact him, especially considering how the major had warned that neither of them must do anything to tip off Lieutenant Colonel Muller about the deal they had made. Something must have happened that would affect tomorrow's transaction. He would have Albert Einstein's head if the little bugger screwed things up.

He issued orders. The officer of the guard snapped a *Heil Hitler!* He and his two *Wehrmacht* turned and, following Brzecki, started briskly into the compound toward Barracks 8 to find the redheaded Jew and escort him to the major's quarters. Major Fischer stood outlined in the bright doorway a moment and watched them go. His suspenders hung from his trousers and the tail of his black tunic was loose and unbuttoned. He went back inside and closed the door behind him.

That was when James's ears picked up the drone of the first approaching Allied bombers. They would be flying relatively low due to the small size of the target and its critical nature, which meant they could be heard coming from a long distance away.

48

By this stage of the war, the Germans were accustomed to Allied bombers pounding their cities. However, bombs were never dropped on concentration or POW camps. Although the SS officer of the guard automatically looked up at the sky, feeling the vibration of all that approaching power through the soles of his boots, he and his men continued following Brzecki toward the heart of darkness, confident that *they* were not the target.

Brzecki knew better; they *were* the target—only not immediately—of the bombers. He cast furtive looks in all directions, as nervous as a beagle passing peach seeds, as obvious as Sidney Greenstreet playing the bad guy in a Bogart movie. Under tonight's prolonged stress, the polished actor had given way to the cornered thief. James feared he would give himself away.

If James noticed it, how much more likely was the SS officer to see it? Allied bombers were nothing to be *this* jittery about. Sniffing a rat in the corn crib, the SS halted his party at the very edge of the night, where starlight, perimeter floodlights, and camp shadows coalesced. Only a few more steps and they would have been in total darkness, out of sight of the gate guards.

The officer glared at Brzecki. Brzecki's teeth chattered. His head bobbed spastically on the thin spindle of his turkey's neck. The SS snatched Brzecki by his shirt front and jerked him close.

James signaled his accomplices: *Now.* They had to move while the Germans' attention was focused on the frightened *kapo.* Grossbert would take the nearest *Wehrmacht,* Eisenberg the officer armed only with a holstered pistol, leaving the larger soldier with the MP-40 assault rifle to James. James hoped the Jews were up to the effort. While the Committee members might be stronger than most other prisoners, they were nonetheless no match in their wasted condition for the well-nourished enemy soldiers.

Wielding sticks and clubs, the three conspirators sprang from the cover of the barracks wall and rushed the Germans. The SS officer glimpsed the attackers from the corner of his eye at the last moment. He released Brzecki and jumped back, going for his pistol. Eisenberg tackled him as hard as is possible for a bag of bones weighing barely a hundred pounds. The SS shook him off and swung his pistol. To Brzecki's credit, the scrawny *kapo* dived to Eisenberg's aid. Together, they took the officer to the ground.

While they rolled about on the ground, meshed in a flurry of flailing arms and legs, Grossbert took down his man with a vicious slash of his club against the soldier's kneecap, dropping him where he could be finished off.

James's target was a broad-faced Prussian with a shovel-like Nazi helmet protecting his head. James got in a quick lick with his sturdy nightstick, crushing the man's shin. The Kraut cried out in pain and crumpled. James stepped in. Gripping his stick with both hands in a police riot-baton stance, he jabbed the end into his opponent's face. Blood spurted. Two more blows with the stick finished the Kraut, with a broken neck.

James wrenched the MP-40 from the soldier's death grip. Just as he jumped back to check on the others, a pistol shot cracked amidst the tangle of arms and legs where Eisenberg and Brzecki struggled with the SS officer. Brzecki screamed and tumbled away clawing at his face with both hands. Grossbert, who had finished his man, leaped forward and clubbed the officer soundly about the head until he lay still, a bloody mess. Panting heavily, Eisenberg staggered to his feet. Brzecki lay motionless, the lower half of his face shot off.

But for the gunshot, they might have gotten away with the attack without alerting the gate guards. The alarm was already sounding. It wouldn't take long before the Elite Guard and *Wehrmacht* rushed the camp.

"Get their weapons," James snapped.

There was no further need for stealth. The fly, as Grams would say, was already in the buttermilk. James took aim at the machine gunner on the main gate's tower with his freshly acquired MP-40. He squeezed off a round and had the satisfaction of seeing the target jolt back and tumble out of the box. The body caught on a wire and it stuck there.

He shot the AG—assistant gunner—with a follow-up round. This fellow jerked back and disappeared inside the box. The machine gun was out of commission, at least temporarily.

High-beam spotlights all around the perimeter immediately blazed and danced blinding light all over the landscape, searching. The escape siren went off with its blood-chilling *Ooo-gah! Ooo-gah!* Eisenberg had the dead SS officer's pistol, Grossbert the *Wehrmacht's* Mauser. They crouched, momentarily stunned into inactivity, watching with fascination as half-dressed guards began running from their quarters, just outside the gate.

Things were getting nasty, damned quick.

The gate sentries opened up, assault rifles chattering. Bullets bruised the air around James's head. Grossbert grunted and fell. James unleashed a burst at the sentries to drive them to ground and delay pursuit. Eisenberg clung to the earth, too terrified to get in on the fight. James shook him.

"Get up! Run!"

"What about Grossbert?"

"Grossbert is dead. Follow me."

James snatched the Mauser from the fallen Jew's hands. Major Fischer's door flew open before James could jerk Eisenberg to his feet and get the hell out of the kill zone. The German had an assault rifle in his hands. He opened up with it.

James faced him. A spotlight flared across his face, exposing him.

"Albert Einstein, you double-crossing son of a bitch!" Major Fischer roared.

Mauser in one hand, MP-40 in the other, James returned fire with both fists, missing in his haste. Fischer sprang out of the lit doorway. Firing as he ran, he raced across the open and merged with the night shadows cast by the warehouses. He dived around the corner of the nearest building, from which he unleashed a series of ineffective sniper shots as James led Eisenberg, zigzagging, deeper into the camp.

Dodging searchlight beams, keeping to the shadows, James made his way toward the crematorium, where Socha should be about ready to light off the goose-shit bomb in response to the approaching aircraft. Eisenberg, weakening rapidly and losing ground, stumbled along behind as best he could. James couldn't wait for him. He had to reach the crematorium with his weapons to cover the escape.

Behind him, sentries and Elite Guard officers at the gate were shooting at shadows. The siren screamed back—*Ooo-gah!*—at unseen bombers, whose throbbing roar electrified the air. Antiaircraft searchlights probed the night sky.

All about him, prematurely, disoriented masses of black-and-white-striped scarecrows milled around the various barracks like terrified zombies, crying out in confusion and terror. They knew they were supposed to do *something*, but for security purposes, the only instruction given even the barracks commanders was to run toward the explosion when it went off.

What the hell was holding up Socha?

He should be setting off the bomb *now*, before death fell from the sky to turn the camp into a conflagration right out of hell's worst chamber.

49

Bomber engines thudded in time to James's racing heart. To his consternation, he found himself short of breath. His thighs and calves burned from overexertion, his limp more pronounced than usual. Days of physical effort, mental fatigue, poor food or no food, injuries and wounds were taking a toll on his battered body. He sucked it up and kept going. His life and the lives of hundreds of others, including Regina, her uncle, little Mimi and her mother, were all on the line.

Gaunt, toothless Eisenberg proved too weak at last to keep going. He must have collapsed somewhere. James wished he had taken the SS officer's pistol from him first; it was another weapon they could have used during the escape rush through the fence.

He kept looking back, half expecting Major Fischer to jump out at him like the boogeyman Grams talked about when he was a little kid. It wasn't in the major's character to give up so easily. James *felt* himself being followed.

There was nothing back there but more darkness, penetrated here and there by searchlight beams and machine-gun tracers. Weapons of various kinds and sizes began hammering at stray groups of inmates.

There was going to be a massacre inside the stockade if Socha didn't set off that damned bomb.

Just beyond the crematorium in the far corner of the camp, irate geese disturbed in their roost were raising a racket, letting James know he had almost reached his destination. He hesitated when he came within sight of the structure. The inward side of the great blocked building facing him lay in shadow, providing concealment from the roving searchlights and the floodlights on the perimeter behind it. It loomed above James's head, as dark and foreboding as Dracula's castle.

He thought he saw movement, but when he snapped his head around to look there was nothing except shadows sent darting and dodging by the ever-restless searchlights.

No time to lose. He sprinted to the front aspect of the crematorium and flattened himself against the wall to catch his breath. Again, he thought he saw something moving.

The voice came from right next to him, not from *out there*. "James?"

"Jesus, Regina! You almost gave me a heart attack."

"You told me to come here and wait for you."

"Where are the others?"

"With Michael. They are on the way. I came ahead to make sure it was clear. Why has the explosion not gone off?"

"That's the big question." He gave her the Mauser and kept the MP-40. "You know how to use it?"

"Naturally."

From fixed, concealed positions out beyond the perimeter, 20mm antiaircraft guns on guard mounts began hurling bursts of bright flames into the sky, even though Allied bombers wouldn't be in range for some time yet.

There was no time for further conversation. Together,

James and Regina entered the crematorium through a door-less opening into total darkness. Flak falling on the roof sounded like hailstones. Even sightless, James knew the way from the days he had spent trundling wheelbarrows full of wet concrete back and forth to conscripted brick-layers. With one hand extended as a guard and bumper, Regina hanging on to his shirt, he found his way past the "showers" and the butcher blocks to the first of eight furnaces arranged in a long row.

He paused to listen. Hearing a sound near the back wall, he called out softly, "Socha?"

"Albert! Back here."

Socha struck a match to reveal where he and Dupre had ripped out an area of brick behind the last steel oven against the back wall. Into that tight space they had stuffed the trousers bomb. Ashes from a burned fuse had blackened the floor. Dupre's goatee quivered in exasperation. Socha turned his scarred and broken face in the matchlight toward James.

"I needed more than a mustard's seed of faith. It wouldn't light."

James's mind whirred as he sought an answer. He reached a hand toward Regina. "Give me the Mauser."

In exchange, he ripped off his striped shirt and gave it to her. "Quickly. Tear it into strings and tie them into a rope."

Puzzled, she and Dupre nonetheless sat on the concrete floor and fell to the task. Socha struck another match in order to provide light while James worked. James opened the top of the first pair of stuffed trousers and, with effort, dug his fingers deep into the hard mass until he located the paper pouch of gunpowder at its core. The fuse had gone out before reaching it. He rammed the Mauser's barrel into the oil-goose manure mixture until its muzzle pressed against the bag of gunpowder. He packed the rifle in until it stood rigid with only its stock and trigger group visible.

"Hand me the line," he said.

Regina and Dupre were still working on it, but he took the loose end of the knotted cloth rope and ran it through the stock sling swivel and from there to the trigger. He made a loop around the trigger and trigger guard, made sure it played freely; then he finished by ensuring the weapon's safety was off and there was a live round in the chamber.

"You *are* a true Einstein, Einstein," Regina approved, understanding.

"The rope has to be longer. It has to reach outside."

Dupre shed his shirt and began ripping it into shreds. Regina tied the strips one by one to the end of her rope as they played it out past the ovens and into the outer corridor. They worked in total darkness. James supposed they would be safe from blowback if they detonated the charge from the vicinity of the mortar-mixing pit outside the building.

"Don't put too much pressure on the line," he cautioned.

So preoccupied were they that the first indication that they weren't alone came from a nearby whisper of sound that was neither one of them nor flak falling on the roof. As they wheeled in unison to confront the intruders, powerful handheld flashlights caught the conspirators in pools of illumination. Cockroaches surprised in the kitchen sink.

Three flashlights blazed. That meant at least three Germans, possibly more, since only indistinct and ill-defined shadows were visible behind the lights. James had been careless in his haste. He should have paid more attention when he thought he was being followed.

A single shriek of juvenile terror raised the hair on the back of his neck. "Alber'!"

The cry was followed immediately by a chilling command issued in the harsh voice of Major Fischer: "Drop that line."

The boogeyman had come.

Regina was in the process of tying off another rag of

shirt when the lights came on. Although Major Fischer might not know exactly what the Jews were up to, they were obviously up to *something*—and it had to do with the cloth rope.

Regina hesitated. They were still in the corridor and next to the "showers," still short of being safe from the explosion. All she had to do was jerk the line to send them all to a better world. If Major Fischer had Mimi, which he obviously did, it meant he also had her mother, Elena, and possibly Uncle Erwein and Michael. All of them would be killed instantly, along with James and Regina, Socha and Dupre.

"I said drop it!"

James nodded at her. He meant for her to yank the rope and set off the explosion. Instead, looking confused, she let the knotted strings of shirt coil out of her hands onto the floor.

"Now the weapon," Major Fischer demanded.

What a sentimental fool James had been. But for his ill-conceived promise to a charitable *Focke-Wulf* pilot, he may have already killed the man and prevented his showing up at inconvenient times.

James eased the MP-40 to the floor and stood back, hands raised to his waist. No sense taking the martyr's route without a purpose—and they were clearly at a disadvantage.

The shadow that was Major Fisher stepped into the light. He was armed with a Mauser pointed at James's chest. He pulled Professor Jahne forward with him. The scientist's sad eyes locked onto his niece.

"What were you preparing to do, Albert Einstein?" Fischer sneered. "It appears you were plotting to double-cross your faithful partner. I would say that this completes our transaction, such as it is, since it appears I have taken the prize. I must confess that you were very helpful, however. I suppose, in a way, I do owe you that much. Your professor and I can now readily disappear in all the confusion you've caused."

Hands reached out and pulled Professor Jahne back into the darkness behind the light. At the same time, a muddy jackboot across Elena's bottom shoved her, stumbling forward, with Mimi clinging to her shirttail. They collapsed in a whimpering heap on the floor. The pathetic little woman's shaved pate glistened in the torchlight. Mimi's big brown eyes, pleading, found James's.

"Like all Jews, Albert Einstein, you are stupid," Major Fischer said. "I'm now officially withdrawing my bid on your life. *Auf Wiedersehen, Jude.*"

50

The moment required impulsive action, not contemplation. James's first impulse was to throw himself at the knotted line that led across the floor to the ovens and the bomb—like a GI who hurls himself on top of a live grenade to save his buddies. There could be no thought of collateral damage such as Mimi or Regina, or anyone else. *Boom!* Mission completed: Scientist and his secrets of the universe destroyed.

Before his body had a chance to respond, however, events erupted with unexpected rapidity and violence, initiated by the quick *Bark! Bark! Bark!* of a pistol. James dived for the trigger line, hitting the floor next to where Elena and Mimi huddled.

That was when his befuddled brain realized that the shooting had come from the direction of the showers and not from the Germans.

Chaos took over, uncontrolled insanity in fast-forward, like a movie projector gone wild. Flashlight beams jerked and stabbed the darkness from every crazy angle. In charged two figures, freeze-framed in the grazing light of a fallen flashlight. One was Eisenberg, the other Michael Grojanowski. Both were shrieking war cries at the top of their lungs, Eisenberg firing the SS Luger that seemed way too large for his wasted frame, Michael swinging a *kapo's* club like a supercharged lunatic.

The Germans returned fire with their rifles, muzzle flames blinking like camera flashes, their discharges deafening in the brick-and-concrete confines.

James felt as if he were inside a tub while a troop of stomp-dancing Cherokees from back home beat on the top of it with steel bars.

He dropped the trigger line and went for his discarded MP-40 instead, slapping the floor in search of it. Finding it, he combat-rolled to one side and brought his weapon to bear against the darkness behind the lights. The scuffling of feet and the continued bark of Eisenberg's pistol made him hold his fire for fear of hitting the two friendlies who had swept into the midst of the Germans.

James glimpsed a third form move past him in a blur, a roar of fury. Light caught big, ugly Leopold Socha joining Eisenberg and Michael in their mad charge. Fire from an automatic pistol caught him in the chest. He jerked as though an unseen puppeteer had gone into spasms on his strings. He dropped hard to the floor, rage unable to carry him the last few steps to reach the throats of the hated enemy.

Discerning a target, James unleashed a burst at the flashing muzzle of the German who took Socha out. That silenced him.

The rest of the fight took place in total darkness behind the reach of dropped flashlights. Eisenberg's pistol barked two or three more times. Michael grunted and yelled as he wielded his club. James heard bodies hitting the floor. Whose or how many he could not tell.

Next to him on the concrete floor, Regina and Dupre covered Elena and Mimi with their own bodies to protect them.

The clash was over as quickly as it had begun. There was no more gunfire. Running footfalls receded up the corridor. James snatched a discarded flashlight off the floor and sprang to his feet. Its beam spotlighted Major Fischer pulling Professor Jahne after him as the pair disappeared out the crematorium door into the main yard.

James started after them. The terrified wailing of the child penetrated his single-task mindset and stopped him. Blood chilled his heart, which he constantly struggled to make hard and uncaring. But there was something especially insistent in the sound—the child's helplessness and dependency upon adults in a world of madness could not be ignored. A single horrifying thought flashed through James's mind, replacing his fixation upon mission.

My God! Mimi! She's hurt!

He looked toward the doorway through which the SS major had fled with the scientist. He looked back at the carnage, cross-lighted by dropped German flashlights, in the midst of which cringed the Jewish child calling out his assumed name in terror and desperation. Professor Jahne was his official obligation; Mimi was his moral obligation.

"Alber'! Alber!' "

He ran back and dropped on his knees next to her. She flung herself into his embrace, clinging to him and refusing to let him go. Fearing the worst, he felt her all over for blood. Miracle of miracles, he detected no wounds. She was frightened nearly to death, so terrified that she trembled all over and couldn't speak for stuttering, "Alber'! Alber'!"

Every time he thought he might have gotten by his personal feelings, tucked them back somewhere where they would stay until after the war ended, they popped up again, at the most inconvenient moments. While he was here on his knees comforting a little Jewish child whose life or death meant not one whit in the greater scheme of the war, the Nazis were getting away with Professor Jahne.

51

Of the Jewish men, only ravaged Eisenberg remained on his feet. Still clutching the Luger he had taken from the SS officer, he staggered over and knelt down where James and the two women, Elena and Regina, were embracing Mimi. Eyes sunken far back into his skull reflected twin beams of savagery and determination. Nearby, James's flashlight revealed Michael lying on his back in a widening pool of thick blood, his dark eyes open, his lips twittering prayers. Psalms, perhaps. He looked a very old man now and continued to age by the second as he proceeded on his journey to meet his Maker.

James longed to tell him how noble and brave and courageous he was this final moment in attacking armed enemy soldiers with only a club, but Michael was slipping into another world and would not hear. He and Eisenberg had most certainly saved the lives of James, the women and little Mimi. How the two of them had linked up and formed a rescue party was a story for another day. James was only glad now that he had not taken the pistol from Eisenberg after all when he couldn't keep up.

James's flashlight beam found three dead German soldiers lying together where they had fallen, like bags of old, bloody clothing. Dupre the Frenchman was also dead, having caught a bullet in the middle of his face. Socha appeared sorely wounded and was pulling himself across the floor with his elbows, dragging legs torn and paralyzed by bullets, leaving a trail of blood on the concrete like that of a garden slug. He glanced toward the light, his scarred and ugly mask of a face looking almost noble. He reached for the end of the string that led to the bomb. Mimi buried her face against James's chest.

Socha blinked at the light. "Albert Einstein . . . ?"

The deep and pained timbre of his voice was startling in the quiet that followed the bedlam of the fight. Even the piston-drum of the leading Allied bombers arriving overhead, exploding ack-ack, *Ooo-gah! Ooo-gah!*, and the clamor of German weapons around the perimeter diminished in comparison to the immediacy of events inside the death furnace.

Socha coughed up blood and phlegm. James ran to him, followed by the women carrying Mimi in their arms. Socha warned them off. The roar of aircraft now vibrated through the crematorium and shook the ground.

"The bombers . . ." Socha faltered. "We must blow the fence before . . . the bombs fall . . ."

He had taken up the slack in the line. It was taut now and twisted around his fist. James's throat knotted when he realized what Socha intended doing. The big, ugly, brave, magnificent bastard was going to blow himself up in order to provide an escape route. His wife and child were dead; he had, on more than one occasion, remarked how his only remaining purpose in life was to kill Germans. And now he was wounded, dying probably, no longer able to maintain the sense of revenge that had sustained him in the camps—and so he would sacrifice the few minutes that remained of his life in order that other Jews might have a chance.

"The old man with the beard . . ." He coughed up

blood. "He must be important for you to . . . have risked so much. Go after him, Albert Einstein."

James and Regina glanced at once toward the door through which Major Fischer had taken the scientist. The old man's unhealed ankle would hold them up, but James had to be going if he hoped to overtake them before it was too late. They would undoubtedly head for the main gate, through which Fischer likely intended to escape with Professor Jahne during the excitement.

Socha's fist that held the end of the line trembled. "Albert Einstein," he labored. "She's . . . still alive . . ."

"What!"

"Gabrielle. I–I didn't tell you before. She escaped from Majdanek. Now . . . Go! Run!"

There was no time to argue, to question further. Socha was right. The device had to be detonated immediately before falling bombs camouflaged the explosion that would guide the barracks Jews to freedom, and before the bombs caught the unprepared inmates milling about in confusion and wiped them out. The escapees needed to get as far away from the camp as they could before it started. Bombing from the air was not a precision operation. At Normandy, bombers tasked with knocking out Kraut coastal defenses had missed them altogether and dropped their loads a mile inland.

That the bombers had come at all, that the Allies were willing to dedicate precious assets to a secret OSS mission of little strategic value, attested to the commitment President Roosevelt and PM Churchill accorded the A-bomb project and the recovery of the scientist most knowledgeable in the field.

James sprang to his feet and cradled Mimi in one arm, in the other hand the MP-40, and made a desperate lunge to break free of the crematorium he had helped build before Socha pulled the string. Elena followed hard on his heels, trailed by Regina, half dragging the exhausted Eisenberg.

The mortar pit was only a few yards away from the front of the crematorium. Hardened excess concrete formed a low bulwark around it. James hurdled it with Mimi in his arms, landing on his bare back to protect the little girl from the fall.

Elena sailed over after him. Hand in hand, Regina and Eisenberg were still leaping for cover when Socha exploded the bomb. The concussion wave caught them and propelled them through the air. James cushioned Regina's fall with his own body. Eisenberg grunted and lay where he hit, too feeble to move.

Dragon fire shot from the building's every opening. The evil structure that was intended to burn thousands of Jews and other undesirables slowly began to collapse with a mighty rumble. First, the explosion hurled a ton or so of brick from the rear wall through the perimeter fences, blasting an opening that trucks could have driven through. Then the roof caved in, choking the air with blinding dust, burying Leopold Socha alive next to the dead Jews and covering up the bodies of Germans he had bitterly hated to the end.

Debris rained out of the sky. James covered Regina and Mimi with his body to protect them. Regina could hardly contain her surprise and excitement. "It worked! You actually did it."

James lifted his head from the ground to watch the disintegration. "Socha did it," he said.

From deep inside the camp and from all about arose a chorus of voices as inmates recognized the signal. Hundreds of stampeding feet pounded the earth as Jews, directed by their barracks commanders, rushed toward the crematorium and freedom. German guards poured lead into the bolting crowds, their fire increasing in fury.

Above them, the night began to wail and shriek as 500-pound bombs fell in clusters. Evacuation of the camp had started a few minutes too late.

"God in heaven," Elena beseeched, lifting her face to the night as the bombs started exploding in the midst of the panicked inmates. "Deliver us from evil, for Thine is the glory and the kingdom for lost souls on earth . . ."

52

The first ordnance detonated across the middle of camp like strings of humongous firecrackers. The bombs were smaller and less powerful than those used in the fire attacks on German cities. Still, the explosions shook the dust right out of the ground. Those caught by them felt the need to grab the earth and hang on to keep from being shaken loose into outer space. Fireballs trod across the compound like the running footfalls of a fiery giant, scorching and bruising, hurling and breaking, back-lighting screaming, ragged inmates as they hobbled, staggered, lumbered and crawled in the direction of the crematorium, where they were promised a chance at salvation.

Machine-gun tracers ripped across the sky like showers of shooting stars. Bombs ignited plumes of flame that irradiated the darkness like great Roman candles. Chunks of steel sizzled as they sank into a tree trunk, from which smoke leaked like blood. Three Jews were picked up and hurled against the red water tower. Other people, pieces of people, lumber, clothing, rock and other debris zoomed through the air in the orange light of the explosions and resulting fires. The dash for freedom became a panicked, mindless stampede, the mob trampling and destroying its own even while it was being consumed.

It was barbaric, it was savage. It was war, but beyond war. The great Winston Churchill once asked what happened to a civilized society when it went to war with a barbarous one like Germany? He answered the question himself. If the civilized society was to prevail, he said, it must necessarily and tragically break the "rules" if it hoped to survive, a course that degraded it to some intangible extent. Bombing German cities lay beyond civilized conventions, but *nothing* was as depraved as the Germans around the Nisko compound pouring fire into the masses of unarmed, half-starved Jews, mowing them down, even while bombs fell from the sky.

Things sometimes went wrong in war, as they had tonight. The timing had been imperfect, resulting in delay and the camp's being bombed before the Jews could get out. Such mistakes, oversights, blunders and errors already weighed heavily on James's shoulders and would one day, after the war, pile on years of nightmares.

But there was no time now for regrets and recriminations.

The collapse of the crematorium gave the floodlight in the guard tower beyond free reign to sweep unobstructed over the crowds striving to reach the hole in the fence. It glared through the dust and smoke like an eerie full moon through swamp fog in a horror movie. James ducked and pulled the others down with him behind the concrete berm as the broad shaft of light skimmed over the mortar pit and settled on the tattered ranks of fleeing escapees.

A machine gun gabbled from behind the light. Tracers burned into the Jews. Heavy-caliber bullets thumped into flesh, and flesh screamed back before it went down in disappearing clumps. Bullets ripped apart a bag of bones who almost fell on Elena and Mimi. Both screamed.

James shattered the elevated floodlight with a shot from his MP-40, casting their part of the compound into partial darkness. The machine gun continued its deadly chant. James took aim at the hostile muzzle flicker and fired at the silhouetted head just behind it. That eliminated the gunner. The A-gunner took over and James shot him too, silencing the weapon.

To prevent a massacre like this was precisely why James risked hijacking weapons from guards. Now, he had only one firearm left. He cursed himself for not having had the presence of mind to grab the dead Germans' rifles before he fled the crematorium.

He thrust the MP-40 at Regina. "Give them cover till the Jews break through," he ordered in English.

She knew where he was going. "You don't have a weapon!"

"I'll improvise. You need it more. They'll be sending troops to cork the hole as soon as they figure it out."

She pecked him on the mouth. "You are a good man, James. Bring my uncle, if you can."

"Give me five minutes. If we're not back by then, we won't be coming. Give Jurawski my regards. Tell him he's not too bad for a Polack."

"Mimi and her mother will be all right. I will find Gabrielle when the war is over."

What more could they say? James gave Eisenberg his flashlight. Through Regina's translation, he conveyed orders that the gaunt Jew was to act as a traffic cop and direct escapees through the barbed wire.

"Can you do it?"

"Like through the Red Sea," Eisenberg promised, laboring to his feet.

James reassured Mimi, who clung to him. "Didn't I come back last time?"

Elena ripped the child off him like a kitten off a screen door.

"I love you, Alber'."

James bolted to his feet and headed out, in his limping gait, to cut off Major Fischer and Professor Jahne before they reached the main gate. They had a lead on him, but the scientist's bad foot and the Allied bombing should slow them down enough that James could catch up. He was back in action: impassionate, methodical, controlled.

While James had been a champion boxer and baseball player, had even done well in basketball, he was too small to play football at Oklahoma A&M. Tonight, however, even with his lame leg, the broken field run he made across the concentration camp would have earned him a slot on any college team in the U.S., no questions asked. He dodged explosions, ducking and twisting through ghastly rollers of panicked human beings, attempting to avoid being clobbered by falling bombs. Twice, nearby detonations knocked him to his knees and seared his hair and eyebrows. Once, a crazed prisoner tried to tackle him for no reason at all. James had to punch him in the face to make him let go.

The dead lay scattered about, faces knotted in anguish, lying in vast pools of blood. A weeping teenager immobilized by fear crouched in the open like a hunted animal. Others careened about, blinded by wounds, pain and terror.

God almighty, would there be anyone left to escape?

Fifty-yard line and goal to go. James's eyes darted frantically around the lunatic landscape attempting to find Major Fischer and Professor Jahne. He realized this was his last chance to salvage his mission, knowing he may have already blown it because he wasn't hard enough to do what had to be done at the beginning. Maybe he should ask Uncle Henry for that desk job in London when—if—he got back. Call it a bad case of the nerves. Call it not being cut out for the kind of job that required a man to empty his soul of all compassion. He simply might not be tough enough for it.

He flattened himself against the wall of the last standing barracks this side of the main gate. Ahead, beneath the bright bursts of AA among the waves of B-17s overhead, in the roar of flames bringing day to night, he saw the gate, still upright and intact. This side of it, Major Fischer's little white cabin remained remarkably undisturbed, although there were smoking craters all around it. The SS officer and the two *Wehrmacht* James and the Jews had slain earlier for their weapons still lay where they had fallen.

No sign of Fischer and his captive.

James launched himself off the side of the barracks and sprinted toward Major Fischer's shack, zigzagging to make of himself a more difficult target in case somebody wanted to get in some target practice. He was halfway across the open quadrangle between the barracks and the shack when a sinister little sizzle and a wake of roiled air kissed his cheek, followed by the report of the rifle that had fired the bullet.

He knew not to stop; there would surely be a second shot.

Over in the shadows of the warehouses, Major Fischer was down on one knee, Mauser upraised, working the weapon's bolt to chamber a round. He drew his bead. He was unlikely to miss this time as James wheeled and rushed directly at him.

53

Professor Jahne stood slightly behind Major Fischer and to his right, a confused old man immobilized by indecision and fright, a brilliant academic out of his element in a violent world. He watched helplessly as the mysterious redheaded stranger known to his niece as "James" but to everyone else as "Albert Einstein" ducked his head and charged his abductor, whipping back and forth as he ran to throw off the SS officer's aim. The little man wasn't even armed, not so much as a *kapo's* club. He wasn't even wearing a *shirt*. Yet, here he came as if half of Patton's army was behind him.

James knew it was his only chance, the best defense being a prompt offense. It was either that or run for his life, the other way, like a spooked rabbit—and get cut down anyhow. His one remaining goal was to reach the Nazi's throat; he required no weapon other than his bare hands if he could make the last few feet that separated him from Fischer.

Everything seemed to lapse into slow motion as he

closed the gap. Blossoms of flame from exploding bombs opened around him as in time-lapse photography. A storage building shuddered from a bomb crashing through its roof, lifted slowly off its foundation, then splintered into its component parts, disintegrating sluggishly with a brilliant core.

Major Fischer fired a second shot, but he hurried his trigger squeeze. The bullet grazed James's bare ribs but failed to slow him. He hardly noticed it among the other injuries and wounds he had suffered.

The German shifted the Mauser's muzzle in his hands ever so slowly to compensate for James's evasive maneuvers. In James's mind, he was running directly at the maw of a black tunnel, out of which, at any instant, could roar a supersonic train to smash the life out of him. There was no way Fischer would miss his next shot, not at such close range, not firing a weapon with a muzzle the size of a train tunnel.

His muscles tightened to receive the projectile. The next one had better kill him instantly. Otherwise, he would have Fischer's throat in his hands and snuff the life from him even as he drew his own last breath. Call it mission completed—the scientist free and on his way via Jurawski and Regina to the Allied side—even if James didn't make it. Uncle Henry and Winston Churchill might heap accolades, posthumously, upon the OSS agent to whom mission always came first.

Well, to whom mission *almost* always came first.

A roar—part rage, part defiance, part death knell—shredded the air. James hardly recognized it as coming from the depths of his own throat and lungs. He reached, *reached,* fingers curling. Nazi white-blond hair directly ahead in his path. Blue eyes widening, *widening,* behind the black tunnel.

Gabrielle is alive! flashed through his mind. It filled what he thought was to be his last moment with inexplicable joy.

Major Fischer roared back at the crazy, half-naked man

almost on top of him. His finger tightened on the trigger.

Still in slow motion, James saw Professor Jahne's chunky, crippled body launch itself into the air, even as the SS officer squeezed his trigger. He crashed into Fischer, his white beard and mane blazing almost red in the firelight like an avenging Thor's. The old scientist had finally erupted from the sidelines and joined the war. And not a millisecond too soon.

The Mauser discharged with a ringing report.

Professor Jahne's attack deflected the weapon a critical few inches. That damn bee farted almost in James's face. It was that close.

Then James was upon the German.

Grappling, they rolled across the ground. James drove his knee into the major's groin. Fischer grunted and slackened his grip on the rifle.

Contested weapon in hand, James sprang to his feet. Major Fischer lay on his back on the ground, face contorted in agony, cupping himself with both hands, knees drawn up toward his chin as he fought for air. A man's balls were his most accessible and vulnerable point, and James knew how to dong them.

Panting breaths burning his lungs and throat, he shouldered the Mauser and aimed it at Fischer's forehead. Fire glow washed in waves across the German's raptor face. His blue glare turned to resignation.

"I'm doing the bidding this time," James grated out between clenched teeth.

Fischer collected himself as the pain subsided. "It looks like you hold trump, Albert Einstein."

James began to squeeze the trigger. Professor Jahne, whose ankle had given away and dropped him to his knees, watched in horror and fascination. He squirmed back to avoid getting splashed by blood.

"You deserve to die," James said.

"In the end, Albert Einstein, we all deserve to die."

"I can't leave you behind to come after me."

"I understand, *Jude*."

"Jews will fight. Haven't you seen that?"

More flame light washed across Major Fischer's face. He made an expression of dismissal. "*Are* you a Jew, Albert Einstein?"

"Damn you."

"Kill me, Albert Einstein. You want to. I can see it in your face. How can we properly have a war if we don't kill each other?"

James's trigger finger tightened some more. Major Fischer's eyes gazed up the long barrel into James's. Suddenly, James became the pilot in the Focke-Wulf 190, peering from his cockpit at the damaged torso of the Carpetbagger B-24. He was looking through the owl's eyes at the cowering guinea fowl.

He *must* be getting soft.

Smoothly, without further hesitation, he switched his aim from between the German's eyes to his right knee cap, and blew it off with a single shot. Blood, bone and flesh splattered. Major Fischer howled in anguish and writhed on the ground. That would hold him; he wouldn't be dogging anyone for quite a spell.

"This is the last time we spare each other's lives, Major," James said as he turned to help Professor Jahne to his feet. "Come on, Prof. Thank you. I owe you my life."

"I owe you my soul."

They headed off toward the hole in the fence, James's arms around the old man to support him. Fires crackled and flared all about, smoke roiled, and there were a few rifle shots, but the bombing run was over, the sound of B-17 engines gradually receding. From behind, through unbidden tears of pain, came Major Fischer's parting cry: "Who are you, *Jude*? Who *are* you?"

54

Having anticipated no Allied attack on a concentration camp, the Germans had set up only a couple of Quad-20 AA guns, both of which had been knocked out by the bombing. Most of the watch towers with their machine guns were also destroyed. Elite Guard, SS, *Einsatzgruppen*, camp administrators—including Lieutenant Colonel Muller, if he was still alive—and common soldiers were fleeing into the surrounding hills. *Kapos* threw away their clubs and either hid out or joined the Jewish exodus to freedom, hoping not to be noticed by either side.

It would take days to get them all rounded up and reconsolidated. In the meantime, those inmates who survived scattered into the forests and made plans to reach Allied lines. That so many had been killed by both American bombers and Germans was another source from which James's nightmares would draw once he had time to dwell on his failings and inadequacies.

He and the professor, in whose cause such chaos had occurred, wended their way through the fires and wreckage toward the demolished crematorium. Bodies lay scattered about, lots of bodies.

Regina, Elena and her daughter were gone from the mortar pit when they reached it. Snaggle-toothed Eisenberg, gaunter than ever, teetering on weakened legs, tufts of hair plastered to his scalp, was still directing stragglers toward the hole blown in the fence. He had the empty Luger in one hand and was waving the German flashlight in the other like a traffic cop.

"I urged them to flee when you were long in returning," Eisenberg said of the women in Polish, translated by Professor Jahne. "The pretty one—your woman, Albert Einstein—did not wish to leave, but I persuaded her that she owed it to the little girl. She said to tell you they would meet you, and that you knew where."

He looked at James out of the hollowed, haunted caves of his eyes. Reflected in them were the fires and horrors endured this terrible night.

"Not all made it out," he said. "Many did. We owe our lives to you, Albert Einstein."

And those who died? Do they owe their deaths to me?

"There were mines outside the fences," Eisenberg said. "Many of our people were killed by them, but they cleared a path for others. Stay to the right, you and the old man. Walk where there are the parts of bodies from those who went before and you should reach the forest safely. Go now. Like Moses, you have led us from captivity."

To what end—to wander in the wilderness for forty years?

Jurawski had probably brought two or three vehicles at best, not enough for everyone. Professor Jahne's escape was top priority. Most of the others would have to do the best they could on their own. That was the harsh reality of the escape.

"Scrounge all the guns you can from the dead Germans and distribute them," James advised Eisenberg. He pointed toward the wooded hills to the south and east, where survivors had the best chance of evasion as the

Russians advanced. "Head that way. God go with you, Eisenberg. *Shalom.*"

"*Shalom.* God go with you as well, Albert Einstein."

James clasped the Jew's fragile hand in farewell. "I was wrong about you and the others, Eisenberg. You are a brave people."

"Jews fight when they must, Albert Einstein. It is the times."

James and Professor Jahne left the bony scarecrow still guiding the elderly, the very young, the more debilitated and other stragglers. Most of them would probably die in the forest either from exposure and hunger or from being hunted down or betrayed by anti-Semites, but they would die free, and not in the "showers" next to the Jew ovens.

People were still climbing over the rubble through the hole in the fence. Amazing, what some goose shit and fuel oil could accomplish. A gosling "liberated" with his kin during the bombing ran around next to the fence in confused, terrified circles, alone in the reflected firelight. Socha had said he would be fond of geese for the rest of his life if the bomb worked. James caught the gosling and carried it outside, where he released it.

"Go with Socha's blessings, little one."

It was almost quiet, now that the bombing and shooting had ceased. The drone of departing bombers diminished to a distant hum. Darkness dominated the forest, away from the light of fires in the camp. Major Fisher's Mauser at the ready, James cautiously approached the predesignated point at the crossroads where he was to rendezvous with Jurawski.

From nearby came the sibilant hum of a gasogene vehicle digesting its charcoal fuel in neutral gear. A man with a rifle kept watch in forest shadow. James and the professor took cover in some bushes near the road until they were sure the sentry was a partisan and not German.

Only then did James step out and hail the waiting Poles.

It didn't take long for the family, minus Michael, to reunite in a glade next to where the partisans had parked a captured black German staff car and an ancient gasogene flatbed truck. It was the same one James had seen at the farm safe house abandoned by the guerrillas that night outside Grudwald.

"Oh, Alber'! Alber'!" Mimi cried, running into his arms in the dark. "I prayed. Do you know what I asked God? I tol' him that instead of letting people die and having to make new ones, why didn't He keep the ones He already had. And He did, Alber'. He kept you."

Jurawski joined the reunion, impatiently urging that they be off quickly. The boxer loomed as big, ugly and powerful as ever. He smelled of rotted onions and rotted teeth, but Regina held onto his arm.

"The last time I am seeing you," the prizefighter growled in his broken English, "I am saying it is better nothing is happening to my Regina."

"Or you would be permanently killing me."

Why couldn't he control his bulldog mouth?

"I am not permanently killing you." He extended a hand and crushed James's in it. "You are in saving my Regina and for which you are in having Jurawski's friendship like she is brother."

He handed James a partial pack of C-rat Lucky Strikes, evidently the same pack James had given him after his parachute jump near Grudwald. James hadn't had a Lucky since . . . He couldn't remember the last time.

"I am in feeling like to kiss you, Polack," James cried gratefully.

"You are not daring," Jurawski protested. "Now, you are must be going quick with the uncle. The driver is having a radio for which you are calling to have the airplane coming for you. Is that being good?"

"You'll never know how good."

Jurawski led them across the glade to the vehicles. Partisans and escaping Jews were piling onto the flatbed truck, as many as could get aboard. Two armed partisans occupied the front seat of the staff car. Elena and Mimi climbed into the backseat. James held the door open for Regina, but she remained at Jurawski's side.

"I knew all along Jurawski would come for me, James," she said. "I will stay with him and fight. It is where I belong."

James hesitated. "I understand," he said finally.

"I am sure Gabrielle is likewise waiting for you."

Into his hand she slipped the little blue barrette that had belonged to her mother.

"Remember me," she whispered.

Professor Jahne said goodbye to his niece with a hug and kiss, and slid into the car between the driver and the other fighter. James got into the backseat. The car, lights out, left the glade. Regina and Jurawski stood together. She had changed into clean trousers, her shaved head was bare again, and she carried a Sten submachine gun slung over one shoulder. James thought he would always remember her like that—and like that night in the blanket on the hill above Grudwald. He smiled.

He lit a Lucky Strike and drew smoke deep into his lungs. Little Mimi had already curled up in the protection of his arm. He put Regina's barrette to his nostrils and drew in her lingering scent.

The staff car pulled onto the road and was soon rolling along at a good clip beneath a rising moon. He looked back once. The glare of the fires at Nisko bathed the horizon in a glow of angry oranges and reds. He was sure the camp and the crematorium he had helped construct would never be rebuilt.

AFTERWORD

It always seemed to be raining on the long pier at Weymouth. It was raining now, a gray drizzle that matched the hue of English Channel waters and the texture of James Cantrell's thoughts. James came here often, alone, whenever he was in Britain. It was where he did his best thinking, where he reflected on the meaning of his life and tried to get everything into some perspective after he returned from a mission.

Four days ago, a Carpetbagger flight had plucked him, Professor Erwein Jahne, Mimi, and little Mimi's mother, Elena, out of Poland. Mimi was now safe with her mother in London, living temporarily with a family Uncle Henry knew. James visited the precocious little child every day, and she always greeted him with an aphorism made up especially for him. "Christians have only one spouse. That's called monotony."

Professor Jahne was being treated at a British military hospital for his shattered ankle, after which he would be flown to New York on the first leg of his journey to the Nevada testing grounds to contribute his expertise to the development of the atomic bomb. OSS operatives supplied with the secret location of Professor Jahne's research papers near the Vistula River had gone in, unbeknownst to the Russians who by now had overrun the region, retrieved them, and were back in Italy by the time James was on his way to London.

"All spirits are enslaved which touch things evil and do nothing," Professor Jahne said. "Albert Einstein, please keep track of my niece. She is willful and strong-minded, much like you, and I am exceedingly proud of her. I am proud of you as well. The true Dr. Einstein, I think, would be honored to share his name with you."

When his plane touched down on friendly soil, one of the first things James wanted to know about was the fate of Major Callahan and the B-24 Carpetbagger crew that had inserted him into Poland from their damaged bomber. Sure enough, the airplane had finally gone down, but everyone aboard survived. A Russian patrol recovered them and escorted them safely to Warsaw, where the Soviets finally negotiated their repatriation.

He also wanted to know about Gabrielle. Had there been any word of her?

"Majdanek. You don't say?" Uncle Henry marveled. "A French Jewish woman engineered a successful escape from Majdanek under the assumed appellate of 'Little Wanda with Braids.' She wrote and smuggled out to the Allies one of the first eye-witness reports informing the world about the death camps. The last information we had, she was still with the Resistance in Poland. Do you think Little Wanda may be Gabrielle?"

The great Winston Churchill had launched a message to the world based on "Little Wanda's" report.

"The systematic cruelties to which the Jewish people—men, women, and children—have been exposed under the Nazi regime are amongst the most terrible events of history," he said. "We are only beginning to learn the full extent of such atrocities in the death camps of Germany and Poland. They place an indelible stain upon all who perpetrate and instigate them. Free men and women denounce these vile crimes, and when this world struggle ends with the enthronement of human rights, racial persecution will be ended."

Perhaps Gabrielle and Regina would meet in Poland. James was glad Regina had Jurawski.

Those who held the opinion that Jews would not fight, as James once had, should have met these two brave women. They should also have met the other courageous Jews at Nisko—Leopold Socha; Eisenberg, guiding out the other Jews at risk to his own life; Michael Grojanowski, the timid one who, with a psalm on his lips, charged German guns with a club and gave his life; the chief rabbi at the water tower who gallantly placed the noose around his own neck; Dupre; Horowitz; Grossbert; all the inmates who had died trying to escape or who had fled into the forests to an uncertain fate. And they should have met Elena and little Mimi, who survived.

Though these Jews were peace loving and put their faith in God for their deliverance, they would fight when there was no other way.

Uncle Henry had almost given up on James after weeks of silence from Poland. He had started paperwork listing James as missing in action when the radio message came requesting a bombing run on Nisko. He had also waited at the airfield all night on the night James was supposed to arrive in England. The agent stepped off the B-24, trailed by an elderly man with a white beard on crutches, a woman with her head shaved, and a little girl. The tall, lanky controller abandoned his normal reticence, unlimbered his long limbs, and with a "Bang on, chap!" unabashedly and with genuine affection embraced James hard enough to squeeze the breath from him.

"You look shagged, my boy. Why, there isn't enough left of you to last till sundown. We had better feed you."

Uncle Henry was ebullient not only about James's safe return, but also about the success of his mission. Two SI (Secret Intelligence) agents from OSS and a rep from British MI6 attended the after-action debriefing. James

told them everything from start to finish, eliminating
only the parts about how he compromised himself and
willfully placed the mission in jeopardy because of his
feelings for a little six-year-old girl and his unwillingness
to unnecessarily sacrifice Jewish lives for the sake of the
mission. Those were unforgivable failings in the world
of espionage, subterfuge and behind-the-lines operations.
Mission always came first.

Such failings were why, last night, he had drafted his
resignation from the Office of Strategic Services. In it he
included the parts he had left out of his debriefing. It was
the only honorable thing to do. He had lost his resolve,
his nerve.

Now, standing with his toes on the very edge of the
pier as though preparing to launch himself across the
Channel, he turned up the collar of his slicker to stop
the cold rain from running down his back. His left sleeve
had hiked up to reveal the tattooed number from Nisko
on his arm. Uncle Henry said it could be removed, but
James chose to keep it as a sort of memorial to those who
had died during the revolt and escape. It made of him, he
thought wryly, a sort of honorary Jew.

He shook out a Lucky Strike and attempted to light
it, but the match kept going out in the rain. The cigarette drooped from his lips. The paper wrapping wilted
and tobacco crumbs dribbled onto his chin. Far out in the
English Channel, a convoy of transports streamed toward
France with supplies and troops to hurl against the Third
Reich.

Uncle Henry came down the pier. James wasn't aware
of him until he spoke. "I know I can always find you here,
James."

James looked at him, silently withdrew his resignation
from underneath his rain jacket and handed it to the station chief.

"What's this?"

"My resignation from the OSS. I'm requesting line
duty with the infantry."

Uncle Henry regarded the envelope for a long minute. Rain made wet drops on it. "Is this because of Mimi and the Jews at the camp?" he asked, then added when he saw the look of surprise sweep over James's freckled face, "Professor Jahne and I had a long talk. James, what happened shows you're still human. We must somehow remain human in all this if we are to do what has to be done and conquer our nightmares when it is all over."

He handed the envelope back.

"James, the war is not over. The OSS needs you, I need you—and somewhere over there Gabrielle needs you. It's up to you whether or not I accept your resignation."

James looked across the Channel toward Europe, where the Allies were still fighting. Where Gabrielle and Regina were still fighting. After a while, he ripped up the envelope and let the pieces flutter like wet butterflies into the gray waters of the English Channel. He brought out a fresh Lucky Strike and shielded it between his lips with his cupped hands.

"Got a light?"

ACKNOWLEDGMENTS

This is a work of fiction, and, as such, any resemblance to actual people, other than the historical, is unintentional. However, in writing the OSS Commando series I strive as much as possible to create thrilling tales based upon actual historical events in order to weave into them authenticity and verisimilitude. I would like to express my gratitude to the following authors and published works for helping to provide me insight into World War II, OSS operations, and, most particularly, the Holocaust:

OSS: The Secret History of America's First Central Intelligence Agency, by Richard Harris Smith (The Lyons Press, 1972, 2005); *They Fought Back,* by Yuri Suhl (Paperback Library, 1967); *The Women Who Lived for Danger,* by Marcus Binney (William Morrow, 2002); *Hitler's Willing Executioners,* by Daniel Jonah Goldhagen (Alfred A. Knopf, 1996); *Operatives, Spies, and Saboteurs,* by Patrick K. O'Donnell (Free Press, 2004); *Auschwitz,* by Dr. Miklos Nyiszli (Fawcett, 1960); *The Holocaust Years: Society on Trial,* by Roselle Chartock and Jack Spencer (Bantam, 1978); *What Was It Like in the Concentration Camp at Dachau?,* by Dr. Johannes Neuhausler (Manz, 1973); *Ordinary Heroes,* by Scott Turow (Farrar, Straus and Giroux, 2005); *The Holocaust,* by Martin Gilbert (Henry Holt, 1985); *The Jedburghs,* by Lt. Col. Will Irwin (PublicAffairs, 2005); *The Air War in Europe,* by Ronald H. Bailey (Time-Life Books, 1979); *The Nazis,* by Robert Edwin Herzstein (Time-Life Books, 1980); *The World at War 1939–45,* by Reader's Digest (Reader's Digest, 1998).